The Hidden Island

By
Angela Corner

For my Dad

We all have things we wish we hadn't done. Mistakes we've made that seem irreversible. Not small things, like stealing a bar of chocolate from the corner shop, or breaking a neighbour's window with a misplaced football, but big things, terrible things. We head down paths from where there seems no way back. Unfixable mistakes, things which can never be undone, and can never hope to be forgiven. We follow one mistake with another and another, because there seems no other way. So, why carry on? We can't fix things, or put things back the way they were. But, we can always make things better. Try to be better. And hope those better things are good enough to recompense for the mistakes we made before.

Prologue – 2005

The sea whispered to him, as he directed the boat out past the headland's sharp claws. There was no wind, no waves. The hull pierced the black water, sending out ripples, distorting the moonlight, as it rested on the water.

He glanced back to the Island. Its mountainous silhouette loomed like a sleeping Fiend. Tiny lights dotted the cliffs and hillsides. Lives being lived. Meals being eaten. Life the same tonight, as it was yesterday. He looked away, concentrating. It was cool out on the water, but he was sweating. His stomach twisted and clenched, but it was not from seasickness. Even the weakest stomach would survive a boat trip tonight, the sea being so calm. However, he'd spent most of his summers on boats of one size or another. Winters, too, between lectures. Shouting instructions, winning races. He had never been afraid of water. Yet, tonight, it seemed possessed by a darkness from which nothing that entered could escape.

The tip of the headland revealed another half-moon-shaped bay beyond. This one was different to the one he'd just left. This beach was illuminated; three restaurants elbowed next to each other. He knew each one, and had eaten at all of them, though Stiggies was their favourite. The food at Nemesis was better, the waitresses prettier, too, but someone, no one could remember who, had picked Stiggies as the place the chosen crowd went to. Where the loudest voices fought to out brag each other. He preferred to listen, to learn who people were, what they knew, and gauge who they might become.

He wasn't close enough to see people - his people perhaps - but he could hear the faintest hint of music, so faint he wondered if the music was only in his head, and if, maybe, this whole thing was a hallucination. A nightmare. He jumped. Another boat appeared around the next headland, heading straight for him. His breath caught in his throat. Then, the boat turned for the bay and the embrace of the restaurants. He recognised the flat-sided shape, and the canopy protecting the occupants. It was the Taxi boat, ferrying diners for food and wine, and taking them home again, once they could eat and drink no more. The boat was empty, apart from the crew. This must be the last lift home. Later than usual. Specially paid for, not part of the usual schedule. He could see the faces of the crew shining in the lights adorning the sides of the vessel. He doubted they had noticed him. *Not that it mattered*, he told himself. People stole up and down this coastline in boats, big and small, visiting friends, looking for seclusion, searching for fish, transporting people, and goods. He was doing his own transporting tonight, but no one would think twice about one more boat.

He passed another couple of golden-edged bays, before rounding a sharkfin-shaped outcrop, and heading towards the shore. This was a tiny bay, cloaked in complete darkness. No villas dotted the mountainside, no restaurants. The land too steep, road access impossible. The beach here was small, hidden behind a swarm of sharp rocks. Nothing bigger than a small dinghy or rowing boat could land here, but he wasn't heading for the beach.

He dropped the engine to an idle, and steered left, seemingly heading into the rock face itself, but at the last moment, an opening revealed itself. A sea cave. The entrance was just big enough to manoeuvre the boat inside. Here, without the moon to help, he had to turn on the boat's spot light. The light ricocheted off the fractured walls, but the water grew even blacker. It was deep in here, he knew that, but tonight, it seemed bottomless. Whatever entered the water here would sink forever. He felt calmer now he'd arrived. He killed the engine. It was now simply a job that needed doing. His job to sort things. Tidy messes, find solutions, and clear paths. He did it gladly. When you loved someone, you did those things for them.

He wasn't a tall man, and though he was strong, it was still an effort lifting the package. The black plastic - a tarpaulin found in the old olive press building - was slippery, his hands struggling to grip. The fishing weights he'd added doubled the required effort, but were a necessary evil. He used his legs and thighs to lever against the side of the boat, and force the package upwards. The boat pitched and rolled, but his sense of balance was good. The package. He could only think of it in those terms. A package to be tidied away. With a final heave, he was there, the package resting on the edge of the hull. Five foot four long, about 8 stone, if you didn't include the weights. The path to their ruin. This dark pit the route of their escape.

The last push was easy. Less of a push. More of a release. He let go, and the package dropped into the water. There was a hollow - comforting? – thwack, and the boat bucked with the swell. The sea spat at him, dousing his face in its blackness. Ignoring it, he leaned over the side of the boat to watch the package sink into the ocean and disappear. He tasted the salt, as it trickled down his face. It was done. The last bad thing he would ever do.

CHAPTER ONE
2016

Inspector Beckett Kyriakoulis tilted his head back, eyes half shut under his sunglasses, and stretched his legs out in front of him. He let the conversation of his friends evaporate around him, whilst the warm, soft breath of the sun bathed his face, and the sea whispered back and forth against the shingle. It had been the first really hot day of the year, and even at 3pm, it was still glorious. May could be a fickle month on the Greek Island of Farou. Days teasing of summer, neighbour to days which shut out the sun and hurled rain at the disappointed souls who'd plumped for an early holiday.

Being early in the season and not yet overrun with tourists had given Rocco the time to leave his kitchen at the Sunrise Bar and Grill, and argue with the many friends who had dropped in for coffee. The other voice belonged to Welsh Nik. Tenth generation local, he was also taking advantage. He ran the boat yard across the road, hiring out boats - big and small - to tourists, who fancied themselves as Captain Jacks or Ben Ainsleys.

On the table next to Beckett's now empty plate - everywhere he went on the Island people would make him meals, as if he was a waif and stray needing feeding up, little wonder at his expanding waistline - was his police radio, cackling away like it had been possessed by a witch's coven, and his radar gun. He had more use for it in the summer for stopping tourists, scaring them with tales of cars careering down mountainsides, not being missed for weeks; telling them to count the shrines at the sides of all the Island's roads. Each one marked a fatality. He rarely, in fact had never, given out a speeding ticket. It wasn't that the locals drove more carefully, quite the opposite, but Beckett had learned to pick his fights, and if locals wanted to end their lives in a metal coffin, that was their choice. His two days a week on speeding duty almost always ended up in one of his favourite restaurants drinking coffee, eating, of course, and listening to his friends argue about football, politics, the price of fish, and their recalcitrant women folk. He rarely joined in. Being an old British stronghold, the locals spoke English when being polite, and to tourists, and Greek at all other times. Greek wasn't Beckett's first language, and though he was fluent, when things got heated, and words were shuttlecocked back and forth, it was easier to listen.

The police radio shrilled him into attention, shouting his name.

"Wakey, wakey, Beckett. Mommy is calling." Rocco teased, but Beckett was already on his feet.

"Yep." He turned away from the others.

"Can you get to the Hotel Golden Sands in Nikisiopi?" At the other end of the radio, Police Constable Flolos' voice was tentative. Ordering one of the bosses around did not come easily to her. She was only a year out of the Academy. She made Beckett feel like an old man. One of a multitude of things.

"Sure, what's up?" He moved further away from the table. It was a small Island. People loved to gossip.

"Missing person reported. Female tourist. British. Not been seen for a couple of days. Her friends are worried."

Beckett was in one of the Hyundai patrol cars, rather than his own car. Much better for slowing down speeding cars, but not great for actual driving. Even with the seat shunted right back, it was still a squeeze. Locals tended to be on the shorter side, and his larger frame was not built for small cars. He headed up into the hills, shifting his position, trying to get comfortable.

His legs were too long, and his head claustrophobically close to the roof. It was also a manual, and before he'd even negotiated the first set of hairpin bends on a 25% gradient, his left knee was grumbling.

He passed the turn off for his own village, cursing himself for not returning to the station in town and collecting his own car before making the journey. It was the big night tonight, the Festival of the Flowers. He'd promised his cousins he'd help set things up in the village square. Tables, seating, lights, and lanterns. One of his cousins, Thakis, would be battling the sound system, as he did every year. There can be no festival without music. 'What will people say?' Thakis would wail. 'They will curse me into the ground, and my olives will shrivel on the branches.'

The Golden Sands Hotel occupied a prime position two streets back from the end of the beach, but the salmon pink render was blemished, like that of a small pox survivor, and the sign in the front garden area was missing the 'n' from Sands. Like many hotels, it was suffering after a couple of lean seasons. There was so much competition for cheap holidays, even the more exotic destinations had plummeted in price. It was a struggle to attract holidaymakers, and with the Greek economy in a cesspit, there was no money for repairs or renovations. The manager, Fran Kingston, would not appreciate a patrol car parked outside, so Beckett drove another fifty yards up the road and parked outside a half-finished apartment block, the intentions of a top storey hinted at by the twisted steel poles which poked up from the top of the concrete shell. Nature was swarming back in, grass three-foot-high, bushes erupting from what should have been the reception area, and an elephant-sized grave, half filled with dank water, which would have been the pool. The locals were up-beat, despite how bleak things seemed. It must be a Mediterranean thing. His British genes always seemed to dominate, and he saw only the decay, not the pending opportunities. Next year. Next year.

He disentangled himself from the tin box, but it took most of the walk back to the hotel before his limp disappeared. It never went completely; some days were worse than others. His friends joked he needed a bionic knee. He might consider doing just that, one day.

Fran greeted him, as he walked into reception. She was behind the desk, mobile phone clamped to her ear. She reminded him of a Rottweiler; a mostly friendly one, but the kids who populated her hotel tended to behave. She ended the conversation as soon as she saw him, and came to kiss him on both cheeks, like a true Mediterranean. Her accent was pure Brummie.

"Inspector. It's been ages. You look…" She hesitated. "You look well."

He shrugged, wishing he'd trimmed his beard that morning. His face felt unkempt to his hand. Grey mixed with honey. More grey now. "How's business?"

"Better than bad. Not as great as good. We'll get there. I'm glad you're still here. Everyone is."

"You didn't think I'd last more than one summer?"

"We were surprised you came back in the first place after what happened here ten years ago…" Her voice trailed off as she saw his expression darken. She forced an extra bright smile, "You'll always be a hero to us but for you… finding Chrystos doing what he did when you captured him. No one would have blamed you for never wanting to come back here."

It had been a while since he'd heard the name Chrystos Spiros spoken out loud. The man – the serial rapist - he'd been sent to the Island to catch when the local police had struggled. He hated the reminder.

"He was just another case." Beckett brushed it off, "And an anomaly for Farou. I'm getting old. London was getting too loud and too crowded. I was more than happy to come back and don't intend to go anywhere else now I'm here. A quiet life is what I'm after."

"You've done your 'adrenaline pumping, outwitting the bad guys' bit? For which we are all grateful, of course."

"Ancient history. Now, the missing girl?" He pushed the memories of Chrystos out of his head, trying not to feel resentment at Fran for mentioning him.

"Emmie Archer. Come on. We'll go to her room. The friend who reported her missing is in there." Fran led the way down the corridor away from reception, numbered doors on either side.

"You don't sound worried."

"Her passport and valuables are still in the safe. She's due to get married in a couple of days. Sounds like a case of cold feet and holiday romance to me. The friend who rang you guys is… erm… a sweet girl, but has never been abroad before. Bit naïve about the ways of boys and girls on holiday. I think this whole week has come as a bit of a shock. As worldly wise as a newborn kitten. Not like her mates. I think she's just tagged along. Can't imagine her having much in common with Emmie, or the rest, back at home. They've been out partying hard, as you would expect for a week long hen do. Little Bee's hung around the hotel for most of the week, like a spare part at a Formula One garage."

"Little Bee?"

"That's what they all call her. I think she's a workmate of Emmie's."

They climbed a flight of stairs, and passed more rooms until they reached number 22.

"You think this Little Bee is panicking over nothing?"

"See what you think." Fran rapped on the door and stepped straight in.

Clothes were strewn on the floor and hanging off the wardrobe door, both bed side lamps were listing drunkenly and empty wine bottles were lined up on the dressing table. There was even an unravelled toilet roll snaking out of the bathroom and out onto the small balcony. The room could be read two ways. Either there had been a violent argument or it was a room like a thousand other rooms belonging to wild teenagers-on-holiday in the summer season. Chaotic. Messy. Disgusting even. But, all of this was indicative of nothing more than too much alcohol, and having a thousand or so miles between the occupant and their loving parents. Beckett had seen more than a few, usually when the alleged crime was one of petty theft, but occasionally, something more serious, like sexual assault. No victim here though. Not like last time. He shook away the memory to concentrate on the room in front of him.

Crime scene, or just a crime against tidiness?

"When did you last see Emmie?" He looked at Little Bee. The name was apt. She was tiny. A decent gust of wind would pick her up with ease. She looked barely old enough to be a teenager, face free from makeup, eyes wide, mouth quivering at the corners. She'd refused to sit on the bed, preferring to shift her weight from foot to foot.

"The day before yesterday. In the afternoon. We were on the beach. She said she'd had enough of the sun, and was going for a wander into town."

"Nothing after that? No phone calls, no texts?"

The girl twitched her head, tears not far from the surface, "It's just not like her, you see. She never *doesn't* answer her phone. Or at least text back."

"Don't be a drama queen, Bee. She'll be with that waiter from the Budapest Club. Gorgeous Georgiou. The tall one. They've been flirting with each other all week. She's all in love. Forgotten about us. Her mates. Just like last time." A second girl, maybe a couple of years older, with short cropped, blood red hair and two nose piercings, came into the room, kicking a purple sandal out of the way.

"Jos, don't you care Emmie is missing?"

"But, she's not missing."

"She's done this before?" Beckett cut in.

"A bunch of us were in Mallorca, and she disappeared for three days with a bull fighter called Rui. 'Cept it turned out, he wasn't a bull fighter. He collected the rubbish. A dustbin man. Emmie was well embarrassed when she came back." Jos giggled, and flicked the hair off her face, drilling her eyes into Beckett's. "You a Brit, then? What are you doing out here?"

She was dressed in a barely-there bikini, showing off a belly ring to match those in her nose, and an impressive tan, given her country of origin and the lack of sunshine they'd had that week. She stood in front of Beckett, hands on her hips, smiling, noticing he'd noticed her. She smiled, pupils dilating. Beckett was used to it. He might be old enough to have daughters their age, but on an island of teenage boys and skinny Greek waiters, he stood out, not just in height but in sheer presence. And most of the young women who came here on holiday had only one thing on their mind – sex. Being a thousand miles away from home, with the weather hot and steamy, did crazy things to Western Europeans. His mother had always been proud of his looks, taking after her side of the family, rather than his father's hobbit like appearance, but girls like Jos wouldn't look twice at older blokes like him in a bar in Camden. He shrugged it off, as he always did.

"Isn't she supposed to be getting married in a couple of days?" He looked back at Little Bee.

"Yes. To Warren. Him and his friends are in Rakos – on his stag do. We were all going to meet up at the wedding." Little Bee chewed at one of her finger nails.

"Yet, you think she's ditched all that, and run off with this Georgios?"

"No. She wouldn't do that."

"Why would she want to marry him? He's a dick." Jos

rolled her eyes, and plonked herself onto the nearest bed, leaning back on her elbows. "Specially compared to the locals. Bet you get this a lot. Girls coming here, tapping off with anything Greek, male, with a pulse. You know the type. Not fussy. Anything's better than the blokes at home."

"But, her bloke isn't at home, is he? Why do you think he's a dick?" Beckett looked at her, as she crossed one leg over the other, and flicked one of her sandals under the opposite bed.

"Not very bright. Prefers Sunday morning football to sex. That's what Emmie always whinges about. What sort of bloke would prefer football to sex? Bet you're not like that, Inspector." She kicked off the other sandal, and eyed him like a cat stalking a mouse.

"Could she be with Warren? Perhaps she didn't want to wait another couple of days before she saw him?" Beckett turned back to Little Bee.

"I didn't want to worry him, so I texted one of his friends to see if they'd seen her. They haven't. Definitely not. And she did want to marry Warren. I'm sure. They've been together since school. She's been so excited about coming here. She couldn't wait."

"I'm sure I saw her last night," Jos chipped in. "We were in Cassie's Bar. I looked out, and I thought it was her across the street, in a crowd. It was so busy, by the time I'd got over there, she'd gone. She'll be back when she's sobered up and sexed out. Full of herself and her *Mama Mia* fling."

"I can't believe you're not even worried about her." Bee turned to Beckett. "What are you going to do? Put out a missing person's alert?"

"Keep trying her mobile. And double check with her fiancé. If she's not back by tomorrow, phone me." He rummaged in his trouser pockets, and pulled out a business card.

"Is that all you're going to do?" Bee took the card and

studied the details.

"Have you got a recent photo?" Beckett avoided her gaze.

"Loads of them from this week." Jos flashed another of her smiles at him, "Not all suitable for official police business though."

"I've got some on my phone." Bee glowered at Jos. Beckett felt an ache starting in his left temple. Were young women this bitchy to each other when he was that age and plucking up courage to ask them out? He couldn't remember. His mind drifted to the village festivities and the cold beer that would be in plentiful supply. Time to make a sharp exit.

"Can you text me a couple of good ones Bee? That number on there." He turned to go.

"Please..." Bee's desperation made him stop. There was something about her that made him want to reassure her.

"Call me tomorrow. I'm sure she'll be back by then. Try not to worry. Her phone is probably flat."

"But, it rings out. If it was flat, wouldn't it go straight to voicemail?" There was a tremble in Bee's voice.

"For God's sake. Listen to him. He's the professional. He's heard this story a thousand times. Now, if you don't mind, I need to get poshed up for tonight's challenge. So unless you want to watch me in the shower..." Jos pulled a face at Bee.

"You're such a cow, Jos."

Beckett left them to what he was sure would descend into an argument. He'd been there too long already. It was an hour back to the station, and then another forty minutes to retrace his steps to home.

He told himself it was obvious the bride-to-be had gotten cold feet, and had found a nice warm bed, away from anyone who might talk her down the aisle. Her clueless fiancé was busy drinking himself into a coma all prepared to sober up in a couple of days and enjoy the happiest day of his life. Poor bastard.

As he walked back to the car, Beckett looked across the abandoned building site. Beyond it, and half hidden behind a row of Judas Trees, rose another building–the Sunshine Apartments. He'd forgotten they were so close to the hotel. Three of Spiros' victims had stayed there. Those memories again. He turned away angry at himself. It was a coincidence. Emmie wasn't missing. Nothing bad had happened here today. The Island had already had its monster. The Fiend of Farou, as dubbed by the British newspapers. A rapist and murderer. No one knew that better than Beckett. He'd caught him, ten years ago. The Island had been quiet ever since. That was why Beckett had come back. For the quiet.

CHAPTER TWO

Beckett braced his shoulder muscles, blanked his aching knee, swung the spade, and sliced into the earth at the base of the clump of nettles. Cowering behind was a flatbed trailer, tucked up against the side of the olive press barn. He'd walked past it a hundred times, without ever thinking about it, but somehow, it had registered in his memory. When the crisis erupted down at the village square – someone, no one could agree who, had forgotten to arrange a stage for the band – it had leapt into his thoughts as the obvious solution. Whilst the locals – a good proportion of them being his cousins of once, twice, or more removed – argued in the loud, very Greek way of a barrage of words and waving arms, he drove back up the hill to the farm.

Beckett drew back the spade and swung again. This time, the blade buried itself with a satisfying crunch under the ball of roots, and with a downwards wrench, the nettles were expelled from the ground. There was movement though, from the disturbed soil. He bent down to get closer and narrowed his eyes; it was hard to focus in a low light. What was that? Ants. Black ones. Running around in circles. Disorientated. A few scurried by his boots. Then, without warning, an eruption spewed out from the hole, like black lava. Thousands of ants spreading in all directions.

He recoiled backwards, tripped over a rock, and ended up on his arse. When he got up his hand felt wet. Blood dripped off it, the viscous liquid pooling, hesitating, and then, plummeting to the ground.

"Old fool," he cursed himself.

There was no doubt life was better after a few glasses of Mythos beer. The mind stopped thinking, and the body stopped aching. The more you drank, the better it tasted. Beckett could feel the alcohol seeping through his body, his muscles sighing as they relaxed, and he smiled. What else mattered, other than drink, food and the company of friends?

It was 10pm, and the square was now thronging with people, locals mostly, plus a few of the more adventurous tourists. The air fizzed with their voices. The white plastic chairs and tables, which had invaded the usually tranquil and empty space in front of the butter-coloured face of the Church of St Christopher, had been unoccupied when he'd left to get the trailer. Now, all were claimed. He'd found a lone chair, with a wobbly leg, and had wedged it up against the wall of the old school at the edge of the crowd. There was a low wall to rest his glass and line up the jugs of beer. A few more beers, and he might even feel like dancing.

Every tree and building around the square sparkled with lanterns. The wind was picking up, and the lights bobbed and swayed. The smoke from the two giant-sized barbeques drifted over, teasing noses and stomachs with the scent of sizzling meat. On the stage – the well-disguised, flatbed trailer he'd shed blood for - the band with their guitars, mandolins, clarinets, bouzoukis and drums stood, thundering the whole village in traditional music. Dancers linked arms and swayed like waves on a beach, all moving in the traditional way, whether they were dressed traditionally or not.

Beckett felt an arm clasp around his shoulders. Thakis kissed his head, and sank down onto the wall.

"I told you no one would notice the stage. It works perfectly." Thakis grinned through his pirate-esque beard. If the beard did only one thing to enhance Thakis' appearance, it was to make his teeth look Californian white, and his smile bigger than ever.

Beckett had arrived back in the village later than planned, and tumbled straight into chaos. The chairs and tables had been wrestled back from the residents of Abila, the next village down the mountain, and were being positioned around the square. Vlassis, a third cousin of sorts, was hanging like a spider monkey off a ladder, stringing up the lights, with Tomas, one of Beckett's police sergeants, shouting instructions.

All that was fine, but then someone asked about the whereabouts of the stage. No stage, no band, no festival.

That was when Beckett had asked what they usually did, and when all he got back was blank stares, he'd headed up the hill to get the trailer.

"That won't do, that won't do at all. It won't work." Thakis had sunk his head into his hands in despair, as Beckett had left them.

Surrounded by bales of hay, some empty barrels and pots of flowers, with the band legged up, sound system plugged in, music belting, and the sun retreated behind the horizon, it looked like it had never been anything other than a stage.

"I've been told to get you to dance." Thakis waved across at a cluster of women on the other side of the square. They waved back like a troop of synchronized swimmers. "There are at least five women there who would love to see you dance. Then, Granny Spiro might stop asking me why you haven't chosen yourself a wife. Lots of beautiful women on Farou. And I am getting a headache from people asking me. No one wanted to marry me. I had to plead with Helena. They all want a piece of Beckett Kyriakoulis."

Beckett knew his defences had been lowered by the beer. Sober, he had no desire to complicate his life, but amongst the women Thakis had pointed out was Dr. Elena Mariadas. He hadn't known she was going to be there. She lived in town, and worked at the hospital. Still in her thirties, the Doctor was fourteen years his junior, with an irresistible smile and eyes as brown as conkers. She was the only female Head of Department at the hospital, and the youngest, too. She terrified most of the men on the Island, though they would never admit it. Beckett wasn't scared, but he knew, however hard that smile and those eyes were to remove from his thoughts, he did not need a woman in his life.

"I need more beer."

"Ah harr. Always more beer. And the more beer, the more attractive the women folk become." Thakis sounded like a pirate now, as he grinned, clapping him on the shoulder, and noticing Beckett's beer jug was almost empty, "You need another jug? I'll bring three now. Then, you dance. And then you chose a wife."

Thakis was still chuckling as he was swallowed up by the masses, swaying as he went.

Dancing, like marriage, however infirm you were, was expected on Farou, but more anaesthetic was needed. For the dancing. There wasn't enough beer or even Ouzo on the Island for the other.

"Beckett, come sit with me."

Beckett weaved his way from the bar, yet another jug in one hand, and glass in the other. The voice came from a table, under one of the cherry trees. The lanterns flickered, dancing in the wind, and casting the owner of the voice in light then dark. Beckett recognised him with a smile.

"Father."

Demetri was the village priest. Dressed in his sweeping black robes and long black beard, his orthodoxy was challenged only by the Nike trainers poking out under the hem. In his late thirties, he'd returned to the Island as a newly ordained priest at the same time Beckett had returned to take up the job of Inspector.

"Unruly tourists?" Demetri nodded at the bandage on Beckett's hand.

"Clumsy old policeman." Beckett offered him a drink, but Demetri shook his head.

"How's the job?"

"Looking like it's getting busier." Beckett fished an e-cig from his pocket. It was part of attempt number ten, or was it eleven, to give up smoking, "Do you mind?"

Demetri shook his head. "Summer is here. The Island is waking up. But, you didn't think it would sleep forever?"

Beckett took a gulp of beer.

"Nothing serious?"

"No. I don't think so."

"The museum is reopening next week. You should come. I'll give you a tour. The history of the Island is fascinating."

"Which do you prefer, tour guide or priest?"

"The two are not so different. Ah… I shouldn't really stay for this…"

Beckett realised the music had gone silent, and the square had cleared of dancers, but people lined the edge, waiting for something. He glanced at Demetri, but he showed no inclination to leave.

A lone drum started to beat. Then, another, and another joined in, all following the same revolving rhythm.

"Look, the boubarei." Demetri pointed. The doors of the Church opened, and figures began to appear. Men dressed in white, animal skins cloaked over their backs, hats some adorned with feathers and beaks. Each one had what sounded like a cowbell attached to their belt, and held a stave, waving it aloft, as they danced in time with the drum beat down the church steps. Beckett squinted. All the men seemed to have black faces and hands.

"The goat men. Paganism erupting from the Church of our Lord." Demetri sounded more intrigued than disapproving.

"You had trips to the Island when you were a boy. Did your father not bring you to the festival?"

Beckett remembered now, of course. The goat men. Their strange dancing. The metallic clanking of their bells. Their faces blackened with ashes and grease. He remembered his stomach tightening, the same feeling you got when you jumped into cold water on a hot day. He remembered tears dancing at the corners of his eyes, and looking around for his father, to take his hand, but his father had gone, and when Beckett did see him, he was in the midst of the goat men, having his face smeared with ash, taking hold of one of the clarinets and playing their music.

"Unites us with our primitive past and with nature. They dance around the village, scaring the evil spirits away. Harmless fun."

"Harmless?"

"For those who treat it as such. For those who don't, whatever they chose to believe can be dangerous. Like Chrystos Spiros."

Beckett looked away. What the hell was it with everyone today? Why was Spiros suddenly back haunting him?

"Chrystos was a frightened soul. He'd met the Devil, and survived. But, once you've taken his hand, and looked him in the eye, your mind is damaged. Don't dwell on the past, my friend. You didn't come back here for that."

"Do you believe the Devil is real?"

"Don't you?" There was surprise in Demetri's voice, as if Beckett had said he didn't believe in breathing, or the ground beneath their feet. Then, Demetri grinned. "Come on. Some semblance of sanity has returned."

Demetri was right. The band had taken back control of the music. The goat men had shed their animal skins, and in the camouflage of the evening, had merged in with the crowd. From a distance, you could not distinguish them.

Demetri raised a glass of Retsina, and handed one to Beckett.

"Yamas." Demetri downed his. "Let's go dance."

"Yamas." Beckett threw his head back, and tasted the raw bite of the wine, as it rolled over his tongue, and burned its way down his throat.

"By the way," Demetri dropped into his ear, as they squeezed through the crowd to get to the square. "Those e-cigs. Wolves in sheep's clothing."

Demetri's words were swept away by the music. Beckett linked arms, and joined in the dance. Smiling faces, laughing, shouting. Children and great grandparents, friends, cousins, strangers. Events were starting to dislocate. He danced faster, laughed louder, as did everyone else.

Beckett found himself clasping Dr. Elena, with no idea if he'd grabbed her, or she'd grabbed him. He twirled her under his arm, caught her around her waist, and pulled her close, bending so he could feel her warmth against his cheek. Her eyes on his eyes, firing electricity at him. For a moment, Beckett wished he was sober so his brain could think, interpret, but it was too late for that. The storm was on them, thunder booming around the mountains, lightning cracking above, illuminating faces.

Beckett hung onto Elena, and he felt her hands on his back, each finger a lightning strike, as they whirled on. The band played louder and faster; people around them holding each other, clinging together, moving as one, as if they were a single, continuous living being. The rain finally came, cascading in from the heavens, drenching and soaking all. Even then, no one stopped. Beckett's last clear memory was looking down at Elena, her short, sun-streaked hair dripping diamonds with every lightning bolt. He thought she was the most beautiful creature he'd ever seen, currents of lust coursing through his veins.

His only other memory after that moment was stumbling

out of Demetri's car, shouting a goodbye, and meandering his way to his front door, wondering why there was a cascade of water pooling over his shoes where the path had been. He was most definitely alone.

CHAPTER THREE

The twisted trunks of the trees lean in towards him; branches reach out with twisted, moss-coated fingers to grasp at his arms. It's dark, the light barely breaking through the shield of leaves, and hot. Sweat rolls down his back. Or is it blood? It feels so hot and sticky. There is a whisper, a murmuring. In the gloom, the forest is alive, watching, warning him. He wants to turn around. But, something draws him onwards. He tries to stay silent, as he's been trained, but the forest belies his presence. Branches snap, birds scream.

He reaches the edge of the clearing. He knows what he is about to see, having been here more times than he can count. He doesn't want to look. He doesn't want to step out from between the trees, but he cannot stop himself. He cannot shut his eyes, and he cannot turn away.

There, in the middle of the clearing, Chrystos Spiros. His wild, raven black hair and beard, like a thousand snakes writhing around his face, his eyes staring, full of madness, and his wolf white teeth glistening, as he bites down into the face of another man. The man moans, his legs kicking, as Chrystos rips a lump of flesh from his cheek. The blood dribbles down his chin. He looks Beckett in the eye, and smiles the smile of the monstrously insane.

Beckett snapped awake. A dagger of light stabbed at his eyelids. Where was he? The edges of the dark underworld of sleep and the sun bathed world of reality splintered against each other. The horror of the dream was fresh and vivid. He could still smell the blood. The sweat. His heart was thundering. He took a long breath in. A calming breath, counting to ten, but he only got to three, and there was a shrill noise, like an angry insect.

The real world won. His pillow was vibrating. He pushed the dream away, back into its box. Through half cracked lids,

Beckett sent a hand rummaging under his pillow until his fingers found the phone. His fingers made contact, and dragged it to his ear. His skull felt like it had been split down the middle, and his throat crackled, so he could barely speak.

"Yes?"

A child's voice spoke back to him. "Inspector? It's Police Constable Floros." She sounded scared. This was more than nerves at waking her boss. There was a quiver to her voice. A sickness. Beckett sat up in bed. Nerves firing. Sleep banished. Dread clenching his stomach.

"What's happened?"

"There's a body. Washed up on a beach near Skalia. I'm on my way there now. Sergeant Tomas is already there."

"Sex?" It came out as a whisper.

"Pardon sir?"

"Male or female?" It was a bark this time, betraying his fear.

"Female."

He hung up. "Fuck."

***

Farou was a small island, but there were many places Beckett had never been. There were hundreds of small, secluded beaches on the North East Coast for a start. For many of them, access was such that they had never been developed for commercial purposes, and never would. Many you could only reach by boat, or were privately owned. The body had been spotted washed up on the beach by a passing fisherman, who'd called it in, before continuing on his way to check his nets.

As Beckett drove, too fast, especially considering the amount of water and debris on the roads from the storm, he dialled Little Bee's number. She answered within one ring. The sick feeling was lodged in the pit of his stomach.

"Hello?" Her voice was small, fearful.

"Beatrice? It's Inspector Kyriakoulis. We met yesterday."

"Yes?"

"Has Emmie come back? Got in touch?" He knew the answer, but hoped anyway.

"No. Nothing. You haven't heard anything then?"

Apart from the news the body of a woman had been washed up a few miles around the coast from their hotel? Beckett sighed. "I'll be in touch."

"Thank you. Thank you for calling. I wasn't sure yesterday if you were taking me seriously. The others don't. So, thank you."

There had been many times in his life where Beckett had found cause to hate himself, none more so than now, and always for things he hadn't done. Standing to one side, not acting, only reacting after the event. Leaping in, doing something, was surely better. The times he'd done that he had felt better about. Even if the consequences - his battered body, shattered knee, and termination by the Metropolitan Police - might dispute. Better to do and fail than simply fail. For the first time in a long time, he longed for a cigarette. A living breathing stick of tobacco to fill his lungs, and coat his cells in nicotine. The e-cig was a poor replacement.

Half an hour later, Beckett was barrelling down an overgrown cart track, Grand Canyon-sized ruts sent the car pitching and groaning, like a tall ship in a force nine gale, between the grotesque, twisted trunks of the olive trees. Sergeant Tomas clung to the door handle, trying not to wince, as he was flung against the roof and the dashboard. With a thud, the Evoque's right wing mirror was punched inwards, making Beckett jump. Another few inches, it would have been his front wing versus the tree, but he didn't slow down. He hated the car, but it was the only one which could make an attempt at the track to the beach. The others were parked at the top, just off the road. He hadn't needed Tomas to meet him up there to direct him, but Tomas had thought it would give chance to brief him. As it was, talking was impossible.

Beckett stamped on the brakes, as they came around a bend. The track suddenly narrowed to a few feet. The nose of the car stopped against a barricade of tree trunks.

"We have no choice but to walk from here." Tomas flung himself out, grateful for solid ground.

Beckett found it more difficult. The driving, digging, and the dancing from the day before had taken its toll. After ending the distress phone call, he'd climbed out of bed and collapsed to the floor, his knee screaming. He grabbed his crutch from the back seat.

"Are you going to be okay, sir? It gets steep."

"You lead."

The path was narrow, channels gouged out by winter rain, slippery from last night's storm, and loose rocks. Tomas descended like a mountain goat, using his arms to balance. Beckett used his crutch with one arm, digging it into the rubble trying to find grip, and his other arm to push himself off trees and hang onto branches. It didn't stop him slipping and jibbing. His knee stabbed at every step. The crutch caught on up-turned roots, lost arguments with stones. His back prickled with sweat. His head throbbed, and his stomach churned, the heavy duty painkillers had yet to kick in, but threatened to make a U-turn from his stomach.

"Can I help?" Tomas was waiting for him, eyes clouded with doubt at seeing the frailty of his boss. Tomas had only recently turned thirty. Young for a sergeant but an old head, Beckett's new boss had assured him, with a pedant's eye for detail and procedure, selling him the job, and the team that went with it. "This last bit is…"

"Keep going," Beckett growled between his teeth.

The final ten metres was almost vertical and blocked by

boulders. Tomas clambered around and down, crouching and jumping. Beyond, Beckett could see the golden crown of the beach. Cursing, he javelined his crutch forward over the rocks, and slithered down after it. Dropping onto the beach, he had to take a moment. Tomas held his crutch out to him.

"Just beyond those rocks." He cocked his head, and flicked an imaginary bit of sand off his shirt sleeve. His hand shook, as he did it. Beckett wondered if it was his first dead body. Probably not. There were old people aplenty on the Island, who had a tendency to die at home in their sleep, rather than the Western way, chained up to hospital machines. But, still, a body on a beach. A young girl at that. Tomas' adrenaline was draining away, and shock was taking over.

The beach was a delicate golden crescent, scattered with spears of rocks sticking up from the sand like dragon's teeth. The two headlands leaned in towards each other, perfect twins protecting the bay, making the entrance barely wider than a channel. The sea was peacock blue, as motionless as glass. A miniature paradise.

It would have been very different in the storm. There was evidence on the otherwise perfect beach – piles of seaweed, a tangle of driftwood. And, of course, a body. It, she, was sheltered by rocks, but the top half of Constable Floros was visible wielding the camera, firing off shots. Instinctively, Beckett checked the sand for footprints. He counted three sets going out, and one coming back.

"Yours?" He looked at Tomas.

"Yes. Of course. The body was washed up. No one else has been here. There were no other footprints. I was first one here."

Beckett nodded. He limped towards the rocks, no choice now but to rely on the crutch. Floros looked around, letting the camera strap hang loose around her neck. Her lips moved, warning of his approach. A second person stood up; Elena, Dr.

Mariadas, busy in her role as Director of Pathology. Beckett's stomach flipped over. He forced away the traces of the longing he'd felt for her only a few hours before. She flushed on seeing him, and managed a smile; enough of a smile telling him he'd not stepped out of line last night. He felt conscious of the crutch, his limp, his hungover eyes and mottled stubble. She looked as beautiful as she had at the festival.

"Hello, Inspector."

"Dr. Mariadas." He rounded the edge of the rock, took a moment, a breath, and then looked down at the body.

She was laying on her front, face turned towards the sea, wearing a pale pink summer dress, material so light it was almost transparent. Her hair veiled her face, obscuring her features, the blonde strands crusted with gold and fragments of seaweed. He couldn't see any blood, or bruising. It was as if she'd curled up on the sand and fallen asleep.

He'd seen many dead bodies, too many, more than most people. He didn't mourn for them; how could you mourn for someone you'd never met and didn't know? But, it didn't matter how many, or how culpable they'd been in their demise. He felt the same dark, leaden sadness. The human body, so frail, so easily snuffed out. Just another empty shell, another lump of flesh and bone to be stared at, poked, prodded, and then buried, left to rot, or burned and scattered into the wind, and finally forgotten. It was that utter loneliness in death which caught in his throat; the ache of sadness weighing down on his shoulders, so much so, he thought his feet might sink into the sand. Death was something you greeted alone, whether you ran towards it or fought to escape. In the end, it was just you and death. Inevitable, hopeless, and pointless.

He thought about Little Bee, how worried she'd been, and how he'd fobbed her off. How he'd been more focussed on getting back for the Festival. How much he'd drunk, eaten, and laughed the night before. All that time, this poor girl was dead, or dying.

"Can't tell you much until I do a post mortem, but she hasn't been dead longer than 24 hours. No obvious cause of death, though one would leap to the conclusion of drowning. There is some bruising around her neck."

Elena crouched down, her body language inviting Beckett to join her. He grimaced, but kept the pain silent. With a gentle hand, she lifted enough of the girl's hair to show a dappled reddening of the pale skin under her jaw. *Strangulation marks?* He looked at Elena. She shrugged.

"The sea was violent last night. Tossed around in that, it's hardly surprising she's bruised."

"Except she's not. Apart from that." He had to stand, and put some space between him and the girl. He felt unsettled. It crept under his skin.

"Let's turn her and see." Elena motioned for Floros to help. Tomas was hanging back, and Floros went to pass him the camera. As they waited, Elena gazed at Beckett, the warm welcoming pool of those soft brown eyes, tempting him in.

"Poor kid. She doesn't look much more than a teenager. She doesn't look Greek, so probably a tourist."

Beckett nodded. "There was a missing person reported yesterday. A girl. Most of her friends weren't worried. I sided with them."

"What?" Her gaze tempered. Her body stiffened. A chasm opened up between them.

"They thought, *I* thought, she was having a good time."

"You knew there was a girl missing yesterday, and you did *nothing?*" She did nothing to hide the accusation and disappointment from her eyes. She crouched back down, as Floros re-joined them.

"Ready?"

Floros nodded and gently, as if the body were made from

the finest porcelain, they rolled her onto her back.

Beckett's breath caught in his throat. The girl's hair now surrounded her head like a halo.

"What is this girl's name, then? We can begin to treat her with more respect." Elena's eyes glinted. Her shoulders bristled with anger.

"I don't know." Beckett replied.

"You took a missing person's report, and can't even remember her name?" Floros was looking at him now, too. More accusations. More disappointment.

"The missing girl is called Emmie Archer." He knelt down, even though he was already certain. He had the photos on his phone; the ones sent by Little Bee, "But, this isn't her."

CHAPTER FOUR

ee's knuckles were white on the handles of the moped.
She'd seen locust swarms of people – Island visitors just
like her – buzzing up and down the streets of Nikisiopi
since she'd arrived, brown ankles flying, crash helmets crooked
on elbows. It had looked easy.

Stamatis, of Stamatis' Scooters, had reassured her, as he'd
swiped her debit card. "It's as easy as riding a bicycle." He
beamed at her.

"I haven't ridden a bicycle since I was ten. And I wasn't
very good at it then."

"But, you never forget. Everything will be fine. I promise
you."

It didn't help. In the week Bee had been on the Island,
she'd learned the locals' over riding outlook on life was,
'everything will be fine.' She was convinced even if an asteroid
was hurtling down on them, they would still smile, shrug their
shoulders to the sky, and say, "Don't worry, it will be fine."

Despite his outward optimism, Stamatis had walked her
past a whole row of gleaming mopeds, with shapely curves and
futuristic headlights, and stopped next to a faded pink relic from
Quadrophenia. The paint was chipped and scratched, with a
skull-sized dent on one side, and a rip in the black leather seat,
patched down with duct tape.

"This one is perfect for you."

Bee couldn't disagree. Stamatis had handed her the key,
and helped her push the crash helmet onto her head.

He'd been less helpful with directions to Georgiou's
farm.

He had closed his eyes, as if in deep thought.

"Why do you want to go there? Georgiou works in the Budapest Club. He will be there tonight. You should wait until then. Mopeds are for town and beach, not for the hills."

"I know where he works. I need to visit him at home. See if my friend is there."

"Your friend? What does she look like?"

Bee felt a spike of hope.

"About my height. Long, blonde hair. Green eyes. Pretty. I have a photo. Here."

She pushed her phone towards him. He glanced.

"Very pretty."

"You haven't seen her then? With Georgiou?"

"I see Georgiou with a lot of girls in the summer."

"At his house?"

"Sometimes."

"Great. How do I get there?"

"The roads are steep and dangerous. There are wild animals in the hills."

Shouting from the road behind them made them look around. A jeep flew past, sardined full of at least eight lads, some standing up hanging off the roll bars, arms and legs everywhere, like a giant octopus. The occupants were howling at the sun and barking like hyenas.

Stamatis sighed. "Follow the signs to Massouri Village, then turn right just after the pink house, and go up the hill. Keep going until you find it."

"That sounds easy enough."

"It will be fine."

Bee wobbled up the main strip, impatient cars blaring at her, passing so close, she was almost swept into their passenger seats. A dozen times, she nearly turned back. She would have done, if she hadn't been doing this for Emmie. If the tall, handsome detective, with his kind eyes and sad smile, was making the effort, phoning her so early on a Sunday, then it was only right and proper she did the same.

She'd been worried about him at first, about his abilities. He hadn't seemed interested. Hadn't even bothered to shave. Even whilst he'd been talking to her, he'd seemed absent.

After Inspector Kyriakoulis had gone, Fran had put her arm around her and squeezed, telling her not to worry. Kyriakoulis was the best at what he did. He'd worked all over the world, and before joining the Greek police, had been in the Army, Special Forces no less, and the Metropolitan Police. If Emmie was missing, Inspector Kyriakoulis would find her. Jos had cheapened things, as usual.

"Sexy or what?" She'd smirked after he'd gone. "In a battered, Liam Neeson in *Taken* kind of way. Did you see that scar on his neck? Definitely a knife wound. Bet he got it from taking out some freaking terrorist. He won't take shit from anyone. I quite fancy being a sugar baby. Might even let him fuck me."

"You're disgusting."

"What's his phone number?"

"Like I'd tell you."

"No wonder Emmie's done a runner. Fed up of you sniffing around after her. It was getting on her nerves. She only invited you along as a charity project, because she felt sorry for you. 'Little Bee never goes anywhere. She hasn't got any friends.' You haven't got any friends, because you're a stuck-up bitch. Simples."

Bee spent a sleepless night alone in the hotel, listening to the echoes of music and voices from outside. She was the only person from work Emmie had invited to the wedding. Surely that meant Emmie counted her as a friend?

She'd avoided breakfast, not wanting to talk to anyone. It was only when her phone spluttered into life, and she heard the Inspector on the other end, she had felt motivated to act. His voice was hypnotic and reassuring. Wouldn't he be impressed, grateful even, if she, useless Little Bee, went out, and tracked down her friend? Jos would have to apologise, and Emmie would give her a hug and thank her for caring.

Cars flew past in both directions, sharing snippets of conversations and blasts of music. The sun was beginning to throw out serious heat, and the puddles from last night's storm had all but evaporated, making Bee's progress less like a slalom course. Her confidence was growing, and she even twisted the throttle up another notch. Stamatis' directions were working. The village of Massouri opened up to greet her, a Taverna on one side and a shop on the other, a splash of colours terraced in front – fruits and vegs, flowers, and pots of honey. The road narrowed and started to climb, as it wound between buildings, villas leaned in towards each other, whites, pinks, yellows, and blues, sagging chain link fences holding back empty spaces of weeds. New cars squeezed into spaces next to rusting ancestors, branches and leaves sprouting through windscreens.

Rounding a bend, Bee came nose to nose with a tourist bus. She felt her heart thumping louder than the thunder cracks from the night before. She stopped, the bus stopped, engine growling, the driver's mouth moving in what she interpreted as a curse. The bulk of the bus made the houses look elfin. How could it ever fit between the buildings? She shuffled the moped into the gateway of the nearest villa, tucking herself in as far as she could, closing her eyes and squeezing her shoulders together, as it passed. She could smell the stink of the exhaust, and her skin prickled with the heat from the engine. Then, it was gone, and in front of her was a salmon-painted, three storey villa, sitting on the edge of what, if you were generous, was a side road. 'Turn right at the pink house,' Stamatis had said. This had to be it. There was no signpost, but it climbed away from the village. Bee took a deep breath, and pointed the moped up the hill.

At first, the road was kind to her. The houses disappeared, replaced by olive trees. To her left, between their twisted trunks and branches, she caught glimpses of the sea, falling away below her. She stopped at a clearing, so hot inside the helmet her head was throbbing, and sweat was blinding her eyes. She yanked the helmet off, skin drinking in the soothing touch of the breeze. She absorbed the view below—diamond sparkles of dancing waves, silver trails from jet skis, postage stamp white sails of boats, and the multi-coloured patchwork quilt of parasols on the beach. It made Bee think of the model village her parents liked to take her to when she was small. 'Have a giant time in a miniature world,' it used to say on the sign at the entrance.

"Seasoned moped rider now," she praised herself, as she hooked the helmet through her arm, certain her destination was close. Emmie wouldn't believe her eyes when she saw Bee whizzing into view. On a moped, on her own, miles from the hotel. Bee felt her mouth curl into a grin.

An hour later, she felt like crying. The road had twisted inland underneath the canopy of the olive groves and cypress trees. The branches entwined to shut out the sun, letting only a dust-encrusted, emerald light percolate through. It was like being underwater. Without the sun, her skin tingled with cold. She didn't want to stop in this gloom-shrouded place, almost afraid she'd drown beneath the surface of the leaves. Is this where all the wild animals lived, the ones she'd been warned about? It was too dark beneath the trees to see any movement swimming towards her, but she could hear noises. Disembodied screeches and warning whistles. *Just birds*, she told herself, *just birds,* and kept going.

Eventually, with panic creeping into her throat, she convinced herself she must have missed the turn off to Georgiou's farm. It couldn't be this far. She'd heard him tell

Emmie he lived just outside of town. Without stopping, she traced a semi-circle in the road, sticking one leg out for balance, and started back the way she'd come.

The trees seemed to have leaned even further over the road, their branches pressing down over head, as if any moment, they would swing down to crush her. Bee was cold, but sweat trickled down her back. Then, something green and dragon-like darted out from behind a tree and scurried in front of her tyre. She braked, and yanked the handle bar, twisting one way, and then, as she tried to recover, the other. Balance was gone. She saw a small, green lizard scuttle into the undergrowth, as the moped bucked, wobbled, and flipped over.

It was hopeless. The front tyre was mangled, burst and flapping loose from the rim. Bee hadn't been travelling very fast, and, apart from a graze on her left elbow, was unscathed, but her hands shook, as if seismic waves were coursing through them. The pocket, where her phone had been, was empty, but she saw it straight away, propped up against the snatching roots of a tree. The screen was splintered into a schizophrenic pattern, and there was no response when she pressed the power button. Dead.

"Can I help? Are you alright?" A voice behind her sent her spinning around.

A man, keeping his distance, stood in the road. His eyes crinkled at her, one hand scratching his short, grey beard. He wore a sparkling white shirt, sleeves rolled up his arms, contrasting against his rich man's tan. A heavy gold watch wrapped his wrist. Behind him, was his car. A gleaming crouching tiger. Bee recognised the Porsche badge. *How did she not hear him drive up?* Fear welled up in her stomach.

"Hello?" He stepped nearer, and a sob burst from her mouth. Once the first was released, she couldn't stop the sobs pouring out of her body.

"Jesus. Do you want me to call someone?"

"I…no… how did you… I don't even know where I am." The words came out in strangled gasps.

"Did you hit your head? Were you knocked out?" He edged closer. She stood up, rough skin of the tree pressed up against her back.

"No. I'm fine." Her body screamed at her to run, but it would be hopeless. He was late fifties, but looked fit, like he ran five miles every morning before breakfast. She'd seen enough TV shows to know that being chased through woods ended up with the girl tripping over, crashing to the floor, and then fading to black, as the monster caught up with her.

He was close enough now she could smell his aftershave.

"Your bike looks knackered." He set it upright, examining the front tyre, "Are you on your own?" He was very British, public school accent.

"I'm on my way to my friend's place. He lives just down the road."

"Out here? Are you sure?"

She nodded. The man was staring at her. His eyes were the colour of the sea. The edges of his mouth curled upwards, like he was permanently amused by life. There was something familiar about him, like she'd seen him before somewhere, perhaps an advert in a glossy magazine for posh cars or expensive watches.

"Who is your friend? I might know him. I own a lot of the land around here. In fact, I think you'll find that's my tree."

Bee stood upright.

"Sorry."

"It's fine. I was trying to be funny. Lighten the mood. Failing miserably."

"Oh."

"Your friend's name?"

"Georgiou."

"Surname?"

"Don't know."

"Where's his place?"

"I, erm… I've never actually been. He works in the Budapest Club in Nikisiopi. His family have an olive farm…"

The man grinned.

"Georgiou, the creator of the best cocktails in the North of the Island? I know the family. But, their farm is miles away." He looked back up the road, the direction his car was facing away from. "You were going the wrong way."

Bee felt herself flush, but her heart was slowing, the sense of danger ebbing. Now, she just felt stupid.

"I'll take you, if you like? It's about fifteen minutes away."

"I can't leave the bike. It's not mine." She felt the tears pressing on the back of her eyes again.

"We'll put it in the back of the car. That okay?"

She nodded.

"I'm Mitchell, by the way. Mitchell Troy. Mitch, to my friends." He stuck out his hand. He caught her in his gaze. It was impossible to look away.

They peered into the back of his Porsche. It was a four seater, and the back seats were already folded forward out of the way. It still looked like a 'square peg, round hole' moment.

"Someone at work has one of these," she offered.

"Nice cars. Designed for golf clubs, not stricken mopeds. Don't worry. We'll squeeze it in."

He lifted the bike, as if it weighed nothing, and with a bit of shunting, manoeuvred it as far into the boot as it would go. The tail gate wouldn't shut, but he gave the moped an experimental jiggle.

"It's not going to shift anywhere. Come on. Jump in."

Bee hesitated.

"I won't bite. Promise. Everyone on the Island knows

me. You're perfectly safe."

Cocooned inside, she sunk into the seat, and brushed her hand on the cool, cream leather.

"Okay?"

Bee nodded. Mitchell started the car. Nothing happened. But, they were moving.

"Running on electric."

"That's why I didn't hear you drive up."

"Sorry. Stealth mode. You've got to do your bit for the planet. So you met Georgiou in the nightclub?"

"Not me. My friend, Emmie. I'm looking for her."

"So, you hired a moped, drove all the way out here, not really sure where you were going. Wouldn't it have been easier to give her a ring?"

"She's not answering her phone."

"Signal is usually good up at Georgiou's."

"She's just not answering. She's supposed to be getting married in a couple of days."

"Ah. But, she's fallen for Georgiou?"

"I don't know. I hope so."

"You don't like her husband-to-be?"

"No, because if she isn't with Georgiou, I don't know where she is."

"You're worried about her?"

Bee nodded, watching the trees slip by.

"I'm sure she'll be fine."

"That's what everyone thinks, including the police."

"Who did you speak to?"

"Inspector Kyriakoulis. Do you know him?"

"Of course. We all know each other on this Island."

"You're not a tourist, then? You're from England."

"Business over there. Home here."

"How hard can it be to find someone in such a small place? I don't understand why she hasn't called me."

"I'm sure she just wants a bit of space. Getting married is a big step. I'm guessing she's not much older than you?"

"She's being going out with Warren since they were fifteen."

"Childhood sweethearts, like my parents. Didn't spend more than a day apart, from the time they met at sixteen, to when they died."

"So it can work then?"

Mitchell glanced at her. "Not often. So, Bee, what do you do when you're not on holiday taking part in hen dos?"

"Not very exciting. I work for the Department of Business. That's where I met Emmie."

"Wow. I'm impressed. At the heart of Government."

"Not really. I'm a junior researcher. I mostly make the tea."

"I'm sure that's not true. You're obviously bright and resourceful."

Bee's cheeks felt hot. She turned her head, so he wouldn't see her blushing.

"See much of your boss? The Secretary of State?"

"He doesn't know I exist. Emmie's done some work for him. She's a senior researcher. She's really good. They love her."

"I'm sure they love you, too."

Bee shook her head. She could feel Mitchell's eyes on her.

"Your modesty is quite disarming, Beatrice. Ah, here we are."

The car turned down a gravel track cut between the swamps of olive groves. There was no sign, no name, no number. Bee wondered how Stamatis had thought she would ever find it.

An ancient woman, dressed in black, was sitting on the steps of a low slung, amber-coloured house. Her body was so twisted Bee wondered how she'd ever be able to stand up, and her face so etched with lines, it was impossible to tell if her eyes were open. Her gnarled hands were scrubbing away at a white sheet–the only sign she was alive.

A couple of large, angry dogs came hurtling out from the shade of the trees.

"Stay here. I'll see if Georgiou's around."

Bee wanted to warn him about the dogs, but he didn't seem the sort of person who wanted, or needed, looking out for. At first, Jos found her constant need to look after people funny. After a couple of days, she'd said it was driving her mental.

"Fine if you don't want to live a little, but the rest of us do. You're like a walking health and safety manual. It's really fucking boring."

The dogs charged at Mitchell, but he didn't seem to notice. Their body language changed as they scampered around his feet, tails wagging. He disappeared around the back of the house. Bee stared at the woman. Her hands, like twigs bound together with leather, scrubbing at the cloth, back and forth, back and forth, even though the cloth looked clean. Bee felt fear at the back of her throat, her imagination conjuring up images of witches, cauldrons, and spells.

Then, Mitchell reappeared. The antelope like figure of Georgiou next to him, those magic hands which juggled cocktails waving like flags, as he talked to Mitchell.

"I haven't seen her since Wednesday night. You were all in the Club. You know yourself it was busy. I didn't get chance to talk to her."

Out of the car, Bee felt vulnerable. The old woman had scuttled crab-like off the step, and gone inside, but Bee could feel her eyes on her from one of the dark windows. The dogs weren't so subtle. Lying in a row, heads resting on their giant paws, watching her, looking hungry. But, however creepy the place, she wished Emmie was there.

"You're certain you haven't seen her?" Mitchell cut in.

Georgiou regarded him for a few moments, a flash of

something – irritation perhaps – crossing his face. "Sorry. I have no idea where she could be."

"If you do hear from her, can you let Bee know?"

"Sure."

"And the police," Bee added.

Georgiou's eyes darkened. "The police?"

"I've reported her as a missing person. They're looking for her now."

"Okay. If I see her. Look, I really have to get on. I'm due at the Club in a few hours, and I have jobs around the farm to do first."

As they drove away, Bee watched Georgiou's reflection in the wing mirror. He stood, a dog on either side of him, all three staring at the car.

"They're a good family. If he knew where she was, he'd tell you."

"But, if she's not here, where is she?"

"I know it's hard, but try not to worry. She might have turned up by now. Do you want to ring Kyriakoulis?"

"I broke my phone."

"You're not having a good day, are you? I think I've got his number."

He pressed a button on the steering wheel.

"Call Beckett Kyriakoulis."

"Calling Beckett Kyriakoulis," a polite, digital woman replied.

A dial tone pulsed out over the car speakers. There was a click, and another polite, digital woman answered. "You have reached the voicemail of Beckett Kyriakoulis. Please leave a message."

"Beckett. This is Mitchell Troy. I'm with Beatrice. She reported her friend, Emmie, missing yesterday. We've been up to

Georgiou Nicoli's place, where Beatrice thought she might be. She isn't there. Beatrice wanted you to know. If you've got any news, please phone Beatrice as a matter of urgency. Thank you."

Mitchell killed the call.

"Kyriakoulis is a competent police officer. He'll find her. But, if you do need any help, give me a shout. I'm good friends with his boss. And his boss' boss."

Mitchell insisted on dropping Bee at the hotel, and taking the moped back to Stamatis himself. As much as Bee tried to argue, Mitchell cut her off.

"He shouldn't have rented you such a death trap. These older bikes are much harder to drive than the new ones. No wonder you had a spill."

Less than an hour later, Bee had just climbed out of the shower, when Fran knocked at her door. "This has just arrived for you." She passed her a box—a brand new Samsung Galaxy S7.

"Who?" Bee blinked at her.

"A lad who works in one of the phone shops in Farou Town. Said he'd been told to deliver it here. Who's buying you mobile phones, Bee?"

Bee shrugged and shut her door. Sitting on the bed, she prised the SIM card from her shattered phone, and transferred it. The new phone woke up, and smiled at her. She tapped in the number from the business card Mitchell Troy had pressed into her hand when he dropped her at the hotel, and typed, *Thanks. I'll pay you back. For everything. Beatrice.*

Within a few seconds, the phone pinged back with the message. *No need. Happy to help. Keep in touch. M.*

Bee lay on her bed, phone clasped to her chest, and drifted into a fitful sleep, full of lurking monsters and dark alleyways with no escape.

CHAPTER FIVE

"So, we've got an unidentified girl, who drowned in the storm last night, washed up on a beach, and a missing British tourist? And they are definitely not one and the same person?" Hydna Petrakis, Chief of Police and Beckett's boss, leaned her elbows on her desk, and pierced his eyes with hers. She wasn't happy.

"We don't know the cause of death, yet. Not until we've got the results of the post mortem. But, definitely not the same person."

"She was found on the beach. Most likely an accidental drowning, then? Too much to drink, fell off a boat, swept away by sea, and then, onto the beach."

"Most likely, but there's some bruising around her neck. I'm not sure. It doesn't feel… right."

"We don't work on feelings, Beckett." She sent her chair skidding backwards, and started pacing the office. "This is not good. This is not good at all."

She was about to turn sixty, but looked ten years younger. A blanket of mahogany hair framed her masculine face. She'd once been described to Beckett as having the ability to charm the birds from the trees, before crushing them beneath her fists. Nothing he'd experienced so far made him doubt that for a minute.

Beckett wished she get on with whatever she wanted to say, and let him get on with his work. The situation was starting to spin out of control. He should have had a grasp on things by now, the scene, the victim, the way forward, but he felt only panic, spreading like a spider's web in his gut.

"Who is she?" She parted the Venetian blinds with two

fingers, and peered down to the street below.

"There was no form of ID on the body. We've taken fingerprints and DNA to see if we can run a match on any of the databases. If nothing comes back from that and no other missing person is reported, we'll have to go public. Put out an appeal. And an appeal for the girl we know is missing, Emmie Archer."

"Not a chance." The blinds snapped back like a whip cracking. "We can't have this splashed all over the papers and the web. Publicity like this, it'll scare off the tourists. The Island can't afford it. We are struggling already. You've heard of the economic crisis we are having?"

"But…"

"We can't have people scared of coming here, cancelling holidays. You know how it was last time. It destroyed the tourist season. You might have caught the Fiend, but the damage was done for many. And memories are long. One whiff of something, and the journalists will be dragging up his name, and we'll have a deserted island for the summer."

"But, if this was an accidental drowning, as you think…"

"I know you, Beckett." She sat on her monolithic desk next to him, voice softening. "Your instincts. If this doesn't feel right, then… God help us."

She went back to the window.

"You're the most talented detective I've ever worked with. Figure out who the dead girl is, and what happened to her. Track down this Emmie Archer, and deliver her back to her husband-to-be, in time for the wedding. And make sure this Island has a peaceful, and profitable, summer."

"If the dead girl's death wasn't accidental, if Emmie Archer hasn't simply got cold feet, or if there's any connection, we need to find Emmie, and we will need the media's help."

"No." Petrakis' eyes flashed. "You will *not* go to the press, until I *say* go to the press. Find another way."

***

Beckett rested on his stick in the corridor, and listened to his voicemail from Mitchell Troy. He replayed it a few times, as white-coated people hurried by; his brain wouldn't process what he was hearing. Mitchell Troy. He recognised that self-satisfied tone, without the need for any introductions, but not on his phone. And not in connection to this mess. How the hell did he know Bee? Did that mean he knew Emmie, too?

"Hey. Kyriakoulis." Elena stood, hands on hips, a few feet away. "Are you interested in this post mortem, or not?"

"Sorry." He hobbled towards her, "Voicemail message from Mitchell Troy. You know him?"

"A little. Everyone knows Mitchell, don't they?"

"Not if they've got any sense. He's been out looking for the missing girl."

"Good, as the police don't seem to have been doing much." Elena held open the door to the Pathology department.

Beckett ignored the remark. "I don't know how he's connected. Nothing's been made public yet."

"Why the hell not?"

"We don't want to cause a panic. Not yet. Not until we know more about what's going on."

She gave him a dark look. Her opinion of him as a human being was rotting away. "Perhaps this will focus your mind."

He followed her into the autopsy suite. They were in the basement of the hospital. Light hazed in from frosted windows running around the top of the walls. Gunmetal grey cabinets lined one wall. Sinks, work surfaces, mysterious tubes, and a sadistic array of tools lined the other walls. In the middle of the room, the body of the dead girl rested on a table under the arm of a giant spotlight, almost like a sacrifice to the forensic science gods.

The post mortem had been completed. The Y-shaped

incision, which ran from both shoulders and down to her pubic bone, had been stitched back in place, and the flesh cleaned. The floor glinted, having recently been cleaned, and the blood washed away.

Elena stood at the far side of the body. Beckett hung back.

"No match on the finger prints or DNA, but this might help you." She beckoned him forward.

Embracing the victim's left breast, was a tattoo. A grape vine was rooted underneath, and unfurled its tendrils up and around the nipple, carrying fists of bursting, succulent grapes. Each fruit looked so ripe, like you could reach down, pluck, and eat them. Anchoring the vine was a brown staff, topped with a bristling pinecone. The death of the canvas had done nothing to dull the vitality of the artwork. In fact, the paleness of her skin served only to enhance it.

"This is high end work. Very expensive. Not many tattoo artists have this much talent. I'm pretty sure none of the tattooists on the Island could produce work like this. You'd have to go to Athens, London, Paris, for something this good."

"How does that help me? You've just widened the search to a global scale."

"You put a photo of that tattoo out on the web, and you'll have the artist within a few hours."

"What else have you got?"

"These are definite ligature marks." Elena flicked on the spotlight, and pulled it closer to the body.

The marks were obvious now the girl was laying on her back, sand washed away.

"See how the imprint is pointed in an upwards direction. She's been hanged; the width of the ligature marks indicates quite a wide cloth of some kind. Not a rope or a cord. But, strangulation is not the cause of death. There's no damage to the trachea. It was done carefully, to avoid permanent damage. And this bruising is a few days old, certainly inflicted well before she died."

"Why would anyone do that?"

"Erotic asphyxiation is a possibility. She'd certainly had sex at some point in the last 48 hours. We found semen. We should have the DNA profile within a couple of hours."

"Forced?"

"No bruising or tearing, but there were high levels of dimethyltryptamine in her system."

"Dimethyltryptamine? DMT?" he cut in.

"Yes." She frowned at him. "Mean something to you?"

He shrugged it away. It did mean something, and it sent a chill through his veins. "Her grasp on reality would have been…?"

"Tenuous, to say the least. It looks like we weren't the only ones partying hard last night. But, the DMT wasn't the cause of death either."

"She did drown then?"

"Yeah, but not in the way you're thinking. She was dead *before* she went in the water. I didn't spot it until I opened her up. Cause of death was a haemothorax; She drowned in her own blood. It's obvious when you look at her lungs, but the cause is much harder to find. The tattoo doesn't help. Look. Here."

Elena touched her gloved fingers to the skin, just under the left breast, stretching it taunt. Beckett bent lower. He'd never have seen it, if Elena hadn't pointed it out. Camouflaged by one of the wine-coloured grapes, a circular wound, only a few millimetres across, punctured the skin, angled upwards towards the lungs.

"The weapon was long, thin, and very sharp. Like a knitting needle or a skewer? It penetrated the thorax, ruptured the serous membrane, and into the lungs. Blood loss was massive. It spilled into the pleural space, effectively drowning her. She would have been dead within ten minutes, or so. And if that hadn't killed her, the blood loss would have done."

Beckett stared down at the body. The girl's voice was silent, but everything about her told a story.

"She would have suffered a great deal. Her lungs would have felt like they were being crushed, her heart about to explode, and the panic, as she tried to breath and couldn't—the most primeval of instincts denied to her. It's a horrible terrifying way to die." Elena's gaze pierced into his soul. "Find out who did this to her, before they do it to someone else."

"There's no reason to think this has any connection to the missing girl." Beckett said it as much to persuade himself Emmie was safe and happy, as it was to convince Elena. He failed on both counts.

"How can you know that, when you don't even know who this is? I thought this work was important to you? I thought the victims were important to you? This isn't about what your boss wants, or what might be the best for the tourist industry. This is about one murdered girl and one missing girl. And you. You have to find who did this. And stop them." Her eyes burned at him, her whole body radiating anger.

Beckett knew she was thinking he wasn't the man she thought he was, the big brave cop, the man who had saved people. Not anymore. He bowed his head, wishing he didn't now have to ask her a massive favour. He hated to do it.

"I need you to do something for me."

Fifteen minutes later, they were in a treatment room in the part of the hospital where the living, not the dead, hung out. He was sitting on the edge of a bed, in his boxer shorts, and Elena was drawing some clear liquid into a small needle.

"Forget about the anaesthetic." With his trousers draped over a nearby chair, he felt pathetic and vulnerable.

"Don't be an idiot. I'm not going to swoon over your bravery." She jabbed his knee with the local, and then turned to prepare the steroid injection. He turned his head away, not wanting to think about the size of the needle.

"I'm not happy about doing this."

"You said."

"When did you last have your knee injected?"

"About a month ago."

"You know they give less relief the more you have."

"I know."

"And using them too often can damage the cells that manufacture cartilage, making your long-term pain much worse."

"I know that, too."

She gave him a look, as if to say the consequences would be nothing less than he deserved. "Okay, ready?"

He nodded, and gripped the edge of the table with both hands.

***

In the hospital car park, Beckett dialled Little Bee's number. The pain in his knee was like a thousand razor blades being jabbed in and twisted around, but he knew in a few hours, the pain would dissolve away. Relief was temporary, but should last long enough to deal with this case.

After a few rings, it clicked over to voicemail. "Beatrice, this is Inspector Kyriakoulis. I need to update you on a few things. I'll come to the hotel. I'll be there in a couple of hours. Apologies for it being so late."

He rang off. He'd wanted to warn her off Mitchell Troy, but didn't know what to say. In his job, you dealt in evidence. Facts. Physical events. *How did you explain you had a "feeling" about someone?*

At least he had some facts to tell her. Beckett needed to forewarn her about the dead girl. Reassure her there was no known connection to the whereabouts of Emmie, though he was getting increasingly worried. He'd sent Tomas to Georgiou's place, who'd confirmed what he'd told Mitchell. Tomas was certain there was no cause to doubt him. Georgiou was from a good family, not that it meant anything. Beckett had been told that before. The Spiros had been a good family, poor but respected on the Island, but they had still produced a son like Chrystos. This was different, though. He knew Georgiou – not well, but enough to have an idea about the sort of man he was, and what he might or might not do. Chrystos Spiros had been in trouble with the police practically from when he could walk. Only petty crimes like theft, hurling stones at dogs, peeping through windows but petty crimes often escalate and Beckett's instinct had pointed him towards Chrystos from the first time he'd picked up the case files.

The tourist police in Rakos had spoken to the hotel where the fiancé was staying. They'd flashed Emmie's photo around. She definitely wasn't there. No one recognised her, but they knew Warren. He and his stag mates were raucous and visible. It was safe to say, Emmie hadn't stolen her way down there, because she couldn't wait until the wedding. She was nowhere. And Mitchell's voice on his answer phone wouldn't leave him alone.

"Lovely to see you as ever, Beckett." Kandace Anastas, editor-in-chief of the *Farou News*, kissed both his cheeks before sitting down. He'd lead her to a table in the back of a café on the main street. "And I would never complain about getting a phone call from you on a Sunday evening, but this is all very mysterious. I'm still a married woman."

She said it with a playful grin. Her pupils and the flush of her cheeks told Beckett she'd been drinking. She was mid-seventies, as glamorous as a Hollywood actress, and her husband, number four, was younger than Beckett. She'd been one of the most vociferous journalists in Athens. Taking over the *Farou News* was her version of retirement.

"It's good to see you, too, Kandace. Life treating you

well?"

"Better than you, I see. You're lamer than when I last saw you. You really need to get that knee fixed."

"One day." He shrugged. He could feel the steroids starting to work their magic fingers. The knee already felt looser. In a few hours, his limp would be almost gone.

"And stop throwing yourself off buildings."

He felt himself go cold.

"Once a journalist, always a journalist. Not relevant to the here and now, though, is it?" She touched his arm, "So, what can I do for you?"

"I need your help. And your discretion."

"This is a story, I take it? I might be an old woman now, but I'll die a journalist. The story always comes before discretion."

"A few hours are all I need."

"Go on. I'll do what I can. What's happened?" The flirtation had gone. Her face pressed towards his, eyes hungry for the story, her journalist synapses firing into life.

His phone burst into life. It was Tomas.

"Sorry." He held up his hand in apology, and turned his head away.

"Boss, a guy has just come into the station to report his girlfriend is missing. He's been on the mainland for the last few days. Got back this morning. Says she hasn't been at work, and none of her friends have seen her. She's not answering her phone. He's very worried. It's not like her, he says. I asked him what she looked like. Twenty-three, blonde, about five foot one, and has a tattoo on her chest."

"I'll be there now."

Beckett hung up. His heart racing.

"Well?"

"I've got to go. I'm really sorry, Kandace." He got to his

feet.

"What about my story? What were you going to tell me?"

"I promise. I'll speak to you tomorrow. Please. It's nothing. Until I speak to you again."

"Inspector!" she called after him, making the other diners turn their heads, but he barely heard her. The adrenaline was coursing through him. Finally, something he could do.

CHAPTER SIX

Beckett watched the man for a moment through a crack in the blinds. The door to his office was closed, and Tomas was sitting in Beckett's moth-eaten chair, waiting. He had told Tomas to use his office. Both official interview rooms were slate walled, slit windowed boxes in the basement, not conducive to a relaxed or informal atmosphere, especially to someone who was already on edge. The man, the boyfriend, was drumming his left foot on the floor, his hands alternately in his lap, on the desk, scratching his head, rubbing his thighs. The snapping open of the door made him start, head swivelling. Tomas jumped to his feet.

"Hello. I'm Inspector Beckett Kyriakoulis." Beckett offered his hand. The man half rose, and shook it. His palm was clammy, grip uncertain. "You are Patrick Gruenanger?"

The man nodded. He was late twenties, square jawed, with close cropped hair and a zig zag nose.

"Has Sergeant Tomas offered you a drink?"

"Yes. Thank you. I'm fine." His English was natural, but spoken with an accent.

Beckett located it straight away. "You're Serbian?"

Patrick's eyes widened, and his mouth twitched.

"I've spent some time in that part of the world." Beckett dismissed it with a flick of a hand. "Thank you, Sergeant. I'll take it from here."

Tomas' face slumped with disappointment, but he left without a word.

Beckett wheeled his chair from behind the desk, so he was sitting almost knee to knee with Patrick. "German father?"

"Austrian. Look, I'm sorry. I'm not sure of the relevance. I came to report my girlfriend missing. No one has seen or heard from her in a couple of days."

"My apologies, Patrick. I can call you Patrick? You don't mind?"

"No… I…"

"Where people come from interests me. The globalisation of backgrounds. My father is Greek, from right here in Farou to be exact, my mother is Danish, but I was born in London, and raised in Copenhagen. Mostly. And, now, I'm back here."

Patrick chewed on his jaw.

"Your girlfriend is…?"

"'Danni, Daniela Deacon." He jutted his jaw. "She's British. English. Born and bred, I think." He was making a point.

"You think? How long have you been together?"

"A couple of years. We met In Brazil. I taught her how to dive."

"You're a dive instructor? Interesting career choice, for someone from a landlocked country."

"But, we do have airports."

"You work here on the Island? Which dive school?"

"Poseidon's at Yianiki. I got the job last summer. Danni came with me."

"Is she working, too?"

"Waitressing. Which she should have been doing this weekend, except she didn't turn up for her shifts."

"Where is that?"

"Taverna Nemesis, Nikisiopi."

"Nikisiopi?" The same village where Emmie had been staying. Taverna Nemesis wasn't in the village itself; rather, it nestled in a sheltered bay, just around the headland from the main village. Still, it was a connection.

"Yeah. Most people have heard of it."

"Okay, no problem. And where have you been?"

"My friend needed help crewing his yacht. Tuesday morning, we sailed to Patras. I jumped off there; he carried on. I got the ferry back, arrived early this morning."

"You went home, and no Danni?"

"Sometimes, she works late, and stays at one of her girlfriends' places. When I woke up, I noticed there were some messages on the answer phone. They were from work, asking where she was. She'd done her shift on Wednesday night. Thursday was her day off, but when she didn't turn up on Friday, they were worried. No one has seen her since she left work on Wednesday, and she's not answering her phone. I called the hospitals. Nothing. So, here I am. Please fill in whatever forms you need to, and let me back out there to look for her. We are wasting time! I don't know where her car is. She could have run off the road. She could be out there injured." The muscles in his jaw were twitching. Any moment, and he'd be on his feet, and out the door.

"Okay, Patrick. I will help you, but you need to calm down. You told Sergeant Tomas that Danni had a distinctive tattoo?"

"Yes. Yes, I did." He blinked at Beckett.

"I have to tell you a body of a young woman was found this morning who matches the description you gave to Sergeant Tomas."

"I'm sorry. I don't understand."

"We have yet to identify her." Beckett held out a colour print out of the photo of the dead girl's tattoo. It was zoomed in, the rest of the body not visible. Just the tattoo, as vivid as he remembered.

"Is this Danni's tattoo?"

"Where did you get this?" Patrick recoiled away from the

photograph.

"Is it Danni's?"

"Yes." His voice broken into a whisper.

"I'm very sorry, Patrick. This, along with the rest of your description, means we have reason to believe the body found this morning is Danni's."

"Body? She's dead?"

"I'm afraid she's been murdered."

"Murdered? I don't understand. Who would murder Danni? I mean, she's beautiful and gentle, and everyone loves her. You must have got it wrong. It can't be Danni." Patrick leapt to his feet, sending his chair skidding backwards. For a moment Beckett thought Patrick was going to attack him as anger coursed through the younger man's body.

"Sit down, Patrick." Beckett ordered. The anger suddenly evaporated from Patrick's body and he sank back down into his chair, shoulders slumped. Defeated.

"I have another photo." Beckett held up a face shot. She looked peaceful, hair swept back like a golden halo. She could have been asleep, if it wasn't for the metal glint of the autopsy table beneath her head. Patrick stared at the photo, and his face crumpled. There was no doubt. He sank his head to his knees, staccato sobs bursting from his lungs.

Danni Deacon. Beckett was back on the beach, staring down at the body. She'd looked so lonely, laying in the sand. Did it make things different, now she had a name? A life? Parents, boyfriend, a job, and friends? It gave him a place to start. But, all those connections she had to the living world changed nothing. None of them had helped her.

He saw Tomas at the door, peeking in through the blinds, and Beckett nodded. The swing of the door snapped Patrick from his grief. He wiped the snot from his nose with the back of his hand, shaking his head at Beckett's offer of a box of tissues.

"Where is she? Can I see her? I need to see her."

"You will. Soon. I promise. But, you understand, in these circumstances, the nature of her death, I have to ask you certain questions."

"You should be out there, finding who did this to her."

"You were her boyfriend. The person who knew her better than anyone."

Patrick's face changed, hardened. "Oh, I get it. The boyfriend did it. That's what you think. That's why he's in here now." He cocked his head towards Tomas, who was leaning against the wall.

"I'm not saying that, Patrick. But, you've been around. You've seen the TV shows. I have to start with you. And, if you want me to find out who killed Danni you'll cooperate, won't you?" Beckett leaned towards him, elbows on his knees, eyes searching out Patrick's eyes, which flickered and wavered.

"Yes. Yes, of course. Whatever you need."

"We'll need to take a DNA swab. Standard procedure. That'll be okay, won't it?"

"I guess."

"So, Tuesday morning, you boarded your friend's yacht? What time, exactly?"

"I don't remember exactly. Around 11. We were definitely on the water by midday."

"And when was the last time you saw Danni?"

"That morning. She'd worked until the early hours at the restaurant. Got home about 3am, I guess. We woke mid-morning, and had breakfast at home. That's where I left her."

"You live in Nikisiopi?"

Patrick nodded.

"Did she say what she was planning to do the rest of the day?"

"Not really. We don't... didn't," his voice broke, "police each other's lives. She'd go shopping. Or meet friends at the beach or their places, swim, sunbathe."

"We'll need a list of those friends, and where they live. And the name and contact details of your yacht owning friend."

"Sure, but he was heading east. It might be hard to get in touch with him."

"We will still try. So, you arrived in Patras. When?"

"Thursday morning. Marco, my friend, stayed until Saturday, before he headed off. Kythira was going to be his next stop, then onto Santorini, I think. But, he changes his mind. He could be anywhere."

"And you got the ferry back?"

"The overnight ferry. Left Patras at 8pm Saturday."

"You have your ticket stub?"

"I don't know."

"Credit card receipt?"

"I paid cash. Look, I'm not lying."

"We have to check these things. Standard procedure. You didn't talk to Danni on the phone, by email, or Facebook after Tuesday morning?"

"No. As I said, we don't police each other like that. We're not some old married couple."

"What was your relationship like?" Happy?"

"Yes, of course. I loved her."

"She loved you back?"

"Yes. Very much."

"Plans to get married?"

"We never talked about that. But, maybe, one day."

"Did you ever argue?"

"Show me a couple who never argue. They don't exist. But, we were happy. Yes, very happy. We live in paradise. We do jobs we both enjoy. We aren't rich, but we have enough not to worry."

"I'm sorry, Patrick. I know this is upsetting. Can you think of anyone who might want to hurt her? At work, friends, anyone?"

"No. Everyone loved her. She'd do anything for anyone. Help anyone who needed it. She didn't fall out with people. She was just…"

"An ordinary girl?"

"Not to me, but… yes… there was nothing in her life that made her stick out."

"Apart from that tattoo? When did she get that done?"

"End of last summer."

"His and hers?"

"What? No… I was away when she had it done. On a diving course."

"Did she tell you she was having it done?"

"No. She'd always wanted one. I'd said I'd pay for one, for her birthday."

"Must have cost you a bit."

"She wouldn't take any money. Told me to buy her a dress to go with it instead."

"And that didn't piss you off?"

"No…"

"Okay. We'll leave it there. You've been really helpful. I am very sorry about Danni. Tomas will take you to the hospital, so that you can see her. We have to ask you to do a formal identification."

"I want to see her." His voice faltered. "What will she look like?"

Beckett put a hand on Patrick's arm. "The cause of death won't be visible to you. She will still look like Danni."

Except, that was a lie. Seeing someone you knew as being so full of life laying on a slab, an empty shell of death-mottled skin, was always dreadful. You recognised the features, the shape of the nose, the angle of the jaw, the curve of the ears, but the thing which made them human; the essence of the person you loved was long gone.

"How did she die? Where was she found? Our apartment?"

"I'm limited in what I can tell you right now. I can tell you she was found this morning, on a beach on the North-East coast. She'd been stabbed."

Patrick stared at him. No reaction.

"Can you arrange to stay with friends for a while? We can't let you go back to your apartment tonight."

"Why?"

"Danni might not have been found there, but her killer could have been there. We need to get in a forensic team."

"I understand, of course. I can stay with friends."

"And, finally, for now, Danni's parents, family? They'll need to be told. Are you in contact with them?"

"They hate me. Can you tell them?"

"Why do they hate you, Patrick?"

"Because I'm not a nice, middle class, English boy. Because I'm Serbian. We are all war criminals." His voice was laden with bitterness. "Even though I was a tiny kid during the war. They think it runs in the genes."

"People find it hard to forget. Tomas will take you to the hospital now."

Beckett nodded at Tomas to take Patrick out. "One last thing. Do you know a British girl called Emmie Archer? She's been staying in Nikisiopi this last week."

Patrick's brain scrambled to make sense of the change in subject.

"She might have been to the dive school, or you might have met her out at night? Or someone Danni met?" Beckett held up his phone, the photo of Emmie smiling out at them.

"No… no…" Patrick glanced at the screen, but Beckett could see his thoughts were now only of what lay ahead at the hospital. He should have asked the question sooner. *Idiot.* He was out of practice. He needed to sharpen up, and do it fast.

Beckett watched Patrick leave his office, an automaton in Tomas' wake. He made a convincing representation of a shocked and grieving boyfriend, but, as her boyfriend, he had to be the main suspect until his alibi could be verified. He was left feeling unsettled. There had been information not offered, and half-truths told, Beckett was sure of that much. But, it didn't make him a killer, however much he fit the profile, however economical he was with the truth, and how much Chief Petrakis wanted it so.

CHAPTER SEVEN

It was a press scrum outside the Old Bailey. Voices shouting, elbowing for room against the barricades. Uniformed officers stood, shoulders set square, ready for trouble, but the atmosphere was triumphant, not resentful.

The BBC camera focussed in on the group, as the door opened to release them. A silver-haired woman in an expensive suit strode out first, eyes searching for the camera. In her wake, a grey couple, who seemed shrunken and stooped into their Sunday best, grasping each other's hand, like hostages just released from captivity. Camera flashes fired and snapped at them, instructions, requests shouted. They recoiled even further into themselves.

"I'd like to make a statement on behalf of Jodie Cox's parents, in light of this afternoon's very welcome verdict of guilty to murder," the silver-haired woman pronounced, silencing the crowd. She paused; anticipation crackled. "Jodie was the shining light of our family. She had her troubles, but she would help anyone. She was our angel. Her murder, on 24 August last year, has left our family shattered and broken. Today, finally, justice has been done for Jodie, and Michael Digby's other victims. It will never bring Jodie back, but the knowledge the monster who ended her life so young is behind bars, is some comfort. The streets of Bethnal Green are safer once again. We would like to thank the Metropolitan Police, the Major Incident Team, and, in particular, Detective Inspector Harper. Without his diligence, hard work, and determination to get to the truth Jodie would never have received justice. He never judged Jodie, or the other girls, and he never gave up on them. The Metropolitan Police has come under much criticism over the years, but if more officers were as compassionate and dedicated as Detective Inspector Harper, there would never be cause to complain. Thank you. We won't be taking questions. The family now requests to be left in peace."

***

In his dad's front room, Detective Inspector Lee Harper stared at his dad watching him on the TV. It was the opening story on the six o'clock news—BBC not ITV in this house, of course. His father's face was still, as he listened to the solicitor's statement. His skin was pale, almost translucent, like the grease proof paper his mum had used when baking her special cakes. Harper would sit on a stool, in the kitchen of their cavernous Victorian house in Heswall, his legs dangling, watching her work. He didn't care about baking. He didn't even care about licking the bowl, but it was better than frowning at his homework.

The picture on the screen flicked, and then cut to a close up of Harper, also outside the Old Bailey. It was strange seeing himself on camera. His accent, the burr of a near Liverpool upbringing, a posh plastic scouser, his mates in the city called him, sounded broader than he recognised, and what was going on with his hair? The curls headed north, like an exclamation mark, but the money spent on the suit was worth it. Too many officers appeared on camera looking like they'd crawled out of an Oxfam donation bag. At least they had some seniority on their side to make up for it. Lee wanted to look good, but he also *needed* to look good, to look serious. Successful. Prime time news coverage.

The picture snapped off. His dad put the remote back on the table and picked up his copy of the *Times*.

"What did you do that for?"

"I thought it had finished." He was perusing sports pages, pretending to read. Henry Harper hated sport. Harper

63

reached for the remote. Henry moved it out of reach. "It will have finished now. I prefer to read my news, not have it talked down to me."

No doubt the papers would have lurid headlines about the case tomorrow. His dad would probably put those pages straight in the wood burner.

"We think Digby killed at least another four girls. We're hoping he might confess now. We'll work on him, for sure."

"Prostitutes, though." Henry Harper flicked through the paper, and found the page he had been pretending to look for.

"They still deserve justice."

"I thought police resources were over-stretched. They're always complaining about it." Henry folded the paper into half and then a quarter, and put it on his knee, crossword face up. It was already half completed. Harper could see his father's arthritic scrawl. "18 across, 'be conscious of the sea, perhaps, aboard ship,' eleven letters."

"I did good here, Dad."

Henry tapped his pen against his lips, eyes narrowed.

"Aren't you interested?"

"Shearwaters… of course. Hear waters. SS being the ship prefix. Do you know what SS stands for?"

"No." It was wrong to want to take your own father by the shoulders, and shake him until he listened. Until he looked at you. Until he acknowledged you.

"Screw steamer. A ship driven by propellers or screws." Henry chiselled the letters into the tiny squares. "Not very clever, really."

"I'm on my way into Scotland Yard now. My presence has been requested by the Assistant Chief Constable."

"Are you sure? He'll be on the golf course by now. Or," Henry chuckled, like a wheezy old car, "he'll be strapped to the headboard in some sleazy hotel, being spanked by one of those prostitutes you're so fond of defending. God knows why you have sympathy for them."

"You can listen to the voicemail, if you like." He sounded like a child, trying to wriggle out of some misdemeanour.

Henry wafted a hand at him, gaze fixed to the crossword.

"They've got something big they want me for. I can't tell you what, because it's not in the papers and won't be, not for a while, but it's ultra-sensitive. They need someone they can trust. That's what they said, Dad."

"Have you asked yourself why they want you?" Henry put the paper down, and looked at him. "If it's so high profile, they must have hundreds of senior officers, with years more experience than you, that they could send. You only graduated out of their little college a couple of years ago." It had been six years, not that he'd expect Henry to know. He hadn't bothered to come to the ceremony. 'Not like a real graduation,' he'd said.

"Because of my work record. Because of the Digby case. You heard what the parents said about me. This could mean I'm up for promotion. To Detective Chief Inspector. It's almost unprecedented for someone under thirty."

"*Almost* unprecedented. Besides, they'll tell you anything to get their own way."

"What does that mean?"

"You're supposed to be street-wise, dealing with the underbelly of society. How can you be so naive about the world?"

"Do you ever actually listen to the drivel that comes out of your mouth?"

"People above you in the hierarchy. Your boss, his boss, and his boss after that, all the way to the top. Those grateful parents criticised the entire Metropolitan Police. They didn't praise the police force, they only praised and thanked you. You think your bosses will have enjoyed that? You think your bosses like you making them look stupid?" Henry slowly shook his head, and raised his eyebrows.

Harper wondered how many of Henry's under-graduates had been subjected to that withering look, being made to feel as intelligent as an amoeba. Henry was bitter. As a teenager, Harper hadn't realised it. His dad was a nasty, vindictive bastard. End of story. After his first couple of years in the Force, Harper had seen enough, met enough, and heard enough people with stories to tell, that he understood his dad better.

His father had been the bright, young academic at Oxford, with his doctorate in Classics, and his beautiful wife. But, he liked to give his opinion to everyone, on everything, and he'd failed to get a permanent position. He'd got a Reader position at Liverpool University, the beautiful wife had two beautiful children, but he was passed over again and again for professorship. The beautiful wife died, and the professorship was only gained by a move to a former polytechnic in London. So, Harper could see the bitterness. As Detective Inspector Harper, he could understand the bitterness. As Lee Harper, the son, he found himself visiting less and trying less. He wasn't even sure why he'd stopped in that evening. Only that he had an hour to kill. He should have gone to a bar, but smelling of alcohol and aftershave wasn't the right image. His team had gone out on the piss with their old boss, finally let out on good behaviour by his wife after an ill-timed heart attack.

"It doesn't work like that in the police, Dad. This isn't academia."

His father flicked a twisted hand at him, as if batting away a persistent fly. "It works the same everywhere. It's why I convinced your little sister to start her own company."

A lie. When Tanya had announced she was setting up a computer software company, Henry had tried to talk her down. Far too risky.

"Have you spoken to her lately? She's up for an Innovation in Industry award. She said they'd given her the nod that she's won, but, obviously, she has to pretend to be surprised at the ceremony. The awards are being presented by Prince Charles. *Prince Charles.*" Henry stressed each word, and glowed as he said them.

"I thought you hated the Royal family. I thought you wanted us to be a Republic."

"When did I ever say that?"

Repeatedly, when they were growing up, Harper thought.

"Jealousy such an unattractive quality. You should be proud of your sister. Her company has got contracts coming out of their ears. She's just been to China. Off to India next month. She was always such a bright child."

His voice dripped with honeyed pride. Married, too, and a mother, to Meg, who'd found her land legs, and was in to everything. There were photos of the happy family splashed indiscriminately around this gloom ridden room. Nicotine-yellowed curtains were glued across the windows, keeping Henry Harper in his own private universe, orbiting his star daughter, her barrister husband, and his beautiful granddaughter.

There was simply no room for Harper. He knew it, was reminded of it at every visit, and after every visit, vowed never to return. Did that make him a masochist? *At the very least, a fucking stupid idiot*, he told himself, as he got into his car. He glanced at the faded green door, with the peeling paint, the withered front lawn, beaten down by North London pollution, the glow from behind those thick curtains, and wondered what it would feel like to never see them again.

CHAPTER EIGHT

Little Bee wrestled the tears back behind her eyes. The aging, fat police officer at the reception desk, whose skin oozed grease and sweat, had rattled Greek words at her like a machine gun. Eventually, in cracked English, he'd told her Inspector Kyriakoulis was far too busy to see her, and that she should leave.

"He hasn't got time to see little girls like you. You must leave."

"Please, please, can you tell him I'm here? I'll wait. I don't mind. He phoned me. He wants to see me. It's my friend, the one who is missing," she pleaded, leaning over the desk, trying to block out the stale smell of sweat. She could feel the hot acid of angry tears advancing, and fought them back. She would not let him make her cry.

He stood up, his belly shaking, as he berated her with another tidal wave of Greek. It didn't make any sense. The Inspector had left her a message. She'd used the last of her euros to pay for a taxi into town, to save him the journey and save time. It was Sunday evening. *What could he be busy doing?* Unless Emmie had been found. A chill grew from the pit of her stomach. *What else could it be?* Her face began to crumple, the tears erupting, and she couldn't hold it back. A whimper escaped, and she turned stumbling over her own feet. A hand caught her elbow.

"My darling, whatever is the matter?" A woman was looking at her, eyebrows knotted together, gripping her elbow, as if fearing she might fall over. Little Bee hadn't realised anyone else was in reception. She must have come in, whilst she'd been arguing with the officer. Little Bee stared at her, vision warped by her tears, but she could smell Chanel No 5, the scent her mother wore. "My darling, are you alright?"

"No… I don't know what I'm supposed to do…" Bee's words tumbled out.

"Come on now. You will get nowhere with Constable Paxos. He's an oaf." The woman glared at the officer. "Let's get a coffee. I'm sure I can help. I'm Kandace Anastas."

CHAPTER NINE

"This is as high profile as it gets, DI Harper." Assistant Commissioner Edelman bobbed his head. "The situation is frankly a disaster waiting to happen. The Vice Consul and Chief of Police out there have filled us in with the details, and they've managed to keep it from the press so far, but we need to contain the situation quickly, so when it does hit the media, we are already on it. Even better that we have someone charged and locked up. We have to be seen to be proactive."

Missing holiday makers, murdered waitresses. On the same Island where, eleven years previously, another British girl had gone missing. The victim was never found but it was presumed she had been killed by the Fiend, who, a year or so later, had gone on a rape spree. 'Return of the Fiend of Farou,' 'Terror Island,' 'Paradise Lost'—it was the sort of story journalists dreamed about. Harper had little time for journalists. They seemed to think they had an automatic right to know everything, and share it with the world. Most of the ones he'd had to deal with on his cases had been young, generally attractive, women. They were easy to control. You dropped your voice a couple of octaves, gazed into their eyes, and smiled. You promised them they could have it all, and they went away hearts thumping a little bit faster, and a little bit louder.

"Of course, sir." Harper loved the AC's office. It was at the top front of the building. Behind Harper's back were the whites, greys, and blacks of London's skyline, cut in half by the river, and shaped by spires and domes, by shards and impossible curves.

"We need someone to go out there, and sort the mess out. It needs sorting quickly and quietly, and we believe you are the perfect officer for the job."

"Me, sir?"

"That false modesty is quite disarming, Detective Inspector." The man standing at the window spoke for the first time since they'd been introduced. He was Sebastian Wolf from the Home Office. Harper didn't trust him. He didn't quite meet your gaze when you looked at him, and when he had shaken his hand, it was ice cold. He was obviously high up and influential, otherwise he wouldn't be in the Assistant Commissioner's office, "But, not necessary in this room. You couldn't come more highly recommended. Time is marching on, and we need boots on the ground over there. We need to know if you'll accept the assignment.

"It's bread and butter to you, DI Harper. You've run several major cases. The only difference with this one is it's on foreign soil. You won't have the backup team you have here, though you will have full access to all forensic analysis and databases." The AC clasped his hands together.

"The challenging part will be working with the local police, but I'm sure you can handle them," Wolf added.

"Who will I be working with?"

"Interesting chap. I don't think your paths ever crossed, but he used to be one of us. Inspector Beckett Kyriakoulis." The AC glanced at a thick file on his desk, pinned under his elbows.

"The name rings a bell."

"Highly intelligent, and years of exceptional service behind him, but he took the job on Farou as a kind of semi-retirement. Went back to run the family olive farm. Not to be saddled with cases like these." The AC pushed the file to one side. "That's why we need you out there, as soon as possible."

"But, where have I heard that name before?"

"He ran the Fiend case out there a few years ago." The AC was starting to sound uncomfortable. The connection now made sense, but that wasn't where he'd remembered the name from.

"Wait… Beckett Kyriakoulis… wasn't he involved in the death of a suspect here?" It was coming back to Harper now. He'd been a raw detective constable at the time, out trying to make sense of the sewers of Lewisham. An armed siege, the death of a suspect, and near death of an officer was fodder for the station gossips.

"Strictly confidential, of course, DI Harper, but Inspector Kyriakoulis suffered a breakdown, and that's why he left the Met and went to work on a peaceful little holiday island." Wolf pulled a chair up next to Harper and sat down, close enough to make Harper want to shuffle back a couple of inches. "Before he joined the Met, he served in the Army. Did tours in Croatia and Bosnia. Army Intelligence. Bit before your time, I know, but you'll be aware of the atrocities that went on out there."

Wolf leaned in even closer. Harper could feel his peppermint breath on his cheek and the hint of an expensive cologne – he could have sworn it was Tom Ford London. He'd only smelt it once before, but it was never forgotten.

"You don't see what he's seen, and do the things he's done, without being affected. It does something to your mind. Skews it, twists it, damages it beyond repair, until eventually, it breaks completely. And once it's been broken, the mind is left weakened, brittle, less able to cope with stress, without breaking again."

"You think he's unstable?" If the gossip was true, Kyriakoulis had gone onto the roof of an apartment block, where a gunman was threatening to shoot a woman and a young child. The boyfriend was already bleeding out on the floor. Kyriakoulis had sprinted across the roof, tackled the gunman, and sent them both plunging over the edge, in an act of either insane bravery or fantastic recklessness, depending on whose opinion you asked.

"No, nothing like that. We're just worried he won't be as focussed as he needs to be."

"So why don't the Greek Police replace him themselves?"

"It's a possibility, but he's a local hero. He has much support out there. They'd only replace him, if he messed up. We can't let him mess up. We don't have that luxury. And we don't really want them replacing him with an unknown quantity."

"And how is he going to feel with a Met Officer working his patch?"

"Grateful, if he's got any sense left."

"And it's exactly what he did on the Fiend case." Edelman nodded, "They requested help, and we sent him. So, he knows the score."

Wolf pushed his chair back and got up. "I'm flying out there," he glanced at his heavy gold watch, a Rolex, Harper noted, "well, now actually. They must be gunning the engines, as we speak. I will oil the wheels, and explain to them the situation is non-negotiable. If you accept, you'll follow me over on the next available flight out there, ready to start doing your thing tomorrow."

"And if they say 'no'?"

"I hope they understand the term non-negotiable better than you do, Detective Inspector. Let me put it like this. We, the Government, the Prime Minister, want the killer of Danni Deacon and the abductor of Emmie Archer to be found quickly. There's already a prime suspect in Deacon's boyfriend. We can rely on you to stay focussed, look at the evidence and not be tempted off on any flights of fancy. I'm sure you'll have this wrapped up in less than a week. And when you return to your duties here, you may find yourself waking up each morning, looking in the mirror, and finding the youngest DCI in the history of the Met looking back at you."

"What do you say, DI Harper?" the AC asked.

This was the case he'd been waiting for. He had been personally selected by the Assistant Commissioner, and given the nod by the Prime Minister. He was being flown in to sort out a crisis, and would be returning the hero. The case did not sound complicated. All he had to do was find a connection between the missing girl and the dead girl, not hard on a small island, and bingo. His brain was already whirring through the processes and procedures he would need to put in place, the questions which would need asking. He was so good at this job; it came as naturally as breathing. Harper felt himself smiling, as the adrenaline started buzzing through his body. He pushed his dad's nagging suspicious tones out of the way.

"When do I leave?"

CHAPTER TEN

"This is a beautiful house." Little Bee's gaze swept the room.

It was like an interior from one of the glossy lifestyle magazines she flicked through at the hairdressers. Homes for millionaires. From the outside, it had appeared to be one of a terrace of slender but unremarkable houses, in varying shades of butter yellow. Inside, it was all polished oak floors, grand vaulted ceilings, and soft furnishings so opulent the reds, purples and golds seemed to ooze out of them. The interior and exterior of Kandace Anastas' house matched perfectly. Bee had never met anyone quite so glamourous. She wondered if she was a famous Greek actress, but didn't like to ask, in case she should have recognised her. She was being so kind, and Bee didn't want to risk offending her.

"That's very sweet of you. It was a rotting shell when we bought it. Luckily, my husband is an architect." The husband, who was at least twenty years the junior, had taken Bee's hand to greet her, and then made himself scarce, "I thought we'd be more comfortable here than in a restaurant. People have a habit of staring when someone is upset. Please sit. I will make the coffee."

Bee perched on the edge of a hulking crimson sofa. The cushions were so huge, like great red clouds. She was afraid if she sat back, she'd sink so far in that she'd never get out.

The room she assumed was a kitchen was through a double width doorway. She could hear cupboard doors and cups being clanked, and Kandace's voice, talking in Greek. She must be on the phone. Her tone was insistent, and even though Bee couldn't understand a word, she seemed to be asking questions of whoever was at the other end of the call.

Her own phone started chirping. She still wasn't used to the different ring tone, or how to pick up the call. It kept ringing and ringing.

"Stupid, useless phone," she muttered at it. It clicked as the call connected. Voice activated hands free.

"Beatrice. It's Inspector Kyriakoulis. Were you just at the station?" The call echoed out on speaker phone. Bee searched the screen, but couldn't see how to turn the speakers off.

"Yes. I got told you were too busy to see me. I got your message. I thought I was helping."

"Things are a bit… hectic. I'm sorry. The officer on reception said you went off with Kandace Anastas. Are you still with her?"

She lowered her voice. "I'm at her house. Do you know her?"

"She runs the newspaper. Can you come back to the station now? Or I'll come and get you. I need to talk to you urgently."

"Urgently? It took me over an hour to get here in a taxi. And then, you were too busy. Kandace is being nice to me."

"Of course she's being nice. She's a journalist." His tone was so condescending; she could feel him sneering down the phone.

"She might be able to help me find Emmie. Unless… what's going on? Have you found her?"

"I don't really want to do this on the phone."

"You've found her. Is she hurt? Tell me please."

"No, we haven't. But… there was a body of a girl found this morning. It's not Emmie, Bee. It's definitely not Emmie."

"Are you sure?" Bee felt like the world was spinning around her.

"Yes. 100%. The body… the girl… has been identified.

But, that's why I wanted to tell you in person; to reassure you. We've no reason to think there is any connection to Emmie."

"How did she die?"

Silence.

"How did she die?" Bee heard herself shouting.

"She was murdered," Kandace interrupted. Bee looked up. She'd no idea how long the journalist had been standing in the room. "A contact at the hospital confirmed it."

"Bee. Is this on speaker phone? Please come to the station now, and we can talk." Kyriakoulis sounded calm, but Bee could hear the insistence, the desperation, in his voice. Her thoughts raced. A murdered girl. Emmie was still missing. Perhaps Emmie was dead, too, or would be soon. Or, if there was no connection, then that was bad, too. All the police's efforts would be concentrated on finding the murderer. They'd forget about Emmie.

Kandace put a hand on Bee's shoulder, and sat next to her.

"I can help you. The police have done nothing so far to find Emmie. We need a public appeal. Someone may have seen her. We need everyone on the Island looking for her. The police won't want that. Trust me. They'll want to keep it quiet."

"Bee. Listen to me. I can help. I will help. Please let me," Kyriakoulis pleaded. "Kandace, you promised you'd wait."

"I didn't know the circumstances, then. If your intention was to protect Beatrice, then that need is over. She knows the facts. If your intention was to protect the reputation of the police force, then I'm sorry. You might have a murder victim. We have a missing girl, and we need to find her."

"Bee. Please come back to the station."

The phone felt hot in her hand. Kandace's arm squeezed her shoulders, face was etched with understanding.

Bee hit the end call button. The room went silent for a

moment, but the phone started chirping again. Kyriakoulis' name appeared. Bee's finger squeezed the power button. The chirping stopped, and the screen went black.

"We'll find her. I promise." Kandace smiled.

CHAPTER ELEVEN

Beckett flicked on the lights. The apartment block was one of a cluster of four identical buildings behind a gated entrance. Blocks like these had sprung up all over the Island since the 1980s. Concrete, block, and steel. Giant Lego bricks dumped in the middle of scrub land. Some had fared better than others. The Riviera Apartments squatted amidst landscaped lawns, interspersed with olive trees tamed to provide shade. As he'd climbed out of the car, he'd spotted the black rectangle of a swimming pool.

Danni and Patrick's apartment was on the first floor of the second block. Each block appeared to have four apartments, two on the ground floor and two above, each with either a patio or terrace at the front.

Beckett blinked, letting his eyes adjust to the brightness. The bulb in the stairwell was broken, and he'd had to find his way up in the dark. He also took a moment to clear his mind and focus. Thinking about the impending shit storm would not help. The forensic team would be here first thing in the morning, but he wanted to learn about how Danni led her life, before it was taken apart and altered forever.

The apartment was open plan, the largest area consisting of the living room, with double width doors onto the terrace. A four-seat dining table occupied the far corner, and the back of the room was given over to the kitchen. A corridor disappeared off behind the kitchen, presumably to the bedrooms and bathroom. The floor was tiled, and dressed with ethnic patterned rugs. There were no signs of a struggle. It was all neat and ordered. *Very* neat and ordered.

There was a wooden framed sofa, with tangerine cushions, and two matching armchairs, all facing a large flat screen television. The walls on either side of the TV were lined with shelves—on the left, DVDs and CDs, on the right, books. There were framed pictures on every spare inch of wall. Lots of photos – many taken underwater. Spectacular shots of rainbow-coloured fish, hulking shadows of manta rays, and the delicate tentacles of corals. There were other, more personal, shots of Patrick, in his dive gear, posing with friends after successful dives, standing on yachts or at quay sides, and his dive instructor qualification certificates.

Most of the books were diving related or sports biographies. The DVDs comprised mostly of action movies, and the CDs, heavy metal. Beckett surveyed the whole room. There was nothing here which appeared to be Danni's.

The first door he opened in the corridor was the bathroom. It was small but neat. Bath with shower over, toilet and sink. In a metal shelf unit, by the bath, were the first signs a female was in residence—patchouli and lotus flower shower gel, and Trevor Sorbie shampoo and conditioner for long hair.

There was a mirror-doored cabinet on the wall, by the sink. Beckett snapped open the door. He didn't need to look at his reflection; feeling like a wreck was enough. He knew he looked bad, not quite a corpse ready for Dr. Elena's methodical dissection, but not far off. A headache pulsed behind his left temple, and his knee throbbed. He'd lost count of the number of painkillers he'd taken. He'd been awake over twelve hours, and his thoughts were processing slower than usual. His eyes felt sunken into his skull, as if they were pressing into his brain, his throat was ragged, and his voice fading. The more beard he grew, the greyer it looked. He was aging with every second. He took a deep breath.

"Focus. Come on. *Focus.*"

The contents of the cabinet were more interesting. Alongside the ibuprofen and paracetamol were three small brown prescription bottles. Beckett picked up each one in turn. He had to move under the sharp florescent light in the ceiling to be able to read the printed labels. Temazepan, Zolpidem, and Xanax. The prescriptions were all made out to D Deacon, dated between January 2014 and March 2015. None of the bottles were more than half full. The address on each one was the same address in Milton Keynes Patrick had given to them as the home of Danni's parents. *Did Danni have trouble sleeping? If so, why? What did the young have to worry about that would keep them awake at night?*

He continued down the corridor to the next room. The couple's bedroom. A king-sized bed took up most of the room. A double wardrobe was clearly designated—left side Danni's clothes, right side Patrick's. Apart from matching lamps, there was nothing on the shelves on either side of the bed. It was impersonal. More like a holiday home than a place people lived year round.

The final door was on the opposite side of the corridor.

Flicking on the light revealed everything which had been missing from the rest of the apartment. This was Danni's haven. There was no bed. Instead, there was a sofa, a couple of elephant-sized bean bags, and a large desk wedged under the shuttered window. Whilst the other rooms had views out to the front or side of the village and the sea beyond, this room was at the back of the building, and the view drew you up into the hills and the forests. Even in the height of the day, it would stay shaded and cool. The vegetation outside was so close, it almost felt like you were living in the trees. He could hear the cicadas shrilling their night time harmonies.

The walls were hung with photos of Danni. Danni with Patrick, Danni with friends, work colleagues perhaps, standing in front of a Taverna, all grinning like loons. Photos of her with an older male and female – her parents. There was a grizzled black Labrador with them, the hair around his muzzle tinged with grey. There were prints on the wall, too. One, an identical copy of her tattoo, or, rather, the tattoo was the copy, he guessed. There were more prints of Greek Gods - Zeus, Apollo, Athena, Dionysus, Demeter. Some were traditional, others modern, intensely coloured interpretations of the myths.

There was a book shelf next to the desk, and the Greek mythology theme continued there, along with the more usual chick lit and self-help books. On the desk was a Macbook. Beckett disconnected the leads. He wasn't going to risk leaving it for the forensic team to collect.

He stood back, and looked at the room. All Danni's life was condensed into this small box of a room. Was that her choice, or the boyfriend's? Him controlling her, or her keeping secrets from him? He looked at the door. There was a keyhole. No key. But, it could be locked from the outside, and the inside. A legacy, perhaps, of when the apartment was used as holiday accommodation. The other bedroom door didn't have a lock, but that door was different to all the others. Different wood. Different colour. Different style. It was a replacement. He went back to study the hinges. The screws were shiny. Fairly new. And there was damage to the door frame around the new hinges. At some point, not that long ago, the door had been kicked in, and replaced. From the angle of the damage, it had been kicked inwards. The way Patrick had described their relationship was they didn't police each other. They allowed each other lots of freedom. A modern relationship, or a troubled one?

He was interrupted by a knock at the front door.

He opened it. A pale, chubby-faced man, with a gleaming helmet of black hair, stared up at him, eyes wide, mouth wider. The man looked at the laptop under Beckett's arm, and then back up at Beckett's face. He recoiled towards the door of the opposite apartment.

"I'm calling the police."

"I am the police." Beckett grabbed his ID out of his pocket. "Who are you?"

The man scuttled forward.

"Linus Sang. I live here. Number four. Have you spoken to Patrick? His girlfriend, Danni, is missing. Is that why you're here? He's worried sick…"

Beckett held up his hand to stop him.

"Perhaps we could go and sit down?"

Linus tried to peer around Beckett into the apartment, but he swung the door shut.

"My place?" Linus offered, taking the hint.

"I think that would be best."

Linus' apartment was a mirror image, apart from it looked like a whirlwind had ravaged it. There were books and papers everywhere. Piles of clothes. The smell of garlic and chicken sent Beckett stomach into spasms. A huge pile of washing up sat next to the sink. A white cat, with a black tip to his tail and a black nose, was curled up on the back of the sofa. The TV was on, but the sound muted. Tom Cruise, in his shades and leather flying jacket, was walking towards a fighter jet.

"Sorry. I… I'm not the world's tidiest person." Linus grabbed an armful of papers from one end of the sofa, and spilled them onto the floor. Beckett sat, and indicated for Linus to do the same. He perched on the edge of an armchair. The cat flicked its tail, and watched Beckett out of half-closed eyes. The room was dominated by an oversized desk, housing three huge computer monitors.

"What do you do, Mr. Sang?"

"Linus, please. I gamble. Online. Poker for fun. Stocks and shares for a living. I know… you wouldn't think to look at me, would you?" Linus' eyes shone. There was a fierce intelligence there Beckett had missed at first glance. He really wasn't on form.

"You make a living from that?"

"Not bad."

"What's that accent? New Zealand?"

"Impressive. Most people don't even notice. I lived in London for twenty years. Came out here for a holiday last summer, ended up staying. You have news about Danni? Bad news, I assume, as you are taking her laptop."

"I'm afraid she was found dead this morning."

"Oh. God. That's terrible. How? Car accident? She was a terrible driver. I worried about her driving home late at night. I always felt better when I heard her come home."

"No. It looks like she was murdered."

"Murdered? Bloody hell." He thought for a moment. "Are you sure?"

"How well did you know Danni?"

"As neighbours. We said hello. She looked after Ariadne, if I was away. Removed spiders from the bath for me. I'm phobic. She laughed at my jokes, which was kind, because I'm not at all funny."

"And Patrick?"

"I didn't have much to do with him. We nodded a hello at each other. That's about it. He was just a neighbour. Danni's boyfriend."

"Sounds as if you don't like him."

Linus shrugged, but it was enough of an answer.

"What was Danni and Patrick's relationship like? Did they ever argue?"

"God, yes. Loudly, oftentimes. She was beautiful and popular, had loads of friends. He was jealous. He's very controlling. I think, anyway."

"What did they argue about?"

"I could hear them, but I didn't eavesdrop. What's

private is private."

"She didn't confide in you? Living next door. When she was rescuing you from spiders."

"Only once or twice. She liked to go out, have fun. Patrick's a dive instructor. He often has early starts, and he can't drink when he's diving the next day. His boss is very strict about that."

"Their arguments, did they ever turn physical?"

"Did he hit her? No. I never saw a mark on her. Though, they can be clever about it, can't they? Only bruise where it can't be seen. Though, on Farou in the summer, that doesn't leave much. Do you think he killed her?"

"Do you?"

"No. No, of course not." But, there was carefully placed doubt in his eyes. "He couldn't have done. He's been away. Told me on Tuesday he was heading off on a yacht for a few days."

"And when did you last see Danni?"

"Wednesday, late afternoon. She was heading off to work."

"Did you hear her come home?"

"No… no, I don't think so."

"You're not sure. Only, you said before you always felt better when you heard her come home. You made it sound like you listened out for her."

"She sometimes stays at a friend's, near the bar. Yeah, that's right. I remember now. She said she wouldn't be back Wednesday night, and she was staying at one of her friends. Her car wasn't here Thursday morning."

"What car does she drive?"

"A blue Toyota RAV-4. I couldn't tell you the registration."

"And when she didn't come home the next day?"

"I assumed, with Patrick being away, she'd decided to

stay at the friends. She often did, when he was away. I didn't keep watch over her." Realisation dawned on him, his mouth stretching open, and lips sticking to his teeth, "This is my fault, isn't it? If I'd reported her missing sooner, maybe she wouldn't be dead?"

"The only person at fault is the person who killed her." Beckett's phone bleeped into life. He looked at the screen. It was Petrakis. The storm had arrived. Beckett wasn't sure he was ready to fend it off. He wasn't sure he could survive any of this.

***

It felt like an ambush, with smiles hiding knives. Beckett was sitting on a large leather sofa in Mayor Baptiste Sarantos' wood-panelled office. Oil paintings of previous incumbents stared down, disapproving and judging. Beckett needed to stay alert, but the sofa was like sinking sand, and every move he made he was dragged further down. Mayor Sarantos was sitting opposite him. He was the youngest ever Mayor of Farou. Italian suit and a film star smile. The consummate politician. Next to him, was the British Vice Consul Neil Ticknall. People described him as a weak man. Beckett had met him at a couple of official engagements, but could barely remember him, beyond his fragile handshake. Right now, he was sweating panic, and seemed to be studying the patterns in the carpet.

Chief Petrakis was standing off to one side. She'd glared at Beckett when he'd come in, and he could feel the waves of fury rippling off her. The final occupant of the room stood out of Beckett's direct line of vision. Beckett had never seen him before. He'd been introduced as Sebastian Wolf, a representative of the British Government. He was a short, grey man, with threadbare hair, eyebrows that arched like a pair of seagull's wings, and a lazy eye, which made his whole face look lopsided. But both eyes burned with the same intelligence, and had a darkness lurking behind them which made Beckett wary. He'd

86

yet to speak beyond a mumbled greeting but Beckett could feel him watching. To get here in time for this meeting, he must have come by private jet, and set off almost before they'd ID'd the body. And if he had set off before the body had been identified, how did they know she was British? His brain tried to calculate timelines, but the numbers swirled around, out of reach. He sensed he was missing some chunk of information, but he had no idea what.

"So, we have this going viral." There was a laptop on the coffee table between Beckett and the Mayor. Baptiste spun the laptop around, so Beckett could see the screen. It was the *Farou Times* website. There was a photo of the Island – olive green mountains, shimmering blue sea – and superimposed on top, a photo of Emmie Archer. The banner headline read 'Fear Returns to Paradise.'

"I thought we agreed not to speak to the press?" Petrakis eyeballed him.

"I didn't..." Beckett began.

"You were seen with Anastas in a restaurant, not three hours ago," Petrakis cut in.

"I left, before I told her anything. We had nothing at that point. My priority was ID'ing the dead girl, and finding Emmie."

"So, you would have talked to her, if the boyfriend hadn't turned up?" Petrakis spat at him.

"We needed her help."

"And you think headlines like this are helpful, Kyriakoulis?" The Mayor closed the lid of the laptop. "Are you so out of your depth you have to rely on journalists to do your job for you?"

"Hang on a minute," Petrakis interrupted. "There might have been an error of judgment here, but no one can say Beckett is out of his depth."

"You're always going to defend him. He was your choice

for the job."

"Because he was, by far, the best candidate."

"That was debatable, then. Now? This case has been mishandled from the start."

"Mishandled?" Beckett leaned forward. "What the hell do you mean by that?"

"We have a murder, a missing girl, and the world's media going into full hysterics. Can I remind you it's only been a handful of years since we had headlines screaming panic about the Fiend of Farou?"

"You don't have to remind me. I caught him."

"When no one else on the Island could… yes, we all know that."

"I think a little calm is called for." Sebastian Wolf peeled himself from the wall. His eyebrows arched even closer to his receding hair line. "I'm sure we are all appreciative of the work you did back then, Inspector. No one is questioning your abilities, are they, Mayor Sarantos?"

"But, perhaps, it is time for a fresh pair of eyes." Baptiste shrugged.

"I'm Chief of Police, Baptiste. I decide who polices on this Island." Petrakis' eyes flashed with anger.

Despite the smiles and cheek kisses at official events, Beckett knew they detested each other. The undercurrent was ever present. Gossip around the station favoured an affair which ended badly, though the stories varied wildly as to who put the affair out of its misery.

"Do we like the boyfriend for the murder?" Neil Ticknall asked, distilling the tension, his voice chirping like a cicada. The phrasing grated with Beckett. He'd clearly been watching too many US cop shows.

"He's got to be the main suspect, at this point. His alibi is shaky. We'll be checking it out first thing in the morning." Petrakis perched herself on the edge of the Mayor's desk, knocking over his Mayor Sarantos' name plaque. A muscle in Baptiste's jaw twitched. An image flashed into Beckett's head – Petrakis on the desk as she was now, legs wrapped around Baptiste, as he nuzzled her neck, one hand pushing up her skirt. "Beckett, what did you make of him? Is he capable?"

The image, thankfully, evaporated. He needed to concentrate.

"We're all capable. I'm not sure. There's something about him. About his relationship with Danni. But, why stab her and dump her body on a beach? He knows the Island. He dives all round here. He'd know where to hide a body, if he needed to."

"I thought the body had been washed up on the beach by chance, not dumped?" Wolf asked. His vowels were perfect, and carefully formed. Private school educated, Beckett guessed. Eton, probably. It wasn't just the voice. It was the way he wore superiority around his shoulders, like a cloak.

"That's what it looked like at first glance. Now, I'm not so sure."

"You're not sure?" Wolf rolled the words around his mouth. "Interesting."

"And the missing girl? Any connection to Danni or her boyfriend?" Ticknall chipped in.

"None that we've found so far. Danni and Patrick have been living on the Island for over a year. Emmie Archer has never been here before. She arrived last week, with her friends, to celebrate her wedding, which is due to happen next week. Her fiancé is staying in Rakos. They hadn't planned to meet up again until the wedding."

"You've spoken to him, the fiancé?" Wolf asked.

"No. Not yet."

"You didn't think it a good idea to go and see him?" Wolf tilted his head, and pursed his lips.

"Emmie's friends thought it was most likely she'd got

cold feet, and wasn't ready to tell him the bad news. I had the local police check out his hotel, and monitor him and his friends. There was no sign of her there."

"So, he doesn't know she's missing yet?"

"I'm sure he knows now." Baptiste sneered.

"I've already got an officer on the way to see him," Petrakis said.

"Who have you sent?" Beckett asked, the pain in his temple pulsed. He was losing control of the whole situation.

"Sergeant Tomas. He's going to invite him to come to the station tomorrow, so we can talk to him. The locals are going to keep him under surveillance, as they are doing with Danni Deacon's boyfriend."

"You let him go?" Ticknall rubbed his temple, as if mirroring Beckett's pain.

"At the moment, he's the grieving boyfriend. He came into the station of his own accord. We couldn't hold him without arresting him, and we don't have enough evidence to do that yet." Petrakis shrugged.

"Your resources sound like they are being stretched to their limits." Wolf glanced at the heavy gold watch on his wrist. It radiated expense. "The question is, can you handle what is now turning into a major multi-faceted case, or do we have to take over?"

"Take over?" Petrakis' voice was sharp, worried.

Wolf's rapid presence now made more sense to Beckett. He was a fixer.

"Just as you brought Inspector Kyriakoulis in when you needed to find the Fiend, we can do the same this time. Provide an experienced officer from the Met. It worked well last time."

"Beckett, Inspector Kyriakoulis was different. He might have been a British police officer, but he's a half Greek. He has an affinity to the Island and the people, and they to him," Petrakis added.

"This crime, or crimes, happened on Greek soil, and we have jurisdiction." Baptiste barked, and his left foot started drumming the carpet.

"I'm surprised," Wolf scoffed. "You seem to be the person in this room who has the least faith in Inspector Kyriakoulis being able to conduct this investigation. I thought you'd leap at the offer."

"To bring in another Greek officer, yes. To have your Metropolitan Police take over the case? That would be the same as saying the Hellenic Police Force have no one competent enough. That we are amateurs. No, I will not allow it."

"I have to agree with Baptiste." Petrakis nodded. "Having foreign officers take over the case would not work. It would cause resentment amongst our officers, and hostility with the locals, both of which would get in the way of the investigation."

"I wasn't sent here because I needed a little jolly in the sunshine." Wolf picked up a framed photo from the desk. It was a press shot of Baptiste, shaking hands with the Greek Prime Minister. "As soon as we were told of the British victim, concerns were raised within the Government. And nothing I have witnessed so far reassures me."

"We will handle this ourselves," Baptiste spat his words out.

"I've heard the Chief's opinion, and I've listened to yours, Mayor Sarantos. Perhaps I should ask the Inspector what he thinks." Wolf directed his gaze at Beckett. "Your arrest and conviction record is impressive, both with the Greek Police and at the Met. You've provided many years of diligent service, and I'm sure I speak for everyone in this room, when I express gratitude for that work. However, you are clearly not at full fitness, and this is, I am sure, not the sort of case you thought you'd have to ever deal with again, when you took the job here.

It will be physically and mentally stressful, and no one would think any less of you if you decided to… well… take a back seat. Let someone else take arms against a sea of troubles."

Wolf licked his lips, and his mouth curled into a self-satisfied smile. Did he really see Beckett as the mad Prince of Denmark, who might prefer suicide, or rather early retirement, than chase this case down to the end? But, maybe, he was right? This was only day one, and he was exhausted. His brain felt like it was being embalmed from the inside out. What if he wasn't capable of running this case? What if he'd already screwed it up? What if he'd missed something crucial, and Emmie was dead because of it? If he was doubting himself how could he, with any conscience, carry on? They were offering him an out. Let someone else take the pain because there would be lots of it. What more did he have to prove in his career? This couldn't be about his ego. It had to be about the girls, Danni and Emmie.

In Beckett's mind, he was suddenly back on the beach, but this time, the storm was crackling overhead, the sky swirling with impenetrable blackness, and explosions of lightning illuminated the thuggish clouds. Beyond the rocks, at the mouth of the bay, the sea was a roaring and foaming darkness, and the bay itself gurgled and wretched like a rabid dog. A floating body would be ground and splintered against the rocks, before it was ever pushed onto the beach. He glanced up to the path he himself would half scramble, half fall down, in a few hours' time. Dark water and debris surged down into a waterfall of mud and branches. Impassable either way.

Beckett turned his head back to the cauldron of the sea. How, then? Time fast forwarded to dawn. The storm had subsided. The sky was clearing, and a rose-coloured hue hinted at the horizon. The sea still bucked and swayed, but the violence had dissipated, and the rain was misting down in whispers, rather than torrents. Rounding one of the rocks at the headland of the bay was a small boat. It bobbed its way to the shore, where it ran onto the beach. He couldn't see the detail of the boat or the person in it, but he saw them drag a body out of the boat, a blonde girl in a pink dress, lift her over their shoulder, and carry her to above the water line.

They laid her out, on her front, went back to the boat, and sailed away, as their footprints dissolved to nothing in the wet sand. Beckett gazed down at Danni. Abandoned. Utterly alone. All that she might have become, gone. Her family. Her friends, their lives ripped in two, changed forever. Had she known death was coming? Had she been fearful? In those last moments, had she hoped she would be saved? But, no one came, and no one saved her.

"No one is better placed to know the best approach here. Say the word, and responsibility can be absolved." Wolf clasped his hands together, and waited.

"Beckett?" Petrakis prompted. "What do you think?"

Baptiste clicked his tongue against his teeth.

He looked at them. They stared back at him.

He stood up. He was a head taller than all of them. They seemed to shrink backwards, all apart from Wolf. Beckett directed his gaze at him.

"Thank you for your concern. But, this is my case. I will find who killed Danni. And I will find out what has happened to Emmie." He switched his gaze to Petrakis. "Things aren't going to be pretty. The media attention will only get worse. Innocent people will be affected. But, only so we can catch the guilty. And we will. I just need to know I have your support."

"You know you do. We all want the same thing. Don't we, Baptiste?"

"The Hellenic Police Force will prove itself to you, Mr Wolf."

"Words are worth nothing, Mayor Sarantos. Let me thank you for your candour, Inspector, but let me be clear on where we stand." Wolf rubbed his hands together, as if they were cold. "The British Government is nervous, after certain recent cases, and wants to be seen to be proactive in looking after its citizens' interests abroad. But, we, of course, respect your sovereignty. However, perhaps I can suggest a compromise? Would you at least let us send an officer over here? To work *with* Inspector Kyriakoulis. It would still be your case. He, or she, would have no jurisdiction, beyond what you choose to give them. An extra pair of very well-qualified hands, to use as you think fit. What do you say?"

"It's really not necessary…" Petrakis began.

"It would look like we were not confident of solving this ourselves. It would make us look weak." Baptiste nodded. "If we were to bring in anyone else, it would be from within the Hellenic Force, not from outside."

"I'm afraid we really must insist. This comes from the Prime Minister himself. He has discussed this with me, and…."

"Actually, another officer on the team would be helpful," Beckett cut him short. "My officers are keen and dedicated, but lacking experience. Someone who has worked major cases would be an asset I could use on my team."

"Excellent. Well said." That curl of a smile crept over Wolf's face, but Beckett could feel Petrakis and the Mayor's disapproval simmering from across the room. "I'll get the necessary in motion."

"Beckett might be able to suggest some possible names?" Petrakis offered.

"I worked with some good officers when I was in London…" Beckett nodded, starting to sift through names and faces in his head.

"Oh no. You don't get to choose. We've already handpicked the best person for the job. He'll be flying out tonight, and be with you early tomorrow morning. Don't worry. You won't be disappointed." Wolf smirked, satisfied. "Trust me."

That phrase always reminded Beckett of his dad, who'd once said to him the last person you should ever trust was the person who said 'trust me.' There weren't many things his dad said to him that he paid any attention to, but this was one which had always stuck in his head.

Petrakis waited until the door had shut behind Wolf and Vice Consul Ticknall, before turning on Beckett.

"On one hand, you stand up and shout about your confidence in yourself, and on the other, you bow down to them, and admit you cannot cope on your own." Santos shook his head. "They will try to make us look stupid. Like your predecessor and my predecessor did, when you caught the Fiend. Their man will report back every little detail, every little mistake."

"And then, take all the credit when the case is solved. We will be made to look like peasants," Petrakis joined in.

"You didn't seem to have a problem with me standing down altogether."

"An honourable discharge and replacement with a bright and successful product of the Hellenic Police Force's training scheme. What is not to like in that? But, this? For them to try and take over. This Island is not part of the United Kingdom, however many of their rich and famous politicians, businessmen, and celebrities have holiday homes here. This is Greece, and I am a proud Greek. Can you say the same, Inspector Kyriakoulis? Which one of your passports means the most to you? The British one, or the Greek one?" Santos paced the floor underneath the portraits of serious faced mayors of the past.

"Right now, all I care about is finding Emmie Archer, and arresting whoever killed Danni. And I will do whatever I have to do to make that happen. Is that acceptable to you both?"

Petrakis nodded. Beckett looked at Baptiste.

"They don't fly someone as senior as Wolf over here in

a private jet, unless they are going to impose certain things on us. If we'd said no to all offers of help, that jet would be heading off to Athens. You'd be overruled, and we'd all be side-lined."

"How did you know he came on a private jet?"

"He couldn't have got here *that* quickly on a scheduled flight. This case is shaking some big trees in Westminster. If we want to keep control, this is the only way to do it."

Baptiste held his gaze for a few long moments before looking away. "Just do your job. And whoever they send over, put him in charge of making the coffee, and mopping the floors."

Outside the City Hall, Petrakis hesitated at her car door. The night air was heavy with humidity and the heady scent of cestrum flowers.

"You really are up to this, Beckett?" The anger gone, instead, Beckett sensed desperation. "I never told you this, but you were my choice for the job, not Baptiste's. He'd got someone else in mind, probably the same person he'd bring in now to replace you on this case. He took some convincing. He wasn't sure any connections to Chrystos was a good thing… and with how things worked out in London for you… Don't prove him right and me wrong. Please. Agreeing so quickly to the Met sending someone in makes me worry you doubt yourself."

"You backed me for the job. Nothing has changed since then. Trust me."

There was that phrase again. He said it without thinking, but as it left his mouth, he thought again of his Dad.

"Okay. I do. Now, go home, and get some sleep. You look like shit."

CHAPTER TWELVE

Harper was not in the best of moods. The Easyjet flight from Luton had been crowded with comedy t-shirts, flip flops, and too much makeup. Most of the passengers had checked in their bags, then gone straight to the bar. By the time the plane was accelerating along the runway, the alcohol fumes were already being recycled by the air conditioning, and the squealing from the women and the hollering from the men had practically burst his ear drums. He'd never understood the desire people had to get totally and utterly wasted, especially on holiday. Why travel thousands of miles to get so drunk, you have no idea where you are? And getting yourself to the point you had no control and no memory of what you were doing…

He couldn't get the image of Sebastian Wolf sitting in a private jet, sipping an expensive single malt, out of his head. Wouldn't it have made sense for him to travel on the same plane, rather than this airborne cattle truck?

As they came into land, the lights of the Island sparkling below, the bleach blonde stick, with the baby blue eyes sitting next to him, who'd tried her best the whole flight to attract his attention, grabbed his hand.

"Really sorry. I hate landing. Especially here. Do you mind?" She squeezed. The scent of Calvin Klein Eternity wafted up from her cleavage. Harper forced himself to smile, and turned his head to look out of the window. He wished he hadn't. They were about to ditch into the sea.

"Jesus." He found himself squeezing back, as the plane

dipped, swayed, and then, bounced its tyres onto the runway.

"See what I mean." The girl untangled her fingers. "You'd think they'd build the runway in the middle of the Island, not in the sea."

It was a stampede to leave the plane. Elbows and shoulders pushing to be the first out, and even then, they seemed to have been abandoned in the middle of the tarmac, and had to wait for a bus. The wall of heat hit Harper as soon as he'd taken his turn out of the plane door. The air was heavy, clogged with moisture, and unfamiliar perfumes so permeated the air, he could taste them as much as smell them.

It took nearly an hour for the carousel in baggage reclaim to creak into life, and start spewing out their suitcases. Some people had fallen asleep, but others seem to have discovered more alcohol, smuggled in from the plane presumably. Two blokes, with identical hairstyles, shaved at the sides, long angular fringe on top, started throwing punches at each other. The girls with them commenced screaming. If this was the UK, Harper supposed he'd have had to wade in, but his jurisdiction here was specific to the murder, and he kept his gaze on the carousel. His head was thumping, and he could feel trickles of sweat meandering down his back.

With relief, Harper grabbed his case, and shuffled, along with the other passengers, down a shabby corridor, with exposed pipework like varicose veins weaving above them, through double doors into the freedom of the Arrivals Lounge. It was chaos. Throngs of people waiting behind barricades, shouting, holding up signs for hotels, travel companies. Holiday reps yelled instructions, trying to herd their respective clients towards the correct shuttle buses, and taxi drivers waving names or just touting for business. After three hours on a cramped tin can, being swept from the cool clear London air to this pungent sponge of a place, the cacophony of noise, the heat, and the carnage felt like a slap round the face. He stood, shell-shocked, with his suitcase, in his suit trousers and casual shirt, feeling like an alien amongst some shorts and sun-hatted species.

Amongst the din, he heard a shout. An arm was waving at him. He stepped forward, and saw a man, amongst the other taxi drivers, holding a piece of paper with 'Harper' written on it, in big, bold letters. The man was a head taller than those around him, and blond, where the other taxi drivers were coffee-coloured and dark-eyed. Harper wondered if they'd specifically selected a driver who stood out from the rest. Made him easier to spot certainly.

"I'm Harper, Detective Inspector Lee Harper. I assume you've been sent to collect me? Do you speak English?"

The man in front of him nodded, and his mouth twitched with a half-smile. There were dark circles under his eyes, and his skin was stretched tight over his cheekbones. Harper wondered if they ever got fed up of late night airport runs, dropping off the hung over, and collecting the drunk.

"Not perfectly, but yes. Please follow me. I'm right outside. Good flight?"

"Now I know what a battery chicken feels like."

The man glanced at him, but said nothing.

"Have we got far to go?"

"Your hotel is about a forty-minute drive."

The glass doors slid open, and the humidity and fragrant aroma hit Harper once more. How did people work in this sort of heat? In fact, how did they sleep? It was nearly 3am.

"We've been having thunderstorms. Feels like we're due another one," the man said, as if reading his thoughts. "Here we are."

The car in front of them bleeped as it unlocked. The Range Rover Evoque was pulled up onto the pavement opposite the entrance, not in the taxi rank. It was a hell of a nice car for a taxi, if more than a bit bruised, but then, most taxis looked like they'd been through a battle or two. A wing mirror missing, gouge on the rear wheel arch. Still, a step up from Mondeos, Mazdas, and black cabs, with their sticky seats, but other countries seemed to use classier cars for their taxis, Mercedes and the like. Harper opened the rear door, and climbed in praying the air conditioning was working. The driver hesitated for a moment then picked up his suitcase, and stowed it in the boot.

Harper drank in the air conditioning, and relaxed into the butter milk leather seat. Occasionally, he saw the driver glance at him through the rear-view mirror, but he tactfully stayed quiet. A good taxi driver was a bad conversationalist in Harper's mind. Negotiating the roads out from the airport was smoothly done, and Harper had to force his eyelids apart. Flashes of imposing, amber-coloured stone buildings, neon lights, and people passed by. It was early morning, but many people were still out partying.

The lights and buzz of the town were soon left behind, but it became harder, rather than easier, to fall asleep. The speed of the car increased, the eager burr of the engine pulling them along, but the road began to twist and turn and rise. Below, to his right, was the black of the sea, as they hair-pinned up and along the coastline. The car rallied around the bends, bounced through craterous potholes, and ducked into impossible gaps when cars and buses came the other way. One turn of the steering wheel too far, one crumble off the cliff edge, one opposing driver with too much booze in him, and they would be plunging down the rocks into the black hole.

Harper was now wide awake, gripping the door handle. Every few miles, they'd pass through a cluster of houses where the road would narrow to barely a car width, round sharp-edged houses, or the road would descend to the shoreline, and pass through villages alive with bars and music and lights and people launching themselves into the traffic with no warning. The driver negotiated it all without stress.

"This is Rakos, where you are staying. Your hotel is at

the far end. It's one of the busier resorts, as you can see. Lots of kids come here, first holiday without their parents. Families, not so much."

Harper could see why. The place was pulsating light and noise. Every building seemed to be a bar or a restaurant, a karaoke palace, or a night club. There were thousands of kids spilling in and out of each one. It was impossible to distinguish where the buildings ended, and the pavement began. Kids were throwing up in the road, pushing each other up against walls, kissing, groping, and laying on the ground wrapped around each other. Drinking, smoking, dancing, pushing, shoving. London night life could be intense, but this was something else. All inhibitions had been left at passport control.

The car stopped. The driver had wound his window down, and was staring outside. He was lost, perhaps understandably. The mass throng of partying kids obscured everything. But, then, Harper saw what the driver had seen. Tucked behind the crowd, at the entrance to a side street was a figure, wearing a black hoodie, with a silver lightning bolt skewered across the back. One-by-one, kids would approach him, hand him something, and take something in return. Impossible to see what, in the gloom, but Harper didn't need to see it to know the man was dealing. It didn't matter what country in the world you were in, the body language of the drug dealer and their customers was the same.

"You fit?" the driver said softly.

"What?"

But, the driver was already out of the car, and weaving through the crowd. Harper hesitated, then followed. The driver was tall and easy to tail amongst the partying crowd. He had a slight limp; Harper had noticed a walking stick in the front passenger seat, but he moved confidently, people subconsciously getting out of his way.

As they emerged from the crowd, the dealer sensed a presence, looked around, and flicked something in his hand. His customers melted away. Neon light glinted on metal. He had a knife.

"That's not very friendly, is it?" the driver spoke. He sounded almost amused.

"Fuck you," came the reply in a heavy Eastern European accent and the dealer was off, sprinting down the side road.

"You go after him. I'll get the car," the driver shouted over his shoulder, as he ran in the opposite direction.

"What?" Harper found himself saying, again. He watched the driver being swallowed back into the crowd, and then, the other way to the dealer disappearing into the darkness. "Bollocks to this."

He started sprinting, after the dealer. He was about fifty metres ahead and running hard. The back alleys and streets were a labyrinth, illuminated only by the flashes and reflections of light from the main streets and bars. The dealer twisted and turned, up alleyways, down roads, doubling back on himself. Harper wasn't gaining ground, but he wasn't losing any either. He was disorientated, his lungs starting to burn. He could hear the throb of music, and something else... cars on a road up ahead. What the hell was he doing pursuing an armed man, on his own, in a place he didn't know? He had no radio to call for back up, and even if he'd had one, who would he call? It was insane.

The man suddenly darted right. Harper followed, and the beach and sea came into view ahead. The man kept running, out of the end of the street, heading for the beach it seemed, but he had a road to cross first. Harper sensed the car before he saw it, and then the man, unable to stop, half jumped, half catapulted over the bonnet, and disappeared over the other side with a sickening thud.

"Shit...shit..." he yelled. He'd chased someone to their death in the first hour he'd been on the Island. His career was over.

Harper stumbled out into the open. The car was familiar. He stared at it. It was the Evoque – the car which had promised him death earlier, had now ploughed down the man he had been chasing. He rounded the front of the car. The driver was standing over the groaning body of the drug dealer. There was no blood, and nothing looked horribly broken. A small crowd was growing, as people spilled out of tavernas and night clubs, to see what was causing the commotion.

"Jesus Christ. Have you called someone?"

"Like who?"

"Ambulance? Police?"

"No need." As the driver spoke, the sound of sirens wailed into earshot, and within moments, police cars screamed up from two directions.

"Great. Now I get arrested."

The driver looked at him with his half smile, which was starting to get irritating.

"Why will you be arrested?"

"We both will. I chased the man, and you ran him over."

"I told you to chase him, and he ran into me, I didn't run over him. Technically, there's a difference."

Four policemen, all four armed, all four looking less than friendly, advanced on them, weapons raised.

"He was driving." Harper half put his hands up. "I'm a British police detective."

"I suppose we'd better get him to hospital. The knife is over by the kerb. It needs bagging."

"Boss."

Harper did a double take. Why was the taxi driver giving instructions to the uniforms? Why were they doing as he told them? He turned to the driver, his heart sinking like a concrete block in his chest, as realisation dawned.

"Welcome to the Island of Farou, Detective Inspector Harper. Chief Inspector Kyriakoulis. Beckett." He stuck out his hand. His grip was strong, and he stared deep into Harper's eyes as he shook. Harper felt his whole soul being assessed in those few seconds, and it made him uncomfortable, "Apologies for the slight diversion. Hotel?"

***

"You can't stay here."

Even with such late notice, there had to have been better rooms available than the one Beckett and Harper were standing in now. To describe it as a lean-to shed was to be generous. Positioned at the back of what was already the cheapest and shabbiest hotel in the town, there was a bed which looked like it had been reclaimed from the dump, the mattress a kaleidoscope of stains. There was a walk-in cupboard missing a door, which, on closer inspection, was not somewhere to put clothes, rather it housed a cracked toilet and a shower head thrusting from the wall like a rotten tree branch. The rancid smell of drains cloaked the room, and stuck in the back of the throat.

The room had been selected specifically to demonstrate how grateful the local police were for the British police officer's presence. Beckett felt ashamed, even more so taking in Harper's reaction. Revulsion had flickered over his face, but then had been pushed away, the man determined not to show his emotions. Beckett figured Harper was well-practised at hiding his feelings.

"It's fine," Harper said, his voice tight. He'd stayed silent in the short drive from the beach to the hotel. He'd run a hand through his hair, and smoothed his shirt, but had otherwise done nothing.

"It's not fine. It's a shit hole. I apologise."

"You seem to do that a lot." Harper regarded Beckett, his gaze measured.

"Do what?"

"Apologise."

"Not something you make a habit of doing?"

"I don't make many mistakes."

"Like failing to recognise the difference between a taxi driver and a senior detective?"

Beckett expected Harper to flush, or at least blink. He did neither.

"You could have introduced yourself. Appearances can be deceptive." Harper stared at him, conker brown eyes hard. "But, if it helps, I apologise."

Beckett matched his gaze for a few moments. Most people were easy to read. Most people gave things away about themselves, without opening their mouths. The young man in front of Beckett was not like that. It was like looking at a blank space; if it wasn't for the fact he was distractingly handsome and dressed in carefully chosen extremely stylish, and no doubt expensive, clothes, you'd could forget he was there altogether.

"Come on." Beckett smiled. "You can stay at my dad's place. It's only a couple of miles, up the coast. He's away so the place is empty."

"Is that appropriate?"

"It's just a place to stay." Yelling erupted outside the shed, the sound of a dozen or so lads returning from their night out off their heads, throwing bottles, and singing tunelessly. "You're going to need to get *some* sleep, if you're to be of any help to me."

Back in the car, Harper fell silent again. When Beckett had been given his name, he'd done what anyone would do. He'd made some phone calls to the friends he had left at the Met and hit Google. The Met contacts had nothing surprising to add to what Beckett had already learned. Harper was bright, ambitious, but wasn't a team player. Officers that worked for him, or with him, did not like him, trust him, or feel like they knew him, even after a long investigation. He didn't adjourn to the pub with his teams. He didn't join in with the practical jokes or bacon buttie rounds. They followed him, because he knew what he was doing, and got results.

Harper had an almost supernatural ability to remember details, and could recite from memory every police manual, procedure, and relevant piece of legislation. He didn't just do things by the book. He *was* the book. No one had ever seen him get physical. He did not get his hands dirty. He was the complete embodiment of a modern detective, so popular with those in charge, those so far removed from the real world, they thought all investigating should be done from behind a computer. The consensus was the bosses loved him, and the rank and file did not.

The description of a man devoid of social niceties was an interesting contrast to the press release from the parents of Jodie Cox. Plus, in the statement made by Harper shown on the BBC website, Beckett had seen emotion. Heard it, too. Perhaps it was reserved only for victims, but it was there, buried behind the protective layers of a computer screen and a television camera.

And he'd certainly got his hands dirty in the short time Beckett had known him. When Beckett had asked him to go after the drug dealer, he'd expected him to refuse, and had been surprised when he gave chase. He was even more surprised to find the man hurtling over his bonnet, with Harper close behind.

"Has the boyfriend's alibi been confirmed yet?"

Harper's voice was so soft, Beckett had to strain to hear him.

"We'll be working on that today."

"The semen found in the dead girl?"

"Danni Deacon."

Harper gave a nod.

"If it's a match for the boyfriend, we will have it confirmed today."

There was silence for a moment. Beckett concentrated

on negotiating the tight bend, and spotting the turn off to his father's villa. It was easy to drive past.

"Murder weapon?"

"Not yet identified."

"Location of the murder?"

"No."

"Whereabouts of the victim leading up to the murder?"

"Not yet."

"You've interviewed the boyfriend, and searched their apartment?"

"Forensics will be in there today."

"And the boyfriend?"

"It's not him."

"When you know so little how can you say that?"

"It was genuine shock when I told him she was dead. He wasn't faking."

"The evidence will decide that."

Beckett pulled into a driveway, and wound his window down.

"Rather than gut instinct?" There's no room for instinct in modern policing. He'd heard that repeated a hundred times back in London, and from his hospital bed, when being told his future with the Met was in a terminal state. Beckett contemplated the security keypad, scrambling through his memory for the code. He hit a few keys, and the eight-foot-high wood panel gates parted like the Red Sea. "Perhaps you're right, DI Harper. And Patrick Gruenanger is not telling us everything. No question there was something off about their relationship, but if the evidence we find points to him as the killer, then we're missing something."

Beckett had given Harper a perfunctory tour of the villa, then had left him to it. Harper was relieved. The villa was mind blowing, and he was struggling to remain indifferent. The gates had parted to reveal a sunken driveway, and rainforest style vegetation banked up on either side, but kept in check by marble retaining walls, embedded with LED lights, which flicked on as they approached. The villa itself was illuminated by the time the car pulled up outside. It was like a modern art installation, carved out of a glacier. Pure white, two storeys, rectangles balanced on rectangles, creating terraces and shade. Even in the pre-dawn darkness, it was impressive.

Harper could have described the interior before the heavy mahogany front door swung open. Creams and whites, clean lines, immaculate maple wood floors. Banks of sofas whispering money, marble clad bathrooms, and with a flick of a switch, a huge terrace, ending with an infinity pool. Beyond the terrace, were the shadows of the cliffs and the dark body of the sea.

"Your dad's place?" Harper had thought of his own father's threadbare terraced house.

Beckett was peering into the huge American fridge.

"Not much in here, apart from beer."

"He doesn't spend much time here?"

"Not much." Beckett was opening other cupboard doors. "There's food in the freezer and some tins. Frozen milk." Beckett waved a carton at him, and put it onto the worktop.

"What does he do? For a living."

Beckett had stopped, and looked at him. That half smile returned. "He's retired."

"Did alright for himself, then?"

"You could say that."

"You don't live here?"

"No. I've got a place up in the hills."

"The olive farm?"

Beckett's smile widened. He was obviously wondering what else Harper had been told.

"That's right."

"There's me thinking this *was* up in the hills."

"Make yourself at home. I'll be back to pick you up in," he glanced at the guitar-shaped clock on the far wall, "five hours? 9am, okay?"

As soon as Beckett had gone, Harper poured himself a glass of beer and did a full recce of the place. He had never enjoyed beer particularly, but his brain was buzzing, and he hoped it might slow things down and allow him to sleep.

The villa was not as massive as it could have been. He counted only five bedrooms, in addition to the one Beckett had suggested he use. Each had luxury, hotel standard ensuites, and they all opened onto private terraces, three on the second floor overlooking the gardens, and three to the sea.

The main body of the house was an open plan living, dining and kitchen area, which all faced towards the glass wall and the terrace. The only other room was down a corridor. There was a door at the end, and a security keypad. Whatever was behind the door was kept locked away. Out on the terrace, Harper could see the room, whatever it housed, had large windows shrouded in heavy blinds. A house like this the room was probably home to an art collection, a couple of Monets and a Van Gogh.

The walls of the large living area were adorned, not with old Masters, but a vast collection of rock tour posters—Pink Floyd, Genesis, Jimi Hendrix, Tempest, The Beatles, Rolling Stones. Harper squinted at them – they all appeared to be autographed. There were also a couple of guitars hanging amongst the posters, again signed, one by Jimi Hendrix, if he interpreted the squiggle correctly. Along with the grand piano nestled in one corner of the room, it was plain Beckett's father was a music fan.

Harper opened a cupboard under the plasma screen recessed into the wall, and found himself smiling. There was a

Bang and Olufsen music system, and a mind boggling collection of CDs and vinyl. A quick flick through proved rewarding. An eclectic taste, but one which reflected Harper's own. He selected one of his all-time favourites, *Blood on the Tracks* by Bob Dylan. The music rained down from every corner of the room from invisible speakers.

He sipped his beer, and studied a couple of photos standing on the mantelpiece of the real wood fire. A young, eight or nine at a guess, blond-haired boy clasping hands with a stunning ice blonde woman in a fur coat. Her natural beauty was quite breath-taking, but the way she looked at the camera, with only the ghost of a smile, suggested an ocean of discontent. The boy, had to be Beckett, alongside his mother.

The second photo was recognisably Beckett, early to mid-twenties, in a military uniform, wearing a green beret. The similarity between Beckett and his mother was now unambiguous. Harper got closer to the photo. The insignia on the beret said, 'Intelligence Corps,' the motto under the photo, 'Knowledge gives Strength to the Arm.' A lesson not to underestimate the now frayed around the edges man, who'd appeared quiet and unassuming, but had already fooled him once into thinking he was a mere taxi driver? Harper sank into the Italian leather sofa, and took another mouthful of beer. He felt uneasy. This was supposed to be his chance to shine.

CHAPTER TWELVE

"You look like shit. And you smell worse." Welsh Nik pushed his sunglasses onto his head, so he could get a better look at Beckett.

"I've had three hours of sleep, and spent half the night taxiing my new assistant around, so unless you've got anything helpful to say…"

Nik had been mercifully quiet up until that point. They'd headed out of the harbour just after dawn, and watched the sunrise wrap its arms around the island in silence. Beckett half thought Nik had gone back to sleep, and had wedged the steering wheel between his ankles.

They were in a medium-sized motor boat, one of the fastest in Welsh Nik's fleet, heading up the coast. It was early, the sun fresh in the lavender blue sky. The air was cool, the sea still, as if the world was holding its breath. The only waves formed were from the progress of the *La Perla*. There was no one else around.

"This'll do. Can you stop for a minute?"

"You dragged me out of bed, told me it was urgent business, and now you want to stop in the middle of the sea?"

"I can't have you being seen with me, if I look like shit. I need to freshen up. If you'd just…" Beckett circled a finger at him. Nik clamped his sunglasses back over his eyes and turned around.

"If I help you to catch this bastard, will I get any credit? Something I can put on my website? As endorsed by etc, etc…"

Beckett peeled off his clothes, piece by piece, t-shirt,

jumper, trousers, and boxer shorts. The air felt like velvet against his skin, his muscles started to unknot.

"Someone is dead, remember."

"Yeah, which is why I'm not in my bed at half past six in a morning. But, business is business."

Beckett shook his head at Nik's back.

"Don't sail off."

He dove into the water. Fingers slicing into the stillness, head, arms, then body and legs enveloped by ice and freedom. It was so cold, his lungs tightened as the air in them contracted, but he pulled himself downwards with powerful strokes. His knee did not trouble him in the water. It felt, too, like the world couldn't trouble him down there in the silence, with the dark below, and the distorted shimmer of light and life above. If he kept swimming down into the peaceful dark, who would he meet?

His lungs started to scream, and survival instinct took hold. He kicked hard with his legs, and burst through the surface, water cascading over his head as he took a deep breath. He climbed back on the boat, and grabbed the towel Nik had thrown for him.

"Feel better now?" Nik was laying on the seats behind the steering wheel, eyes shut, hands behind his head. "Can we carry on?"

Beckett put back on his clothes.

"Much better. Thank you."

They sailed on, Beckett studying a map. He could feel Nik watching him.

"What's he like then, this English policeman?"

"About twelve years old. I think he'll be okay. Though, he did mistake me for a taxi driver."

Nik threw his head back laughing hard. "Doesn't say

much for his powers of deduction. Though, you do look more like a taxi driver than a cop."

"Thanks."

"Well, he better not start throwing his weight around. The days of the British empire are long gone from here."

"You love the Brits. You wouldn't have a business without them."

"Of course I love them. I laugh and talk to them, and take their money. They are my friends, when they are here. But, then, off they go again. That's the way we like it. We don't want them ordering us around."

"That won't happen. I'm in charge, and he's just a kid. He's good, but inexperienced."

"That's what they might have told you, but they will try and take control. That's what they do. They can't help it." Nik frowned, as a thought came to him. "In fact, this British bobby must have left the UK almost before your lovely boss lady had agreed to him coming. They've taken control already."

"Do you want to concentrate on driving the boat? I know you find it hard to do more than one thing at once. We don't want to hit a hidden rock and sink. I might not be feeling generous enough to save you."

Nik couldn't swim; a surprising gap in the skillset of a boat yard owner. One of the phrases he trotted out for the tourists was, 'That's why I have boats. If I could swim, I wouldn't need them,' along with using it as a guarantee about how safe his boats were… so safe swimming skills would never be necessary.

"You'd never let me drown. Hell, you'd save Hitler."

Beckett ghosted a smile, but went back to his map. He didn't save everyone. In fact, as far as some people went, it was quite the opposite.

"Do you know what are we looking for?"

"The bay where we found the body. This one here."

They rounded the headland. From this perspective, it looked even more difficult to access. He couldn't see the golden crescent of the beach. It was too obscured by the shark's teeth rocks.

"We can't get in there in this."

"You'd need a smaller boat?"

"A small rib would do it."

"You wouldn't want to travel far into one, with a body on board you were intending to dump, and the sun coming up."

"No, not far at all."

"So, they probably launched from another bay, either further along or back the way we came."

"Any further, and the coast line is more exposed, more chance of getting seen loading a body into a boat."

"Back the way we came then."

Nik turned the boat around. Beckett looking at the map, and then he shoreline. They passed two more bays, but with no road access. Beckett shook his head, and they sailed on. They rounded another outcrop of rock, and there was a large shingle beach tucked up against a sheer cliff on one side, but a gently sloping cluster of trees on the other.

"This one. Can you land?"

***

Under instruction, Nik stayed by the boat.

There was a road on the map leading through the trees right down to the beach, but the local maps were notoriously unreliable. What looked like a road often turned out to be no more than a rabbit run, perhaps once passable by donkeys. But, rough and pockmarked as it was, this was definitely a road, with a semi-circle of dirt nudging up to the beach, perfect for parking and turning cars. And there were tyre marks—fat, heavily treaded ones, and another set, very different. Much thinner, too thin to be belong to a car. Motorbike perhaps or a trailer. A boat trailer.

Beckett crouched down to inspect them, before

following the tracks, careful not to step in them, up from the beach. The smaller tyre marks trailed the bigger ones; definitely a trailer. He looked back to where Nik was laying in their boat, dead to the world. You could reverse a car and trailer right down to the water. The shingle wouldn't leave any marks, of course, but there were plenty of indentations in the dirt of the road and turning space. They had to be recent. The rain from Saturday night would have obliterated any made before that.

He hobbled back down to Nik. The shingle was uneven beneath his feet. This time yesterday, he'd have been in curled up in a ball on the floor trying to walk across it. Now, it was bearable. Thank god for chemical intervention.

"This is the place they launched from. There's lots of tyres marks on the track above the beach."

Nik opened his eyes.

"Why not dump the body here? Why go to all the trouble of launching a boat, and sailing up the coast? Where's the sense in that?"

"The other beach must have meant something to the killer. Perhaps to the killer *and* the victim. They took a big risk in putting the body where they did, and by phoning us to bring it to our attention."

"I thought you said a passing fisherman phoned in?"

"You can't see the beach when you sail past. You have to go right in, around the rocks. I bet you'd have to be almost on the beach, before you could see it."

"Which means…?"

"The person who phoned in must have been involved."

"They killed someone, and then, rung to tell you where to find the body? They don't sound very smart. You'll have caught them before this English Detective wakes up."

"Maybe. All of this, Nik, the details, are strictly confidential of course."

Nik held his hands up.

"Of course."

Beckett didn't believe him for a second. As soon as Nik was back at base, he would be telling anyone he could collar about his dawn trip to the murder scene. He'd embellish his role, and divulge wild and wonderful theories. It was the way of the Island. Beckett hadn't mentioned the arrival of the English Detective. Nik had already heard that from someone else, before Beckett had opened his mouth.

Keeping anything confidential would be almost impossible, but in this case, it might help. If the information about the phone call, and the boat and trailer, found its way back to the killer, it might unsettle them. And any strange behaviour made them easier to spot, for him, his officers, and family and friends. They might even hand themselves in. Or it could make them panic, and kill Emmie. It was a risk he had no choice but to take.

"You can head back now. I'm going to walk up the track to the road."

"You're done with me? My role as trusty and dependable sidekick is over?"

"Appreciated, as ever."

"Be careful my friend. The murderer might be around. Returning to the scene of the crime." Nik pulled a scared face, then grinned.

"Thanks for the concern."

Beckett kept to the edge of the track. It was drier under the trees, but the imprint of a vehicle and trailer were still visible. Two sets, one up and one down. They'd have to do a search of the track, and into the trees on each side. Back in Athens or London, you'd have a hundred officers all briefed and primed within a couple of hours. He kept his eyes on the ground, but there was nothing. Time of death meant Danni had been killed a few hours before she was dumped on the beach. So, the body would either have been in the boat already, or in the car. If there was any evidence from the body, it would be by the shoreline. He'd seen nothing, but the search would concentrate there.

The track climbed gradually, and wound between the tortured trunks of olive trees. The sun wasn't old enough in the sky to have generated much heat, and it was icy cool under the canopy. The shattered light, refracted by leaves, had a green hue. It was a different world to the brash yellow and blue of the beaches. There was no sound, no breath of wind. But, there were creatures out there. The Island teemed with wildlife, feathery, furry and scaly, with wings or legs, or without either. Thousands of pairs of eyes, perhaps watching up from the gloom. This was their place, not his… so why were they so silent?

Beckett thought he heard something ahead. The sound of a car engine, slowing down, stopping. A door slamming. He'd called Tomas from the beach, and organised a patrol car to meet him at the top. He didn't want any tourists or locals deciding today was the day they wanted to visit the beach and destroy evidence.

He could see the black ribbon of tarmac through the trees, and as he rounded the last corner, he could see the car. A blood red hatchback parked across the entrance to the track. Not a patrol car.

Another two strides, and he could see someone hunched down in the gloom next to the trunk of an olive tree. *What were they doing? Stopping for a pee?*

"Hey there," he called.

The person was on their feet, and back in the car. Beckett started running. The engine fired into life, and, with tyres spewing out muck and gravel, accelerated away. Beckett reached the tarmac, as the red car disappeared around the corner.

He turned back to the tree. There was a bouquet of flowers, yellows, pinks and blues, tied with a red silk ribbon. He crouched down, and skimmed the note – a hand-drawn love heart and one word, 'Danni.' There was something looped around the ribbon—a bracelet. Beckett pulled latex gloves from his pocket, snapped them on, and lifted the bracelet away from the bouquet. It was a leather friendship bracelet, with three silver beads, each one engraved with an intricate design. The light under the trees wasn't bright enough to see the detail, but he didn't need to. He'd seen a bracelet just like it once before. *Found* a bracelet just like it once before. His stomach clenched.

CHAPTER THIRTEEN

arper stood on the terrace, gazing across the pool to where it merged with the ocean and with the horizon beyond. The ferociously blue sky, the deeper blue of the sea, and the aqua of the pool melded together beautifully. Green clad cliffs rose and fell to his left and right, rocks jutting out into the blue, with tantalising hints of gold. Tiny silent boats passed beneath, leaving their white trails behind. He'd never stood anywhere more beautiful or breath-taking. He felt an urge to phone someone, tell them where he was, take a photo with his phone, and text it. But, he didn't know anyone who would care.

The heat was starting to build. He could feel it stealing into his skin. He was tired. A few hours on one of the sun loungers beckoned like a drug, but Beckett was due soon. He'd found an iron in one of the kitchen cupboards, and easing all the creases out of his clothes felt like a priority over more sleep.

Back inside, Harper started the search for an ironing board. He remembered what he thought might be a walk-in cupboard in the corridor leading to the locked room – perfect place for an ironing board. He dropped a hand to open the door, but his attention snapped to the keypad of the locked room. The red 'locked' light, which had sparkled on the keypad, was now shining green.

He approached the door. Hesitated. Listened. The house was silent. He was sure he was alone. He put his hand on the door, and pushed. It gave to his pressure, and swung open. Noise exploded back at him, so loud, so intense, it stunned him for a moment. Then, it dawned on him. He had walked into a recording studio. He was in the control room, the mixing desk arcing out in front of him. Beyond, was a huge glass window. The noise, a searing, majestic, squealing electric guitar, was blasting through the open door from the studio room. A man, short, stocky, with a mass of curly, silver hair, was firing the fingers of one hand up and down the neck of the guitar, plunging at the strings with the other hand, creating a magical thunderous incredible sound. He was completely immersed in the music he was creating. Harper drank in the sound with awe. The range of sounds one man could conjure from a simple guitar and a set of amps always astounded him.

The noise built to a crescendo, and the man spun around, as if the music was surging up from the floor through his body and out through his hands. He was the music. He grinned and nodded at Harper, and continued playing, clearly loving having an audience. Harper felt like he'd slipped into a parallel universe. He recognised the man. The crooked nose, the mouth, which seemed to take up half the face, the ever-present dimples, and the blue eyes, which always seemed to be laughing. Harper had watched the face age in fast forward. Album covers, videos of concerts from the last few decades, interviews on TV. There was no mistaking him. This was Faulkner Lis, lead singer and guitarist with one of the biggest prog rock bands of all time, Tempest. A rock god was playing right in front of him.

Harper's mind ran through the rock posters on the walls, the luxury of the villa, the slight reticence of Beckett when asked what his father did for a living. *Why the hell had no one thought to tell him?* Beckett Kyriakoulis' father was Faulkner Lis. *How could he not have known?* In the back of his head, where all the music trivia was stored, a little voice popped up, reminding him that Faulkner Lis' real name was Constantinos Kyriakoulis. He was born in Farou, moved to London in his teens, started the band, and changed his name, in tribute to his favourite writer, William Faulkner.

"You must be Harper." Faulkner put the guitar to one side, and offered his hand. Harper shook it, trying to organise his thoughts into something sensible. "Beckett sent me a text to say you were staying. Think I probably forget to text him back to warn him I was on my way."

"I'm sorry. I'll pack my things; I've used some milk, but…"

"Shut the fuck up," Faulkner cut him off, clapping him on the shoulder, and grinning. "You're more than welcome to stay. Hate being here on my own. And you're obviously a music fan, unlike my son. Do you play?"

"No. A bit. Not really. Not like… that…"

"It's just practise. We'll have a jam sometime. If Beckett lets you out to play. How… erm… is he? This, erm… dead girl… the case… it's not… he's, erm… Look, d'you fancy a coffee?"

As Beckett drove to his dad's place, winding the car up the cliff road, he could not get the image of the bracelet out of his head. The last time he'd seen it, or rather its twin, he'd been sitting in the Chief's office, with Rosie Payne's parents, explaining to them the bracelet had belonged to their daughter, and had been found in the possession of the man suspected of killing her. Beckett hadn't told them Chrystos Spiros had been wearing the bracelet. That he collected jewellery from each of the women he'd raped, and was wearing every piece when Beckett had found him. He also didn't mention how when he had crept into the clearing in the forest where Chrystos had been hiding, the Fiend had been eating the flesh from around the cheek bones of Panos Myron, a local man who'd chosen to conduct his own manhunt, and ended up in one of the bear traps Chrystos had set up around his camp.

There was no evidence Chrystos had intended to use the

traps to kill people; they had been for catching food. When Beckett had found the camp, Panos was alive, but he was certainly, in Chrystos' head, classed as food. Beckett had witnessed things in his military career, in Bosnia and Iraq, which could give birth to nightmares, things which twisted and warped the mind until it snapped, but the image of Chrystos chewing human flesh, blood dribbling down his chin, eyes wide with innocence, the women's jewellery hanging around his wrists and neck, had never ever left him.

Every other piece of jewellery had been returned to the victims, who, though mentally and physically scarred for life, managed in one way or another to resume their lives. All had been brutally raped by Chrystos, but always released when he'd finished. A week or so later, he would select another victim. Rosie, however, was different. She'd disappeared one day, and that was that. The fact Chrystos was wearing her bracelet was enough for everyone to conclude he had committed the crime. Though a body was never found, everyone was convinced he'd murdered her, and hidden her body somewhere on the Island. Enough for everyone, except Beckett. Chrystos was sent to a secure mental institution on the mainland, and the case closed.

But, now, an identical bracelet had been found. He was certain Patrick and DNA tests would confirm it had belonged to Danni. His stomach stung with sickness. Of course, when Emmie went missing, when he had the call about the dead girl on the beach, he'd thought of Rosie, but he'd pushed those thoughts away. It was impossible to do that now. He'd never believed Chrystos had killed Rosie.

As he let himself into the house, Beckett could hear voices drifting in from the terrace. The soft burr with the rounded vowels of Harper, and the flat Greek, mixed with London tones of...

"When the hell did you get here?" Beckett stared at his dad, who was holding court at the large outdoor dining table.

Harper sat opposite. Faulkner had somehow managed to conjure up a luscious fruit salad breakfast, with croissants and Danish pastries. He had always been able to magic things into existence. On his ninth birthday, Beckett had longed for a bicycle, but his mother had refused to buy him one. He hadn't seen or spoken to his father for months, but Beckett had woken up on the morning of his birthday to find a bicycle, tied up in ribbons, leaning against their front fence—the exact model he'd wished for, but never told anyone. How had his dad known which one to buy?

Faulkner leapt up, and grabbed Beckett in a bear hug.

"Flew in a couple of hours ago. I could have given your lad here a lift, if I'd known. Saved him the Queasyjet experience."

"I didn't know you were due over." Beckett backed out of Faulkner's reach. He had to admit, he still looked great for his seventy years. The effect of years of partying and touring had been shed with a few years of a more relaxing lifestyle. The familiar irritation Beckett always felt when near his dad started to niggle around the edges. He circled his shoulders, as if to rid them of tension.

"I wasn't planning on it. I just thought you might need some moral support." Faulkner dropped his voice so Harper couldn't hear.

"Moral support. Why?"

"You know… with the case."

"You think you being here will help me do my job better?"

"Well… I… a friendly face, and all that."

"Which faces out here aren't friendly?"

"The longer it takes… if things don't go… I just want to help."

Faulkner's eyes were shining, animated with concern, his mouth open, desperate to conjure up some more convincing words, and his arms almost twitching with the need to grab Beckett in another comfort hug. Beckett looked past him, to where Harper was sitting, gaze fixed out to sea, pretending he wasn't listening.

"We're going. You ready, Harper?"

"Of course. Yeah."

Harper jumped up. Beckett turned to go.

"Perhaps we can talk tonight, son."

Beckett kept walking.

In the car, Beckett could feel the anticipation fizzing from Harper, like a shaken-up bottle of pop. It wasn't an unfamiliar experience.

"Go on, then," Beckett said.

"Go on, what?"

"Whatever you're desperate to spit out."

He could feel Harper look at him, consider his options, and then…

"Your dad is Faulkner Lis. How did I not know that? Why didn't anyone tell me?"

"Because it's not relevant."

"But, it's the sort of thing people gossip about."

It was impossible to work in any police force, and not be subjected, willingly or not, to endless rounds of gossip. He knew Harper wasn't the sort of man who went down the pub with the rest of the team after a shift to share titbits. Beckett had never talked about his dad, so doubted other people did either.

"I'm sure people have enough to say about me, without analysing my family tree."

That shut Harper up for a moment.

"What was it like growing up with him? Did you get to go on tour?"

"My parent's split up when I was eight."

"You must have been the coolest kid in school."

Beckett shrugged. He'd never told school friends about

his dad. They'd all assumed his dad was the man who picked him up every day, who'd taken him to football camp, who went to his graduation. Growing up, Beckett had tried to forget there was another man who had biological right to claim the title.

"I asked about getting you a vehicle whilst you were here. There's no budget, apparently, but I've got a pick up you can borrow. It's a bit battered, but it works. We'll pick it up later."

"Thanks." Harper hesitated. "He says its fine for me to stay on. Is that okay with you?"

"Sure. I told you. He loves guests." Beckett tugged on the steering wheel, as a tourist bus swept wide round a clifftop corner. Harper gripped the door handle, and sucked in his breath. Beckett almost felt sorry for him. This was a long way from his comfort zone.

"Assuming we survive the drive, where are we heading?"

"To see the boyfriend. While you were sleeping, I took a boat out to look for where the body was loaded from. We know she must have been transported into a boat, and taken out to the beach where she was found."

"I take it you found it?"

"Not just that. Someone was leaving flowers. They disappeared when they saw me. We're trying to trace the car, and the flowers. And they left this."

Beckett passed him the bracelet, cocooned in an evidence bag.

"Definitely Danni's?"

"That's what we're going to check now. I had a car outside the flat where Patrick Gruenanger stayed last night. He didn't leave there all night, or this morning."

"But, you think he might have snuck out somehow?"

"Unlikely."

"He's still the most promising suspect."

"There's something else."

Harper was studying the bracelet, turning it over in his hands.

"I've seen a bracelet identical to this one before. Rosie Payne had one."

He had Harper's full attention.

"Identical? How can you be sure? That was years ago."

"I'm sure, because I found it."

"It's just a coincidence. That case is closed. It's of no relevance to this."

"You think?"

"You don't?"

"The bracelet is not the only similarity. Danni had a tattoo."

"I've seen the PM photos."

"Rosie did, too. Grapes wrapped around a staff. Same as Danni."

"Rosie's body was never found. How can you know the tattoos were the same? There were no photographs from before she went missing. All you had was a description from a friend. And I'm not convinced you can say for certain the bracelets were the same either. Not after so long. It's a distraction. White noise. We need to stay focussed on the evidence in front of us. You know that as well as I do."

Beckett said nothing. For someone who was so certain the past was of no significance, Harper had enough knowledge of the Rosie Payne case to make it clear he'd at the very least been briefed, but more likely, had read copies of the case files.

"Any news on the missing girl?"

"The tourist police are handing out her photo. People have obviously seen the media coverage now, too. No sightings, as yet. There's no evidence of any connection between Danni Deacon and Emmie Archer."

"You think it's a coincidence a girl goes missing, and another ends up dead?"

"White noise, maybe?"

Harper bit back whatever he was about to retaliate with.

"If the two are connected, then finding out who killed Danni will lead us to Emmie."

"If it is the same person, Emmie Archer is likely dead by now anyway."

"Are you always this positive?"

"Realistic. Patrick Gruenanger's alibi?"

"Sergeant Tomas is checking out the CCTV at the port, to see if Mr. Gruenanger shows up arriving back in Farou early Monday morning, as he said. We've got people doing the same on the mainland. No response – either phone or email – from the friend he claims he sailed with last week. Forensics are down at the beach where we think the body was launched from. Tyres marks should be traceable to a make and model, and they'll do a fingertip search for anything else. And we should get the DNA results later today to confirm who Danni slept with before she died. We're also analysing her laptop to see if that can give us anything, as well as the forensics from the apartment."

Harper nodded.

"If you think I've left anything out…"

"Don't worry. I'll tell you, if that happens."

"You leapt at this opportunity?"

"I'm sorry if my presence makes things awkward for you."

"Some advice?" Beckett glanced at him, that blank face, the guarded expression. There was a slight shrug of the right shoulder. "Don't ever apologise, unless you mean it. And never take a case because you think it will bring you glory. Those are the cases that'll sucker you in, chew you up, and spit you out."

"You got your glory. You caught Chrystos Spiros. You're still the local hero."

As if to prove the point, a faded Land Rover passed

them, its side panels crimped and bent, headlights blinking, and the driver waving. *Local hero*, thought Beckett. *How much longer?*

CHAPTER FOURTEEN

Nikisiopi was emerging into consciousness, as Little Bee left the hotel. No one else in the hen party had surfaced. Even the news about the body on the beach, and Bee's assertion Emmie wasn't with Georgiou, hadn't much shaken their faith Emmie was simply warming her cold feet with another man. The wedding was due to happen the following day, and that evening was to have been the last big night out for the girls. They'd booked a table at their favourite restaurant, Stardust, and Jos was 100% convinced Emmie would make a dramatic entrance. 150%, Jos had expanded. Bee pointed out it wasn't possible to be more than 100% sure of anything. Jos had waved her away. Emmie loved to be centre of attention… a 150% of the time. Bee had gone back to her room, and slammed her door.

She hadn't been able to get hold of Kandace, despite leaving several messages. She guessed if there was any news, she would have called her back. She didn't dare phone the Inspector. He'd be furious she had talked to the press. He'd probably arrest her, or worse, get her extradited back to London. She couldn't stay hidden in her hotel. She needed to be doing something, and if the only thing left was to walk the streets of Nikisiopi, with a photo of Emmie, and ask each and every person if they'd seen her, then that's what she'd do.

Bee turned right out of the hotel, then left onto one of the bar-lined main streets, and straight into the path of Warren. Her mouth dropped open, and her stomach clenched with fear. His mouth was drawn into a snarl, his eyes wild. He looked like a bull, ready to snort and charge at her. Behind him were three of his mates, their faces all etched with the same animal aggression. Bee felt like an ant, caught in the middle of the street.

"Where is she?" Warren roared at her.

"I don't know. That's why I reported her missing." Her voice sounded tiny in her head, like someone had stolen the volume switch.

"The first thing you should have done, the very first thing, you stupid little cow, is to tell me. She is my fiancée. I had a right to know." He was right in her face now. He was over six foot, and when she looked up, all she could see was his nostrils flaring like a bull.

"We didn't want to worry you. Jos thought that…" She realised what she was about to say.

"Jos thought what?"

Bee backed away a couple of steps, but Warren grabbed her shoulder. His fingers dug in like claws, grating against the bone.

"Jos thought what? That she was slagging about? Emmie isn't like you lot… not that anyone would want to stick anything in you…"

"Do we have a problem here?"

Bee hadn't heard the car drive up, of course, and out of the corner of her eye, she could see Mitchell Troy.

Warren pushed Bee out of the way.

"Who are you?"

"A friend. You should be thanking her. She's the only person who's been doing anything to find Emmie."

"Friend? Shagging her, are you? Paedophile. You're a fucking pensioner. Disgusting."

"You're the one who's disgusting. Just leave us alone." Bee pushed at Warren, flushing with embarrassment. He brushed her away.

"I think you should leave." Mitchell stood between Warren and Bee. Bee could see the muscles either side of

Warren's jaws twitching.

"Please, just go," Bee pleaded.

"Tell me where Emmie is," Warren roared at her, sidestepping Mitchell. Bee could see the veins in Warren's neck, and the spittle spraying from his twisted mouth.

Mitchell put a hand on Warren's chest. Bee felt herself go cold, as Warren grabbed Mitchell and hurled him into the kerb. Mitchell hit the ground so hard Bee heard all the air whistle out of his lungs. Warren turned back to Bee.

"Now. You and me are going to have a discussion."

Bee could see Mitchell crawl to his feet. She wanted to scream at him to stay down. This was her problem. She didn't want him to get hurt, and saving someone once was enough. But, the words wouldn't come out of her mouth. She felt tears on her cheeks, and sobs building in her throat.

"What the fuck is wrong with you?" Mitchell yelled at Warren. Warren swivelled. A car pulled up behind Bee, though she barely registered it.

"What the fuck is wrong with you, old man?" Warren raised his fist.

Bee wasn't sure what happened. It was a blur. Suddenly Warren was on his knees, his outstretched arm twisted at an impossible angle behind his back, screaming for mercy. A tall hulk of a man standing over him, gripping the arm. Inspector Kyriakoulis.

"Are you okay, love?" a gentle British voice was asking her. Through her tears, she saw a pair of brown eyes under a floppy fringe. "Come and sit down." She let the man lead her to the pavement, where a seat miraculously appeared. She realised she was outside a bar. Mitchell sat down next to her.

"Are you okay?" He smiled, brushing the dirt from his shirt.

"I'm really sorry."

"You don't have to apologise to me. The guy is a thug. I take it that's Emmie's fiancé?"

Bee nodded. A patrol car had arrived, and two uniformed officers were prising a now handcuffed Warren into the back seat.

"Beatrice?"

She blinked into the sunlight, holding a hand over her eyes. Inspector Kyriakoulis was smiling at her, worry clouding his eyes. Next to him, there was a shorter man, the one with the soft brown eyes and floppy fringe, and a face which made her stomach flip over.

Kyriakoulis crouched down, so he was at eye level.

"Are you okay? Do you need to see a doctor?"

"He didn't touch me," she managed to whisper. "But, he hurt Mitchell."

Kyriakoulis' eyes flicked to Mitchell. She saw his expression change. His jaw clench.

"Only my pride is bruised." Mitchell winked at her, and smiled at Kyriakoulis. There was something in his smile she didn't recognise. She felt like she was in the middle of a conversation she didn't understand. "Good to see you, Beckett, even if the circumstances are less than agreeable."

"Mitchell. Why are you involved in this?"

"Right place, right time? Or wrong place, right time? Did you get my voicemail yesterday?"

Beckett stood up, face turning back into shadows. "You'll both need to come to the station to make statements."

"I don't want Warren to get in trouble. He's upset, because I didn't tell him about Emmie. It's not really his fault." Bee's voice trembled.

"Seems he learned about it from the internet. Not the best way to learn your fiancée is missing," Mitchell said, shrugging.

"We'll still need those statements," Kyriakoulis replied stiffly. "You're sure you're not hurt, Beatrice?"

"Positive."

"I'll look after her, Inspector. I'm sure you've got more than enough on your plate. Is this the cavalry?" Mitchell held out his hand to the brown eyes with the floppy fringe.

"Detective Inspector Harper, Metropolitan Police."

"Mitchell Troy. Let's hope you catch the bastard who killed that poor girl and find Bee's friend, before anyone else gets hurt."

"That's why I'm here, sir."

"Polite as ever, these British bobbies. Makes me miss home."

Bee looked at Beckett. His face was unreadable. When he walked away, she noticed his limp was nearly gone.

"If you need anything, or you feel at all threatened, please call us."

Bee realised the Detective Inspector was talking to her. She nodded. By the time she thought of saying thank you, he was getting into Inspector Kyriakoulis' car.

CHAPTER FIFTEEN

"What do you want to do with Warren?" Harper asked, as he climbed into the car.

Beckett pulled away from the scene slowly. "Give him time to calm down. We'll interview him this afternoon."

Harper nodded. Beckett was watching his rear-view mirror. Harper glanced back. Mitchell Troy was still talking to Beatrice. He had an arm around her shoulder.

"What's the deal with you and Troy, then?" Harper asked.

"Deal?" Beckett angled the car around a corner, and was back to concentrating on the road ahead.

"I thought you were going to let him get smacked."

They'd been at the apartment where Patrick Gruenanger was staying. He was in a bad way, the friend putting him up had said, so much so the doctor had prescribed sedatives for shock. No way had he left the apartment that morning, the friend confirmed. He could barely raise his head, and conversation was a jumble of words and silence. He'd identified the bracelet with a nod of his head, before curling up, arms wrapped around his knees.

Harper had seen guilty men play the grieving boyfriend before. Some even managed to convince themselves they truly were the devastated innocent party. Tears and tablets didn't impress him. He had been running through the evidence in his head, as they had driven away from the apartment, and around the corner to where Beckett had to brake to avoid Warren throwing Troy to the ground. Beckett had jumped out, as Troy clambered to his feet, and Warren had turned, with his fist raised.

Warren was a hulk of man. Rugby player, Harper had guessed. Twice Harper's size both in height and width. Not a man Harper would think about tackling alone. He'd looked across at Beckett, expecting him to wade in, being of similar size and, obviously, army trained, but he had hesitated. Beckett seemed to have sensed Harper's stare. Their eyes had met. The gaze had unnerved Harper, but in the next moment, Beckett had sprung forward. He'd grabbed Warren's fist, twisting his arm around and back, hyper rotating the shoulder. Warren had screamed like a wounded animal, as Beckett had forced him to his knees, smart enough to realise the more he struggled, the worse the pain would get.

"That's what you thought?" Beckett murmured, eyes scanning the road.

Harper pressed on. "Who is he?"

"He's a businessman."

"What sort of business?"

"You should ask your friends at the Met."

"What's he been done for?"

"A few misdemeanours, when he was younger. Nothing that's ever stuck since. He'd tell you he's in the legitimate import-export business. He's won awards. Met the Queen. Advised your Government."

"You think he's importing what? Drugs? People?"

Beckett shrugged.

"Based on what evidence?"

Beckett didn't reply. The single-track road had narrowed even further, as it wound steeply down wrapping around the bottom of a silver boulder the size of two double decker busses. The forest was thick, trees leaning over the road, turning the day into night.

"What's he doing mixed up with the missing girl?"

"I don't know."

"Is he a suspect?"

"When I found Chrystos, he was camped out in the forest. On land owned by Troy."

"What are you saying?"

"Chrystos Spiros worked for him for a while. Cleaned his pool, tended his garden, general handyman stuff. The Troys used to host parties at their villa. If Chrystos met Rosie, then that's where. We know Rosie was on the guest list. Troy knew her. Not well, he said. She was a friend of his wife."

"You think Troy was involved? That Chrystos wasn't working alone? Did any of the rape victims mention a second man?"

"No."

"And Chrystos admitted to all the offences? He didn't mention Troy."

"He didn't admit to killing Rosie Payne."

"But, he was found with her bracelet."

"That's not the same thing."

"You think Troy killed Rosie?" Harper couldn't keep the incredulity from his voice. "Why?"

"For the same reason he killed his wife. He's a sociopath."

Harper snorted. He looked across at Beckett, whose eyes were fixed on the road. "What makes you think he killed his wife? You got a body?"

"She took their boat out one night, and jumped overboard. There was a half empty bottle of whisky and an empty bottle of paracetamol."

"Note?"

"A brief one. Typed on a laptop. Sorry to her kids. Sorry she couldn't cope."

"You investigated?"

"I was back in London. The locals looked into it. The verdict was suicide. She'd been treated for depression. It was no great surprise to anyone."

"Apart from you."

"Troy's a sadist."

Harper felt himself smiling. "You *are* crazy."

Beckett snapped on the brakes. The car lurched to a halt on a blind bend. The ground to Harper's left fell away vertically between the trees. "That's what they told you was it?"

"Who?" Harper kept his eyes to the front, not wanting to face the death plunge. All it would take was one car, travelling a bit too fast, to come around the bend, slam into them, and take them spinning down into the pit.

"Your bosses at the Met."

"Drive, will you?"

Beckett shrugged and drove on.

CHAPTER SIXTEEN

The road down to the Bay was not for the faint-hearted. Coaches and buses didn't ever attempt it, and most people opted to arrive by the boat taxi. Beckett always thought the drive was worth it. To emerge from the depths of forest, and find yourself in a different world. The horseshoe-shaped bay with the radiant sand, and the diamond sparkle of the sea beyond. It was no surprise a visit to the Bay, and one of its three tavernas, was on most of the wealthier tourists' to-do lists.

Beckett tried to push thoughts of Mitchell Troy out of his mind. He knew it made him sound paranoid. He didn't blame Harper for scoffing, but it still hurt to know people he'd worked with in London, some of whom he'd thought respected him, even liked him, not only thought he'd lost the plot, but were warning people about him. Perhaps they were right. He was a joke.

"Very nice." Harper said, as they drove out of the trees, and down the dirt and gravel track to what passed as a car park, shared by all three tavernas. The tavernas also shared one jetty, jutting out into the water like a beckoning finger.

"Kensington on Sea central." Beckett got out of the car, and stretched his back. He had to admit, pacifying Warren had been enjoyable. The familiar buzz of adrenaline. He might not be as fast across the ground as he'd once been, but the technique was still there.

Harper raised an eyebrow.

"Mitchell Troy, and my dad for that matter, aren't the only wealthy ex-pats who have the Island as a second home. There are hundreds of luxury villas dotted around this part of the

Island. CEOs, actors, politicians. People say, during the busy months, you see the same people you'd bump into in Kensington."

"Not sure that's a selling point."

"For you and me, no. But, they bring lots of income to the Island. Attract many others, who want to brush shoulders. And this is where they like to eat."

Taverna Nemesis was the largest of the three clinging onto the right-hand edge of the Bay. It had a two-layer terrace wrapped around the front and side, the front terrace almost kissing the sea and the side terrace stepping up and into the rock face. There were already a dozen customers drinking coffee and chatting. Beckett caught Harper glancing at the menu displayed next to the front step. The prices wouldn't look out of place in Kensington High Street. The tourists who came here didn't fly in on middle of the night charter flights in flip flops and cheap sunglasses.

Michale Bakas, the owner and chief chef, took them up into the cliff terrace, and hooked the rope barrier across the steps. Beckett hadn't come across him before. He was from the mainland, and had bought the restaurant a couple of years prior. He came with a wealth of kitchen experience, learned in some of the top Michelin starred restaurants in the UK, and even some minor appearances on television. Impressive, for a man in his early thirties. He exuded confidence.

"We use this as a private function room/VIP area when needed. I thought we might not want to be disturbed." Michale had triangle of raven black hair under his bottom lip, and a head as bald and shiny as a chicken's egg. He sat at one of the tables. Beckett took the chair opposite.

"We'll want to speak to your staff as well." Harper stood off to one side, where he could see the beach terrace below. Michale kept flicking his gaze over to him.

"Of course. No problem. I can't believe what's happened. Danni was a lovely girl."

"Everyone is in shock." A woman stepped onto the terrace. British, her accent was bland, hard to locate, flattened out by a public-school education. She was petite and very blonde. Disarmingly beautiful. She glanced at Harper, then fixed her gaze on Beckett, "We were all very fond of her."

"This is Sophia, my wife." Michale half stood. "Inspector Kyriakoulis from the Island police, and DI Harper from the Met in London."

Sophia smiled at them both. "Do you want me to stay?" Beckett noted she did not look at her husband once.

"Please, sit down," Beckett instructed. She took the seat next to Michale. He reached out, and squeezed her hand.

"What do you want to know, Inspector?" she asked.

"When was the last time you saw Danni?"

"She worked her shift Wednesday night. Finished about 1am." Michale nodded in agreement with his wife.

"You didn't see her after that? Or speak to her?"

"It was her day off Thursday," Sophia said. "And she didn't turn up for her shift on Friday lunchtime."

"We were worried. I phoned her at home and on her mobile, but no response," Michale leaned towards Beckett, eyes imploring. "I even went around to her apartment. Knocked on the door, but no answer. Her car wasn't there, either."

Beckett caught the glance Sophia flashed at him. That was news to her.

"Has she done that before? Not turn up for a shift?" Harper cut in.

"Once or twice," Sophia said. "Staff forget shifts, go out partying, and sleep through. Decide they'd rather spend the day on the beach. One of the curses of being an employer."

"But, you were still worried enough to go around? Why?" Beckett asked Michale.

"I was in town anyway. She's a good employee. She'd been working really hard. We catered a big party Tuesday night, and we didn't get finished until about 5am. She worked a double shift Wednesday. I thought I'd check, whilst I was there, just in case."

"Just in case, what?"

"She'd overslept, or wasn't feeling well."

"And when you confirmed to yourself she wasn't at home, what did you think?"

"I assumed she'd gone away with Patrick." Michale shrugged. "She'd said he was heading for the mainland for a few days."

"Did you know Patrick?"

"Only through Danni. He dropped her off sometimes. Occasionally came in for a drink. Not often though. I'd say hello, if I saw him in the street."

Beckett looked at Sophia.

"Same. We were fond of Danni, but she was staff. We didn't socialise."

"You must have an opinion of him. Was he friendly, happy, quiet, reserved, rude, helpful?"

"As I said, I really didn't know him."

"I always thought he seemed…" Michale hesitated. "Rude… well, maybe not rude… unfriendly… He never said much when he came here."

"Did Danni and Patrick seem happy?"

"You think he did it?" Sophia sat up in the chair.

"Why would you say that?" Harper stepped closer.

"Because the police always suspect the boyfriend, or the husband, first," Michale said to Sophia. He turned back to Beckett. "I think their relationship was like most people's relationships. Sometimes, good, sometimes, not so good."

He glanced at Harper, who paced around the back of

Beckett to stand by the roped-off entrance.

"I think he was quite a jealous person. I'm not sure he liked her being a waitress," Michale added.

"Did she tell you that?" Beckett asked. Sophia was watching her husband. Michale rubbed a hand over his skull.

"She said something one night. End of last season, October time, just before we shut for the winter. Said she might not be able to come back this year. It was causing fights with Patrick. He didn't like her working late so many nights. He didn't like the way the men here looked at her."

"I thought you said he rarely came in. How did he know *how* people were looking at her?" Harper asked.

"I'm not sure. I think it was more in his imagination than anything."

"But, she did come back this year?"

"I asked her if it was okay. She said it was fine."

"Where did she work over the winter?" Harper queried.

"People here tend not to. You make your money in the summer season. Some people pick up odd jobs, but most go on holiday, or go home. I have no idea what Danni did." Sophia's voice sharpened. Beckett wondered why she was getting impatient.

"No. Sorry." Michale shook his head.

"Their neighbour, in the opposite flat, said he heard them arguing, loudly, quite often," Beckett said. "She never mentioned arguments? Came into work upset?"

"Linus Sang?" Michale asked.

"You know him?"

"He comes here quite a bit. I always thought he had a bit of a thing for Danni. She felt sorry for him, I think."

"He makes my skin crawl. He's a weirdo," Sophia added. "Maybe you should be looking at him as a suspect."

"He's a bit odd, but I think he's okay. Danni said he was a good neighbour. Used to look out for her." Michale gave her a dark look.

"Was Danni interested in Linus? Sexually, I mean."

"God, no," Michale snorted. "He was her pet project. She wanted him to find a girlfriend. Get out a bit more. She was like that. I think she enjoyed playing Cupid."

"You never heard Danni talking about other men? Perhaps someone she met here?"

Sophia's gaze flicked to Michale, then to Beckett. "It's possible. We have a lot of rich and powerful men who come in here. Danni was a pretty girl."

"So, Patrick did have reason to be jealous?" Harper asked.

"Danni was always the complete professional when she worked here," Michale snapped. The tension between him and Sophia now palpable.

"Were you having an affair with Danni?" Beckett put his elbows on the table leaning forward.

"What? No." Michale pushed his chair back, horrified. "I'm a happily married man. My wife is sitting right here, you bastard."

"When I think people are keeping things from me, I ask difficult questions."

"We're not keeping anything from you," Sophia said. "I trust my husband. He was not sleeping with Danni."

"You said Tuesday night Danni was working for you, catering a large private party?" Harper asked, calming the situation. "Do you have many private functions here?"

"It wasn't here. We get a lot of bookings from people who want to hold parties at their homes. If they're prepared to pay, then I'll do them. Danni usually volunteers." His voice tightened. "Not because she wants to spend time with me, before you insinuate anything, but because the tips tend to be very generous."

"The one Tuesday night?"

"It was an eighteenth birthday party."

"Where?"

"At Mitchell Troy's place. For his kids. They're twins."

"And Danni was there, with you?" Beckett could feel his heart rate accelerating. He could also sense Harper staring at him.

"We've done a few parties up there. He likes my food."

A connection. Danni at Troy's two days before she disappeared. It was as tenuous as it got, but it was still a link.

"Thank you for your help. If you think of anything else, please let us know. Can we talk to the rest of the staff now? The ones that are here. We'll need a list of the rest." Harper's clipped English tone permeated his thoughts.

They learned nothing new from the working staff. Most had only started that season, and didn't know Danni well. One of the sous chefs, Carlos, who worked at Nemesis for years, was the most helpful. He had no doubt in his mind.

"Her boyfriend was a thug. They argued a lot. I heard he got into lots of fights in the resorts. He's no good. You need to look there first. Danni liked to have a good time, but she was a nice girl. She didn't deserve what happened."

"Was she seeing anyone else? Did you ever hear any rumours? Someone she met at work, perhaps?" Beckett had asked.

Carlos had known exactly who Beckett was referring to. He tilted his chin and his eyes grew cold. "I have no idea. People gossip. But, I don't."

That was all he would say.

Back in the car, Beckett hesitated before starting the engine. "You think there was anything between Danni and Michale?"

Harper suppressed a smile. "Do you?"

Beckett ran his thoughts through his head. There was something not being said. Michale was closer to Danni than he was letting on, and Sophia was not the happy, doting wife.

"Everything would suggest yes." And yet, he couldn't see it.

"I think they were friends. I think they may have confided in each other. But, they weren't sleeping together."

"You can say that so definitively?"

"Michale's gay. I'd stake my life on it."

"He's married." Even as the words came out of his mouth, Beckett knew how ridiculous and out of touch they sounded. "Obviously, not openly gay. So, why do you think he is?"

"Because it takes one to know one."

Now, he felt really stupid and awkward.

"You never said," he added quickly. "Not that it matters."

"Why would you assume I was straight?" Harper seemed to be enjoying Beckett's discomfort.

Beckett started the engine. "You're sure about Michale?"

"You mean how accurate is my gaydar?"

Beckett glowered at him. "I'm sure it's not fool proof."

"I know what it means when a man looks at me, like Michale was looking at me. Don't tell me you didn't notice? Do you get the vibe when a woman gives you that 'look'?"

"Sometimes."

"To be fair, women are harder to read than men. I'm… 97% sure? Is that good enough?"

"Does Sophia know?"

"She's pissed off at him, for some reason. Either she's fed up of being the beard, or she thinks like you did; that Michale was shagging Danni." Harper lifted a shoulder noncommittally.

"If Danni was cheating on Patrick, it wasn't with

Michale."

"But, if you suspected it, and Sophia, too, then Patrick might have assumed the same. That's motive. We need that alibi confirming. Or rather, not. Where now? The station? We've still got Warren locked up." Harper clearly wanted to change the subject.

"A small detour first."

Harper glanced at him, about to protest.

"We need to see if Troy wants to press charges, before we decide what we do with Warren."

Harper shrugged. Not happy, but with no argument he could make.

CHAPTER SEVENTEEN

Harper thought about protesting against the visit to Mitchell Troy's, but figured Beckett would go with, or without, him. Better to be with him, and know exactly what was said, so he could report back accurately.

Beckett flicked on the radio, as they headed back up the impossible road away from the Bay. His mood was dark. Conversation not encouraged. Surely there had to be more going on here than Beckett disliking Troy? Whatever Beckett had been through and done, he was clearly an intelligent and perceptive man, not given to random vendettas and conspiracy theories. That didn't seem to fit his profile at all.

The music on the radio was traditional Greek bouzouki songs. Harper wasn't sure which was worse. The music itself, each song a slight variation of the one which came before, with a slow hypnotic beat and wailing voices, or the crackle, buzz and screech of the terrible reception. Nothing set Harper's teeth on edge as much as a badly tuned radio.

"You got any other music?" he asked.

"There might be a CD in the glove compartment," Beckett muttered at him. "I don't really listen to music."

"How can you not love music when your dad is Faulkner Lis?" Harper asked, clicking open the panel in front of his knees.

"Because we don't have to be like our fathers."

Harper thought of his dad. He'd be sitting in his front room, having walked to the news agents for his paper. Cup of stewed tea on the side table next to him, adding another circle of damp to the collage of Venn diagrams. BBC news would be flickering on the television, volume set to mute, so that he could shout at the news reports with anyone challenging his views. As the day progressed, he would flick channels to find his favourite knowledge-based quiz shows, where he would answer all the questions correctly. If the quiz show host declared a different answer, then he was wrong and a fool, and a letter of complaint would be fired off to the production company. He hoped Beckett was right.

Harper craned his neck, and put his hand into the glove compartment. His hand alighted on something smooth and square, which felt like a CD case. He pulled it out and something heavy came out with it, thudding to the floor.

The CD was one of the Tempest's – their fourth album called, *The Lion Whispered.*

Harper eyed Beckett, who glanced at it.

"Faulkner thinks it's hilarious to put his CDs in my car."

"You never listen to them?"

"I think I used it to scrape ice off my windscreen back in London."

Harper couldn't tell if he was joking or not.

"Do you mind if I…?" He waved the CD case at Beckett. Beckett shrugged, and the silver disk slid into the stereo. Within seconds, the sound of waves crashing over rocks and the distance beat of drums filled the car. Satisfied, Harper bent to retrieve the object that had fallen to the floor.

It was a handgun, encased in a battered leather holster. A Glock 26.

"You might want to put that back," Beckett said, his tone flat. "So I know where it is, should I need it."

Harper stowed it back in the glove compartment, and sank into his seat. He hated guns. Even thinking about them gave him a burning sensation in the pit of his stomach.

He'd done the firearms training. Not because he'd wanted to, but because his superior officers had wanted him to, and he wanted promotion. The training officers down at the MPSTC at Gravesend had been impressed. They considered him an excellent shot, he topped his class, and the instructors had recommended him for further training. But, despite the ease with which he'd picked up the skill, the way the grip seemed to mould into his palm and the trigger mesh with his finger, and how effortlessly he found the target, as if his thoughts alone were carrying the bullet wherever he wanted it to go, he went away feeling sick.

Hitting paper and card targets, shaped in vague resemblances of human beings, was one thing. It didn't matter how many bullets you put in them, the expressions on their faces never altered. The thought of a small, lead bullet tearing through skin, exploding blood vessels, splintering bone, thrashing and shredding flesh and muscle, horrified him. That he, with the neat metal tool, could inflict that damage, so easily, simply by squeezing a trigger with one finger. He did not want to be the person who squeezed that trigger. He did not want the responsibility. But, for the man behind the steering wheel, it seemed to be as casual a happening as paying for a loaf of bread. He kept his gun, that small piece of death, in his glove compartment. Like a box of tissues… or an unwanted CD.

Harper knew from what he'd been told of Beckett's history using a weapon was something he'd had to do a lot. He'd killed people, put bullets in them. Dealt death. Hard to imagine such a quiet man, who seemed more attune to this little Island, shooting anyone. It was only in a few unguarded moments Harper had seen the killer behind the eyes—seeing Mitchell about to be flattened, tackling Warren. When listening to Beckett talk about Troy, to Troy, he saw flashes of it, but it went just as quickly.

It was impossible to imagine what it must feel like to kill someone. *Did it get easier the more people you killed, to the point where you were prepared to hurl you and someone else off the top of a block of flats?* Harper was pragmatic. There needed to be people like Beckett in the world, to protect others, people like him, who didn't want to do the dirty work. The soldiers in war zones. Even the specialist officers in the Met. He didn't want to be one of them, and wasn't sure he trusted a man who had travelled so far along that path. At least the officers in the Met had a massive organisational and procedural structure behind them. And soldiers had their battalions and regiments and their superior officers.

Out here, on this little Island, far away from the limiting force of British regulations, in a place where he did not know the rules, he felt vulnerable. Now, he understood why being chosen for this job was not necessarily a vindication of his ability. Maybe it was more because he was expendable. They'd taken advantage of his ambition. *Well, damn them.* He wasn't going to let that happen. Beckett might think he was in a Western, bringing the man in the black hat to justice by whatever means it took or destroy what was left of his career trying. The only option left to Harper, as he saw it, was to keep the investigation legitimate, identify the killer, and get him charged as quickly as possible. What Beckett chose to do once Harper had left the Island was entirely up to him. He just had to keep control of him until then.

Mitchell Troy's place was about ten miles from Beckett's farm, further south down the Island. He owned about 500 acres in total, which included olive groves and a vineyard. The land extended from the forested hills in the north, down to a fertile valley, which ran down the middle of the Island. Over the years, Troy had purchased more and more land from the locals, spreading his domain wider and wider. The villa itself was nestled into the last of the hills, so it looked out over the flat expanse of the valley. With the land jutting up almost vertically up behind it, the two squat, square towers at both ends, and the battlements on the roof terrace, it looked more like a fortress than a Greek Villa.

The hulking iron gates at the bottom of the drive were guarded by bronze griffins, perched on massive gateposts, and an electronic keypad. Beckett didn't recognise the disinterested voice, which crackled through the speaker, and then, without acknowledgment, disappeared. After a couple of seconds, the gates swung into motion, and let them through.

Harper had been quiet since he'd picked up the gun. He hadn't seen a stop off at Troy's as a priority, but hadn't protested. Perhaps he saw it as another opportunity to report back to London on Beckett's mishandling of the case. It would have been more tactical to drop him off at the station, let him loose in the incident room, let him talk to Warren even, freeing up Beckett to prod Troy all he wanted, without prying eyes. He'd never been great at playing games. 'You do what you think is right, and sod the consequences,' was how Faulkner had summed him up. He wasn't sure if it had been a compliment, or a criticism. He'd been in hospital at the time, leg in traction mending, whilst his career was disintegrating around him.

Beckett glanced at Harper, wondering if he needed to brief him, or, at least, tell him to keep quiet. He was taking everything in, the long, winding drive between rows of grapevines, eyes widening when the house emerged like a charging behemoth from the trees above them, as the drive swung northwards.

"I thought your dad had the nicest place on the Island."

"Faulkner's is pretty average. This place is something else entirely."

"He built this himself?"

"There used to be a little farmhouse where the fishing lake is now."

"I guess he wanted a fortress, not a farmhouse."

Garden terraces framed the house, vegetation gushing down lush and flowing with colour and opulence. It always made Beckett think of the hanging gardens of Babylon. Where the house was slab-fronted and brutal, the gardens were an abundance of natural beauty. It was an uncomfortable contrast.

Mitchell was already waiting for them, as they pulled up on the gravel area running around three sides of the house. There was a cluster of parked cars. Mitchell's Porsche, a two-seater BMW sports car, a couple of bulky 4x4s, and a brand new Mini. None of them red.

Mitchell strode to meet them, smiling, arms outstretched. He couldn't look more relaxed or more welcoming.

"Beckett. Good to see you again so soon, and DI Harper. Welcome to my humble abode."

He said it with just the right amount of self-mockery, eyes twinkling. He exuded magnanimity. Beckett half-expected a gaggle of orphans to dash out from behind the house, and erupt into a joyous chorus from *Annie*, with Mitchell as Daddy Warbucks. He shook the image from his mind. One of the horrors from his early childhood, being dragged to the West End by Faulkner, and being left in the auditorium, whilst Faulkner disappeared with a fan – all blonde hair and scarlet lipstick.

"Is this a good time?" Beckett asked, returning the handshake and the smile, though he knew his eyes betrayed him, "We have Warren Nock in custody, and I need to know if you aim to press assault charges."

"I thought we'd been through all this, Inspector? I'm not going to press charges. The man is clearly upset, and not without reason. If you need a statement to tidy up the paperwork, then I will gladly provide one. It seems trivial work for two senior officers, but as you are here, why don't you come inside, have a drink, and we'll get it over and done with. It won't take long. You saw most of it yourselves."

"That would be very helpful, Mr. Troy." Harper nodded.

"Mitchell, please. Come on in."

Mitchell led them through a side door, down a cool marble clad corridor, and out into a huge, glass-fronted living room that, with the glass panels slid out of the way, ran seamlessly outside into a terrace, with endless views down the valley.

A bank of sofas ran around one end of the room, encircling a massive wall-mounted television screen. CGI alien soldiers were silently blasting hideously deformed zombie like monsters at the behest of a lad, late teens, who was sprawled on the sofa, so hypnotised by the battle, he did not notice their presence.

"This is Callum, my son. I'm not sure you've ever met him, Beckett. He'll have been in school back home when you were here chasing Spiros. He's all grown up now… but not so, as you'd notice." Mitchell picked up a cushion, and lobbed it at the boy. It connected perfectly with his head. He spun around, pulling down his headphones.

"Piss off…." His voice trailed away to nothing on seeing the two strangers.

"I'm so glad the extortionately expensive private education has been worthwhile." Mitchell rolled his eyes.

"Yeah, whatever." Callum pouted. He was baby-faced, with arching eyebrows and a dimpled chin, marred by a sullen expression.

"You'd think with all that money they would have taught you how to write the bloody computer games, so you could earn your keep," Mitchell looked back at Beckett and Harper. Beckett watched the colour flush into Callum's cheeks, and a nerve twitch behind his left eyebrow.

"Maybe I should ship him off to join the army. See if he's as good at killing living, breathing alien nations. But, I already know the answer. He's too bloody useless to be any good in the real world."

Callum jumped to his feet, and stomped out onto the terrace to where a girl was swimming lengths of a pool. Beckett could just see her head bobbing up and down.

"I was sitting outside about to eat lunch. Shall we…?"

Mitchell directed them onto the terrace, where a large canopied table housed a tray filled with jugs of what looked like freshly squeezed orange juice. An outsized barbeque housed sizzling meat – kebabs on long skewers, steaks, chicken pieces – and there was already a pile of meat set out on plates on the table and a huge bowl of Greek salad. Becket wondered if Troy was doing the cooking, or if a member of staff would pop out from a concealed door to turn the steaks at regular intervals.

"Please help yourself, if you're hungry. As you can see, there's plenty to go round."

Beckett shook his head.

"Should we come back another time?" Harper pushed his chair back a little. Callum had taken up residence on a sun lounger. The girl swam up to him, he leaned forward to say something to her, and she looked around at them.

"Now is good. But, DI Harper, you have to eat. It's basic human physiology." Mitchell speared a chicken leg, with a long silver skewer, and passed it on a plate to Harper. "Surely you're a little bit tempted, Beckett? A man cannot live off nicotine and Mythos beer alone. Unless you've turned vegetarian. Understandable, after finding Spiros the way you did, I suppose."

Beckett shook his head ignoring the dig.

"Aren't you going to introduce us, Daddy?" The girl eased out of the pool, and drifted over to them.

Beckett knew, because of the party Danni had been working, that both children had just turned eighteen, but whereas Callum still looked like a child, all puppy fat and scowls, the girl was anything but childlike. Her body curved like a pear, her breasts threatening to spill out over the top of her bikini. There was no shortage of confidence, her white micro bikini hid little. She was pretty, but her mouth had a turn to it that made her look permanently displeased, and her eyes were a sullen green. She way she looked at Harper was the way Harper was looking at the array of meats fanned out before him.

"Of course, my darling. These are Detective Inspector Harper, from the Metropolitan Police, and Inspector Kyriakoulis. They're here about that missing girl's fiancé."

"The one who decked you this morning?" Callum had wandered over, picking up a kebab with his stubby fingers.

"This is my daughter, Lily."

Beckett nodded at her. Despite their differences, now they were standing together, he could see the resemblance to her brother. They both had the round, baby like faces, which were almost handsome and almost beautiful.

"We're also investigating the murder of Danni Deacon."

"That girl on the beach?" Lily stared down at him, meeting his gaze.

"That's right. Did you know her? Any of you?" Beckett looked at each Troy in turn. Each one shrugged, and shook their heads. Harper's focus was now on the conversation, not the food. "I am correct in thinking you had a party here last Tuesday evening?"

"That's right. It was the kids' eighteenth," Mitchell answered. He was still relaxed, one arm swinging over the back of his chair.

"Michale Bakas did the catering?"

"That's right. He's the best chef on the Island."

"Danni Deacon was one of his waitresses. She was working here, at your party, on Tuesday night." Beckett waited. Mitchell sat up in his chair, and pushed it away from the table. The kids blinked, not sure what to say.

"That's awful." Mitchell ran a hand through his hair. "Poor girl. I had no idea. There were four or five waitresses serving that night. It sounds horribly snotty, but I don't really notice them when we have events. We have so many guests, and my focus is always on them."

"Are you certain?" Beckett shunted the orange juice and meats out of the way, and put a photo of Danni – a happy, smiling Danni – on the table, "All of you? This is one of the last places she'll have been seen."

"One of the last places, but not the last place?" Mitchell looked at Beckett. All the relaxed friendliness had evaporated from his eyes. The eyes were now shark-like, wary, guarded.

"She worked her shift at Taverna Nemesis on Wednesday, but wasn't seen after that."

Mitchell nodded, and picked up the photo. He studied it for a few moments, and narrowed his eyes.

"No, sorry. If she was working here, I must have seen her, but I don't recognise her."

"You don't eat in Taverna Nemesis? You would have seen her in there."

"If I eat out down there, I go to Stiggies."

"I thought Michale was the best chef on the Island?"

"He is… but I prefer the atmosphere in Stiggies." Mitchell passed the photo to Callum. "Did you see her Tuesday night, or were you too pissed to see the end of your own nose?"

Callum flushed, but took the photo. He glanced, and passed it to his sister.

"I don't remember her. Maybe. I think I've seen her in Nemesis."

"Ever talk to her?"

"Only to order steak, medium to charcoal," Lily mocked her brother, "Yeah, I remember her from Tuesday night. I'm sure I saw you flirting with her, Cal."

"I was not," he spluttered, cheeks red hot.

"Don't mess around, Lil, this is serious. I doubt Cal was flirting with anyone. He wouldn't know where to start." Mitchell shot her a warning look. She rolled her eyes.

"I do remember her, because she spilt red wine on my dress, silly cow. I had to get changed. Wasn't really her fault, I suppose. Some dirty old mate of Dad's 'accidentally on purpose' brushed past her, and his hand accidentally groped her bum."

"Can you give me his name?" Beckett asked.

"Yeah, who the hell was it, Lil? You better not be making this up," Mitchell growled.

"What's his name? Erm… he's the, erm… what do you call him? The Consul guy."

"The British Vice Consul?" Harper glanced at Beckett. "Neil Ticknall?"

"He *was* here. With his wife. They brought their daughter."

"She's, like, twelve. God knows why we invited her."

"She's sixteen, and she's a nice kid. Neil is a good guy. If he did knock into poor Danni, it would have been an accident." Mitchell's voice was constricted with fury.

Lily dropped her shoulders, suddenly looking like a little girl. "It probably was an accident. I bet it was her boyfriend that did her."

"Did you know her boyfriend?"

"No. Why would I? I just assumed she had one."

"Callum? When you were at Nemesis, did you ever see Danni with anyone?"

"I don't even remember seeing her, not really."

"Her and Michale were pretty friendly. I reckon they were banging each other. He's kind of sexy in a weird way," Lily piped in.

"As you can see, my daughter is not necessarily the best person to rely on in your investigation."

"You've been very helpful. We'll leave you to the rest of your day." Beckett pushed himself to his feet. "Oh, we'll need a list of everyone who was here that night."

"We haven't done my statement about the incident this morning." Mitchell also got to his feet.

"You can do it at the station, when you drop that list in." Beckett headed back the way they'd came. "We'll see ourselves out."

"You've forgotten your photo." Callum took a few steps after him, holding out the photo of Danni.

"Keep it. It might jog your memories."

"What d'you make of them, then?" Beckett asked, as he drove the car back through the vineyards.

Harper wasn't sure what he thought. This was a world totally alien to him. The mega rich, with their massive homes and lives, which spanned several countries. Most of the people he dealt with back in London had been born into shitty lives, which only continued downwards as they got older. There was violence, jealousy, drugs, anger, and hopelessness. Bad parenting, or often non-existent parenting, was the common thread. Perhaps here, too?

"The kids are both spoilt. Over privileged, and under challenged. Typical private school educated."

"You don't approve of private education?"

"Why should the amount of money your family has determine the quality of your education?"

"It's a very British thing," was all Beckett said.

"Mitchell hasn't got much time for the son. Thinks he's a waste of space, from what I could see. Dotes on the daughter, though. I suppose it's always going to be a weird dynamic, with a mother who killed herself." He glanced at Beckett. "Even if that's not how you believe it went down, the kids must do."

"Why?"

"Because, if they thought their Daddy had killed their mother, they wouldn't be living in his house, letting him throw them birthday parties."

"Perhaps."

"You haven't forgiven your dad for splitting up with your mother. If you thought he'd killed her…"

Beckett revved the engine, as they waited for the gate to open. "I'd have killed him. But, we all react in different ways."

As they passed through the gateway, Beckett's phone rang. "Kyriakoulis."

"It's Tomas. Where are you?" He sounded excited.

"Heading back to the station, why? You got news?"

Harper could hear the hint of desperation in his voice.

"I couldn't find any trace of Patrick Gruenanger on the CCTV, and neither could the guys in Patras. No response from his yachting friend, either. The Serbian Police have got back to us. He was convicted of physically assaulting his then-girlfriend, when he was seventeen. The Brazilian police, also. He was deported, rather than charged, but again, it was after assaulting a girl, we assume Danni, as that is where they met, isn't it?"

"Yes, that's right. They can't confirm the name of the girl, though?"

"No, but I don't think it matters." The line went quiet, as Tomas opted to build the suspense. "We have an eyewitness who saw Patrick, they think maybe with a woman – not Danni - in Farou town on Wednesday morning. A day *after* he said he'd left on his friend's yacht. I think we've got him. The Chief wants him arrested. Do you want me to go?"

"He is still at his friend's apartment?"

"As far as we know."

"Meet us there. We'll be about forty minutes." Beckett rang off, and glanced at Harper, "You don't get travel sick, do you?"

"No. Why?"

"Good." Beckett floored the accelerator, and Harper was pressed back in his seat.

"It was Patrick doing the cheating." Harper tried to ignore the skull crushing trunks of the olive trees, as they sped past.

"Or, perhaps, they both were. We haven't had the results of the DNA test yet on the semen." Beckett didn't take his focus off the road in front.

"If Danni was cheating, and Patrick found out, that's motive."

"But, if he was also cheating?"

"Wouldn't stop his ego being hurt. He's got a history of violent behaviour towards women."

"It's possible."

Harper felt like banging his head against the dashboard, but he didn't want to distract Beckett. The Evoque whistled around a tight bend, and accelerated down a hill.

"You have to admit, he's ticking all the boxes."

"We have no forensic evidence. We don't know where Danni was killed. Why dump her body on that beach, rather than out at sea, where she wouldn't be found?"

"Maybe he was full of remorse. Maybe he wanted her body to be found, so he could grieve for her. Maybe that beach was special to them, in some way."

Beckett's face broke into a wide grin. "I like those ideas."

"But?"

"No 'but.' I think you are correct."

"I wish you'd make your bloody mind up."

"It still doesn't make Patrick the killer."

"Luckily, we get the chance to ask him."

"I think you should interview him. I've spoken with him already. I think a new face would unsettle him."

"Okay. Yes. Good idea." Harper tried to keep the

surprise from his voice.

"Patrick likes to be in control. He has a short temper. If you want to get a confession, then push those buttons."

"Cheers. After a few hundred interviews, I'm still really unclear about what to do." Harper let the sarcasm leech into his voice.

"Sorry. Just trying to be helpful."

They fell into uncompanionable silence. Harper watched the world flash by outside the car. The endless olive groves, the clusters of multi-colour houses, the tavernas, the tourist buses, donkeys in fields and rusting tractors momentarily impeded their journey, before Beckett overtook them in suicide-like manoeuvres. He missed the crisscross of London streets, the red buses, the rain, the sense you were surrounded by millions of people. He had to get this confession, and he needed to work out how.

Harper ran through different scenarios in his head. Begin friendly or start hostile. Go in, and belittle him, wind him up, get him to lose his cool, or probe gently, hoping to catch him out. He found himself wondering what approach Beckett would take, and what methods he might have used to extract information when he was running around Bosnia and Iraq. Follow the evidence, was what he'd been taught. Let the suspect think you were trying to help them. Present them the facts, and let them explain the variances. Actual confessions were rare. They needed some forensics.

CHAPTER EIGHTEEN

There was no sign of Patrick in his friend's apartment. The officer parked outside hadn't seen him leave but did admit, to his shoes and the pavement, he might have fallen asleep after lunch.

The friend, an Italian called Cellesto, shrugged his shoulders.

"I don't know where he is." But, he shifted his weight, and wouldn't look either Beckett or Harper in the eye.

"I think you're lying." Harper nodded at him, keeping his tone light. "I can understand why. He's your friend. You feel a sense of loyalty. But, he is a suspect in a murder. Did you know Danni Deacon?"

"He wouldn't have hurt her," Cellesto whined.

"If he's innocent, then what's the issue in telling us where he is? If he's guilty, then why would you not want him brought to justice?" Harper glanced at Beckett, but he didn't even appear to be listening.

"I've told you, I don't know where he is." Cellesto turned to Beckett. "I haven't seen him. I don't know where he is."

"Obstructing an investigation is a criminal offence, as is aiding and abetting. I'm sure we can come up with some more." Harper looked at Beckett. "I think we should arrest him. He might be more helpful down at the station."

"You can't arrest me. I start work in half an hour. If I'm late again, my boss will fire me."

"DI Harper seems keen on arresting everyone today," Beckett finally spoke.

"Not me. I've done nothing wrong."

"You're lying to police officers." Harper took a step towards him. Cellesto backed up.

"Children, please. I'm sure we can come to an equitable arrangement," Beckett said and coughed.

Harper looked around, as Beckett picked up a magazine spread-eagled on the kitchen table. Underneath was a bag of cannabis, and some ready rolled spliffs. *How the hell had Beckett known they were there?* Harper turned back to Cellesto, whose eyebrows had disappeared under his fringe.

"I don't know how that got there," he squawked.

"You don't know much today, do you?" Beckett said. "Tell you what. I'll give you a choice. Either you don't know where the cannabis came from, or you don't know where Patrick has gone."

Cellesto's mouth opened and shut, like a goldfish.

"You know how long you'd get inside for even this much cannabis? Come on. Be sensible."

"I tell you about Patrick, and you forget the drugs?"

"What drugs?" Beckett dropped the magazine back onto the table, so the drugs were hidden once more.

"Okay, okay. Patrick left here about an hour ago. He was going back to his place."

"To do what?" Harper asked, a sense of dread spreading from his stomach outwards.

"I think he was going to get some of his things from his place, and do a runner."

Beckett was already five paces towards the door.

Harper growled at Cellesto. "Do not move from this flat. Do not try to warn him."

Beckett bounded down the concrete steps outside the block. Harper had to take two steps in one stride to catch up.

"What about the drugs?"

"You really want to arrest everyone?" Beckett answered,

whilst jumping into the car.

Harper threw himself in, as Beckett gunned the engine. He only just managed to shut the car door, before they flew through the gateway, and bounced onto the street. Harper scrabbled for his seat belt, as Beckett handbraked around a corner. *Sod it*, decided Harper. Beckett never did his belt up, and in less than a minute, they thundered into the grounds of the apartment block.

Patrick was there, stuffing a suitcase into the back of a Mazda. *Red*, Harper thought. *Bingo*. Beckett jammed on the brakes, and Harper had to brace himself against the dashboard. This was why you wore seatbelts. Beckett was out of the car, and striding towards Patrick, as Tomas in a patrol car came screaming around the corner, sirens blaring and lights exploding.

Patrick froze, suitcase half in the boot.

"Going on your holidays, Patrick?" Beckett quipped.

Harper couldn't keep the grin from his face.

It was back to reality at the station. They had arrested their suspect, but Beckett had reiterated he wanted Harper to do the interview. Harper did not feel any less pressured when he found himself in the incident room. In fact, the station as a whole was underwhelming. It was housed in a 19th Century pillar-fronted, grey building off one of the town's frantic main streets. It reminded him of a mausoleum. There didn't seem to be any sign or plaque at the front indicating its true purpose. Reception was cavernous, lines of empty benches and a cubby hole encased in glass, where a police woman was sitting reading the Greek version of *OK* magazine.

The incident room itself was a good size, plenty of desks, but most with an inch of dust on top. What he assumed was Beckett's office – a stud wall and glass-windowed square in the corner—looked like many senior detectives' offices he'd ever seen. Cluttered, chaotic, with a tinge of nicotine coating everything. The incident room was not what he was used to.

There was no buzz of activity, apart from the officer he assumed to be Tomas, who was dancing from foot-to-foot, waiting for his boss to finish reading through the notes left on his desk. There were no white boards tracking the stages of the investigation, target sheets, or in-trays full of to-do actions. Harper wondered if Beckett worked entirely inside his own head.

"The car actually belongs to Danni. At least, it's registered in her name. As well as the RAV-4, that's still missing," Tomas was telling Beckett. "Is it the one you saw at the beach, do you think?"

"Possibly. I only heard it, and caught the colour between the trees. Forensics are onto it?"

"Yes, though, with it being Danni's car, it will be full of her DNA anyway."

"Have we had the make and model back on the tyre treads found at the beach yet?"

"Nope, they're still working on them, but the lab results are back from the semen found in Danni..." Tomas' voice died in embarrassment. "Anyway, it's not Patrick's. And we don't have a match on our database."

"Get in touch with Europol and the Met, get them to run it through their databases," Beckett instructed.

"Do you think Patrick knew she was sleeping with someone else?" Tomas was almost panting with excitement. Harper figured they were about the same age, but Tomas was like an enthusiastic puppy. This investigation was the biggest thing he'd ever worked on.

"That's what Harper is going to find out."

"You're not questioning Patrick?" Tomas' mouth dropped open to form a perfect O shape.

"DI Harper is itching to have a go at him. You can sit in, Tomas. It will be a good learning experience."

"You don't want to be there?" Harper asked Beckett.

"You don't need me. I want to speak to Warren, and bring the Chief up to speed. Do me a favour, though. Patrick confirmed the bracelet was Danni's, but ask him if he bought it for her, or if she bought it herself."

"You're thinking whoever she was sleeping with might have bought it for her?"

"Perhaps. Any joy with the laptop, Tomas?"

"I sent you a couple of things to look at. Nothing in her emails, 99% spam. She doesn't seem to do social media – not on that laptop. Oh… none of the florists we talked to recognised the bouquet. They all said it looked homemade. Flowers from a garden."

"Good work, Tomas." Beckett nodded at Harper. "Go get him, then."

Harper nodded back.

"It's this way." Tomas spun his back on Harper, and marched out of the room.

Harper sensed the Sergeant was not at all pleased to be paired with him. *Fine, as long as he stayed quiet.* Harper had his strategy lodged in his head. Now, all Patrick had to do was play along.

CHAPTER NINETEEN

Beckett squinted through the slit in the door. Warren was hulked on the plinth acting as the bed. His shoulders were slumped into his chest, like he'd been deflated. Beckett nodded at the guard, and he unlocked the door and swung it open. Warren raised his head, and, eyes widening, pushed himself back into the corner.

"No offense was intended." Beckett kept his distance. "You were about to assault someone."

"You nearly broke my fucking arm. What sort of copper are you?"

Beckett raised his hands. "We got off on the wrong foot. I am sorry you heard about Emmie from the Net. We should have informed you in person. No excuses. But, I want to reassure you, we are doing everything we can to find her."

"You think she's dead, don't you? Like the girl on the beach." Warren struggled to control his face, muscles twitching, eyes shining with tears.

"I've no reason to think that. We can't find any connections between the two cases."

"Emmie is still missing though… she has to be somewhere. Someone must have her."

"We're doing all we can."

"What about me?"

"Neither party want to press charges, so you are free to go."

"Go? Just like that?"

"But, you have to stay away from Beatrice. No more

threats."

"I want to be out there looking for her."

"Stay out of trouble, and you won't have a problem."

"Tomorrow is our wedding day." He gave no indication of moving.

"We'll find her, Warren."

Beckett stood at his office window, and watched Warren trudge out of the station and cross the road to the main street. If he was involved in Emmie's disappearance, then he was the best actor Beckett had ever met. He was a man in shock. The world that he'd been so sure of—mates, booze, fiancée, wedding, meals on the table, shirts ironed, sex on Sundays, and two weeks in the sun each year—had all evaporated. Warren was a thug, and a bully. Probably not a stranger to pushing Emmie around, but he hadn't killed her. He wasn't bright enough to cover it up. The more Beckett thought about it, the more he wasn't convinced the two cases were connected at all. In fact, the only connection the two girls did have was Mitchell Troy. Troy wasn't dumb enough to insinuate himself into Bee's life, if he had anything to do with Emmie's disappearance, but where did he fit into the jigsaw?

He sat down at his computer, and opened his email from Tomas. There was a video file attached. He clicked it, and a grainy image appeared on screen. It was frozen for a few moments whilst it downloaded, and then it started to play.

It was footage taken on a phone. The exposure too dark to see anything clearly, but the gist was soon obvious. In a forest clearing, a group of people in animal masks and cloaks of fur, waved staves aloft, those staves topped with pinecones. Off camera, the sound of drums, thump thump, thump thump, and cow bells clanging. There was a large fire crackling and popping, and the people started dancing.

There was a large wooden casket under a wide-girthed olive tree – a tree so old its branches had doubled back on themselves, and were touching the ground in places. A cloaked figure, with a wolf's head mask, stood before it, and with a jab of his arm, plunged his stave into the ground. The crowd gathered behind him, and started chanting. He crouched, opened the casket, and, with a flourish, lifted out a carved, wooden object, and held it above his head. The crowd fell to their knees, but still thumping their staves to the ground and chanting. Beckett squinted. The wooden object was a phallus. The leader then began to march around the clearing, holding the phallus aloft, and the worshippers followed behind, dipping and swaying in time to the shamanic drumming. They threw their heads back, jabbing their staves into the air and into the earth.

The video ended abruptly, but there was a second one attached to the email. Beckett opened that one, too, and wished he hadn't. The same location, same people, as far as could be told under their masks and cloaks, but later in time. There was drink, flagons of wine being poured down throats, over faces, bongs being smoked, and people having sex, in couples, in groups, large groups, and people being whipped whilst having sex, and as the camera turned, there was a woman, naked from the waist down, being strung by her neck from one of the low branches of the ancient tree. Two people supported her, and a crowd gathered around. The video stopped. There were no more videos to watch, and Beckett was glad of it. He felt sick. There was nothing in the videos to identify anyone. But, he recognised that tree. He'd found Chrystos Spiros sitting underneath it.

CHAPTER TWENTY

Patrick was sitting on the edge of the cheap plastic seat, elbows on his knees, his feet tapping the floor. Aileen Andreas, a local lawyer, was sitting next to him, notepad on the table. Through the one-way mirror from his vantage point in the room next door, Beckett could see the page was blank. Harper was sitting opposite, Tomas next to him. Tomas was scribbling away, despite the fact the interview was being recorded. Harper leaned back in his chair, shoulders relaxed, face welcoming. Harper could have been in a bar, chatting to a friend.

"Why were you running away, Patrick?"

"I wasn't."

"What were you doing then?"

"I needed more stuff. I was heading back to Cellestos' place."

"He told us you were doing a runner. You broke into your apartment, despite the police tape. We caught you loading your suitcase into the back of Danni's car, which, incidentally, you didn't inform us you still had."

"It's my car, not Danni's. Hers is missing."

"You still should have informed us."

Patrick shrugged his shoulders, but his head slumped towards his chest. He was a beaten man.

"In your statement, Patrick, you said you joined the boat of your friend on Tuesday, and you left the Island together that same day?"

Patrick nodded. "That's what I said."

"So, how do you explain someone seeing you in Farou

Town, on Wednesday afternoon?"

Patrick's head snapped up. "They couldn't of… they're lying."

"They are certain it was you."

"They must have seen someone who looks like me, or got the day wrong."

"The problem I have, Patrick, is there is no one to verify your story. We haven't been able to get in touch with your friend. Him and his yacht seem to have vanished. We've checked CCTV at the ferry port in Patras and here, to see if you appear on camera, but nothing. We've asked the crew of the ferry you claimed you took from Patras on Saturday, but no one remembers you."

"There were hundreds of passengers. I was there. I swear."

"I'm pretty sure if one person saw you in town on Wednesday, there will be others who did, too. We are also checking the town's CCTV cameras."

"You won't see me, because I wasn't there."

"The problem I've got, Patrick, is your girlfriend has been murdered. We can't establish an alibi. We have a witness, who has made a statement they saw you on Wednesday, which means that you are lying to us."

"I'm not lying." Patrick gripped edge of the table, pulling the chair forward underneath him. He glanced at his lawyer. "Tell them. It's my word against this witness. Why are you believing them over me? I'm not lying."

But, he was. Beckett could see it, and hear it in the rise and fall of his voice. In the tension down his neck, and into his spine.

"Did you ever argue with Danni?"

The change of tack threw Patrick. He sat upright. For a moment, his head turned towards Beckett. Beckett wondered if he realised he was being watched through the blackened window running the length of one side of the interview room.

"We've been through this. Yes. Sometimes. No more than anyone else."

"We have reports you fought frequently. That the arguments sometimes turned violent."

"Violent? No, never. A few things might have got thrown occasionally. But, I was never violent to her."

"You have a conviction for assaulting a girlfriend when you were seventeen."

"She punched me. I slapped her back."

"And you were arrested for assaulting a girl we believe was Danni, when you were in Brazil together."

"What? No…"

Harper was remaining completely calm and reasonable, his tone unthreatening. They could have been discussing the weather. Patrick was unravelling. Beckett could see his entire body flooding with fear. He could not sit still, but did not dare move from the chair, so he shifted about, as if the plastic seat was too hot.

"Was Danni faithful to you, Patrick?"

"Yes, of course she was."

"Are you certain?"

"Yes." But, his voice betrayed him.

"The evening before she was killed, she had sex with someone. We found traces of semen."

Patrick's mouth opened but no sound emerged.

"The DNA profile doesn't match yours. Have you any idea who she was sleeping with?"

"It must have been the person who killed her. See, it wasn't me. Was she forced? Was she raped?"

"There were no signs of violence. I put it to you, Patrick, that you found out Danni was cheating on you. You couldn't stand it. Your Danni being touched by another man. Laughing at you behind your back. You lost it, attacked her, and killed her. Then, when it was clear your story was going to be blown wide open, you decided to do a runner. Where were you going? Back to Serbia?"

"If I'd thought Danni was cheating on me, I would have killed the bastard, not her."

The door behind Beckett swung open. Floros appeared. "I've put those archived files you requested in the boiler room. Are you sure you don't want them in your office? It's about a hundred degrees in there."

"No, that's perfect. Thank you."

"You should be in there, boss. You'd get him to confess."

"Not if he didn't do it."

"You still would." She flushed.

"We don't really want people to confess to things they didn't do."

"No, of course… I just meant…" Glowing red now, she stumbled over her words. "I'd better get back…" She disappeared, leaving the door swinging.

Beckett took a final look at the interview room. Patrick had curled himself into the foetal position on the chair, both legs juddering, sobs wracking his body. Harper sat impassively, waiting. He was good. Patient, calm, picking and prodding where necessary, but sitting back, and letting the story ooze from the interviewee. It didn't change the fact Patrick wasn't the murderer.

CHAPTER TWENTY-ONE

The boiler room was down a dank corridor, pipes snaking along the ceiling like vines, and peeling paint leaving rusting metal gaping. Floros hadn't exaggerated the temperature, at least not by much. The room itself was little more than a box. No windows, and just one strip light, which shot an eye-squinting, yellow glow across the room. It was the room people came to when they didn't want to be disturbed, whether that was studying for sergeant's exams, phone conversations with journalists, or heat generating trysts with a colleague.

There was a cardboard box on the desk. Beckett placed it on the floor, and then methodically transferred the contents, one-by-one, onto the desk, spreading them out. There wasn't much. A couple of brown files embracing typewritten and handwritten papers. A few photographs. And some items wrapped in evidence bags. A leather-beaded sandal, a gold and green silk scarf, and a bracelet. All the items had been found at Chrystos' hideout. The bracelet had been identified as Rosie's by a couple of her friends, and also contained traces of her DNA. The sandal and the scarf were less certain. Her friends thought they could have been Rosie's, one more certain than the other, but not 100% convincing. No DNA was recovered from either item. It wasn't them he was interested in.

Beckett snapped on a pair of nitrile gloves, and fished the bracelet free from the bag. It was as he remembered it–identical to the one which had belonged to Danni. He bent his head, and squinted. Actually, not quite identical, some of the patterns on the beads were different. But, similar enough to be satisfied the bracelets had been made by the same person. Finding the maker of the bracelet hadn't been deemed necessary at the time. Chrystos was found wearing it. The conclusion was obvious. Beckett had been hailed the hero, and had returned to London, held up as an example of an outstanding Met officer. Things were different now.

He placed the bracelet back into the bag, settled himself in the pockmarked wooden chair, and opened the first file. He found the original missing person's report. Rosie had been gone twenty-four hours, and her flat mate, Kelly, had come into the station. Beckett studied the photo of Rosie, as he remembered from when he looked at it the first time around. A pretty girl, with olive skin, a mane of chocolate and golden hair, and a huge smile. He ran his eyes over the description typed up on the report. Then, read it again. The usual—height, build, colour of eyes, hair, etc–but then the words, 'tattoo, lower back.' He read on. There was no description of what the tattoo looked like. But, he knew the detail had been reported, verbally at least.

Beckett put that file to one side, and opened another. This was his own report on finding and arresting Chrystos. He had to force himself to read the banal words he'd used to describe the horror he'd come across. There was nothing in there he didn't remember. The next page was a medical and toxicology report. The conclusion from the doctor was Chrystos had suffered a severe psychotic episode. *Not a stretch for any doctor to conclude*, Beckett figured. No one in a sane state of mind would eat the flesh of another human being. Something else stopped him dead—Chrystos' toxicology results. High levels of dimethyltryptamine in his system; the same drug they'd found in Danni.

Beckett returned all the contents to the box, and lumped it upstairs to his office. He was stowing it under his desk when Petrakis burst in, her rich floral perfume enveloping him even before she made it through the doorway.

"Where the hell have you been?"

"Chasing some leads."

"Doesn't matter. I thought you'd want to be there when we charge Gruenanger with the murder of Danni Deacon."

"He confessed?"

"Hate to admit it, but pretty boy did good."

Someone cleared their throat. Harper was hovering outside the doorway. "I'm not sure I believe him."

"What?" Petrakis spat at him.

"You're going to pin this on me anyway, so I confess. I did it. I killed Danni." Harper did a pretty good impression of the Serb.

"Good enough for me." Petrakis nodded, head bobbing like a boat on rough seas. "He had motive and opportunity, plus a confession. We're going to charge him."

Harper searched out Beckett's gaze, and gave a half shrug. Harper knew it was bogus. His mouth twisted down at the corners.

Beckett got to his feet. "I think you're wrong."

"I'm your Chief of Police. It doesn't matter what you think. Decision is made. Who wants to do it?"

Beckett gave a half smile. *Not a chance.* Petrakis turned to Harper, who avoided eye contact. "I don't have jurisdiction."

"Fine." She spun out of the door, Harper leaping out of the way.

"Ma'am." Tomas ran into the incident room. His voice was pitched near the ceiling, "A woman has just come into reception. She's saying she's come to help Gruenanger. She's his alibi. They were together from Wednesday night to Sunday."

Tomas had put her in the other interview room. Beckett, Petrakis and Harper stood in the side room and looked through the one-way mirror. The woman sitting on the cheap plastic chair, twisting a lock of blonde hair around her ring finger and glancing repeated to the door, was Sophia Bakas.

"They could be in it together," Petrakis offered.

"What motive?" Beckett asked. He wondered if Michale knew about the affair, or if he even cared. But, if he did know, had he confided in Danni? Even if Danni knew, it didn't serve her to blow the secret. Michale was gay, and had a wife as cover, because he didn't want the world to know. Danni and Michale were friends. Why would she do anything to damage his reputation? Danni was the injured party. It was her boyfriend cheating. And even if she was also seeing someone else, why would Patrick want to get rid of her? She had no money, no assets. They could all have gone their separate ways, and no one would have thought anything of it.

Petrakis shrugged, and rubbed her left temple.

"Danni knew about the affair, and was threatening to tell Michale," Harper offered.

"But, you're certain Michale is gay."

"Wouldn't stop him caring. He's built up this perfect life. Perhaps he'd have chucked Sophia out. Maybe she'd lose her stake in the business."

"I checked. Sophia owns 51% of Michale's company. Together or divorced, doesn't make any difference." Beckett watched the woman in the other room. She got up, and paced the circumference, then sat down again. "Besides, she says they sailed to the mainland together. Tomas is checking out the story, but if their receipts and phone records match, they were hundreds of miles away."

"So, where the hell does that leave us, Beckett?" Petrakis struggled to keep the panic from her voice.

"We need to find out who Danni slept with the night before she died. We know it wasn't Patrick. We doubt it was Michale, but we'll check the DNA anyway. So, who was it? We need to ask Michale; she might have said something to him. And we should check with her neighbour, Linus Sang."

"She could have been sleeping with him," Harper mused.

"I don't think so, but he is a little infatuated with her. He seems to keep a close eye on her comings and goings. He may have seen someone."

"Or been so obsessed with her when she turned him down, laughed at him, he killed her." Harper warmed to his theme.

"Danni was a fit five foot seven. Linus is a geeky five foot of nothing. He might have the physical strength to drug her and kill her, but he could never have dumped the body on the beach."

"He could have got someone to help him?" Harper insisted.

"Possibly, but he strikes me as a loner. I doubt he knows anyone else well enough to persuade them to help him move a body."

"Any other suspects?" Petrakis snapped.

Beckett hesitated, and then went to speak. Petrakis held up a hand. "If the name 'Mitchell Troy' comes out of your mouth, I will snap off each of your fingers, and feed them to my dogs."

Out of the corner of his eye, Beckett caught Harper smiling.

"Danni was at Troy's, two days before she disappeared. We know Rosie was up there, too, the evening she disappeared. The bracelets they wore were almost identical, definitely made by the same person. That's two connections we can't ignore," Beckett continued on.

"How can you possibly know the bracelets are the same after all this time?"

"I had the case files brought out from the archive."

"You did what? Oh, never mind. We know who killed Rosie, and he is safely locked up in a secure hospital. And, yes, I checked. He's still there." The exasperation sprayed from

Petrakis' lips.

"The drug in Chrystos' system was identical to that found in Danni's. That's connection three. Rosie had a tattoo, as did Danni. Connection four."

"Don't you think you're grasping now?" Harper interrupted.

"You know, I never believed Chrystos killed Rosie." Beckett ignored Harper, and focussed on Petrakis.

"He told you he got the bracelet off Rosie's body."

"But, he didn't say he killed her."

Petrakis started shaking her head, like a slow hand clap.

"If I'm right, then whoever did kill Rosie could still be on the island. They've killed once. Perhaps, they've done it again."

"Mitchell Troy, you mean?"

"We need to speak to Chrystos. I need to ask him about Rosie."

CHAPTER TWENTY-TWO

After the altercation with Warren, Mitchell Troy had insisted on buying her a coffee, strong with lots of sugar, which Bee didn't want, and didn't enjoy. She forced herself to drink it, and thanked him over and over. *How far in someone's debt could you plunge?* she had wondered. He seemed such a nice, genuine man, but the encounter with Inspector Kyriakoulis had thrown her. Kyriakoulis was a policeman, therefore had to be a good judge of character. It kind of went with the job. He and Mitchell had obviously come across each other before, and the shape of Kyriakoulis' face had changed, as soon as he saw the older man. Bee was surrounded at work by people who she knew hated each other but smiled, shook hands, grasped arms, and asked all the right questions—partner, kids, this year's holiday. Kyriakoulis had made no attempt to hide his revulsion, she could think of no other word for it, at seeing Mitchell. If Kyriakoulis, an inspector, hated someone so much, there had to be good reason, didn't there?

Mitchell hadn't mentioned it. He'd chatted away, as they'd drunk their coffee. Trying to get her mind off the confrontation with Warren and Emmie, still whereabouts unknown, he'd asked her about work. What it was like surrounded by the machinations of government, what her ambitions were, how often did she get to meet the PM? She'd told him a junior researcher spent most of their time photocopying. Machinations of any kind were reserved to remembering who had what drink. Her ambitions were to not get fired, and the closest she'd been to the PM was when she saw the back of his head across the other side of the office. Mitchell had laughed. She wanted to ask him about Kyriakoulis, but didn't dare, and when he looked at his watch and said he had to go, she'd been relieved.

She decided to do a spin around town. Posters of a sunshine-filled Emmie were stuck on lamp posts and in windows. Occasionally, Bee would stop and ask people if they'd seen her, pointing out her photo to them. She'd got used to the stock response of a smile brimming with sympathy, and a shake of the head, usually accompanied with an 'I hope she turns up soon,' or an 'I'm sure she's fine.' It was disheartening, and after a while, she stopped asking, and just wandered up and down the streets, into and out of the bars and cafes, wishing Emmie would appear in front of her, knowing it wasn't going to happen.

Her aimless wandering found her on a side street. She'd gone into a taverna at the front, and exited at the side. Disorientated as to which direction she should turn, Bee stepped off the kerb and straight into the path of fossilised Land Rover. She stepped back to the safety of the pavement, as the car pulled up in front of her, and a wiry man shot out from the driver's seat. He had a mane of silver hair and a grizzled face, which reminded her of the miniature schnauzer living next door to her parents. He didn't appear to notice her, as he bounded across the pavement into the art gallery occupying the slot on the street next to the taverna.

The Land Rover was rainbow-coloured. None of the four doors were the same colour, the bonnet was faded crimson, and the body a sickly green. It was unique, and a memory triggered in Bee like an electric shock. She'd seen the Land Rover before, in town, prior to Emmie going missing. In fact, Emmie had pointed it out, saying she'd love one just like it.

There was something on the back of the passenger seat. A silk scarf, white with red trim. Bee stepped closer, her heart thumping. On the scarf were delicately drawn flowers, blues and reds, purples and golds, and the strong green tentacles of stems, branches and leaves, entwining each other. Bee opened the door, and reached in to uncurl the bottom edge of the scarf. Her hands were trembling as she revealed the word 'Valentino.' It was Emmie's scarf. Bee had been with her when she'd bought it six months previously at Liberty's. Emmie loved that scarf. She took it everywhere, wore it everywhere. It was too much of coincidence there were two identical scarfs on this small island. Surely?

Bee glanced into the back of the car. There were no seats just boxes, blankets, a chainsaw, and a tarpaulin. Nowhere to sit, but plenty of places to hide. She scurried to the rear door. It resisted, then opened. She scrambled in, shut the door, and buried herself under the tarpaulin. The smell pierced her nose. Musty, yet sweet. It felt damp, and her scalp felt itchy. She wriggled into the foetus position and waited.

A couple of minutes later, she heard the driver's door open, and the man grunt as he got back in. He was humming, but not a tune she recognised. The sound of her heart beating was so loud she was sure it would give her away, but the Land Rover shuddered and spluttered into life, and with a crunch of gears and a jolt, they were moving.

The Land Rover's suspension was so unforgiving, and the roads so potholed and subsided, that Bee's spine cracked and groaned. Her left shoulder was pressed up against a hard piece of metal. At every recoil, it dug further in. The smell from the tarpaulin was making her eyes water, and she so desperately needed to cough.

The man's humming turned to singing as he swung the car around a sharp bend. A passable version of Nessum Dorma echoed throughout the car, but she still didn't dare make a sound. Her mobile phone. The thought of its presence in her pocket made her go cold. If it rang now, she would be in trouble. It was in her front trouser pocket, stuck between her leg, and the floor of the car. She tried to move an arm to get her hand in her pocket, but it was impossible. She was wedged in. To get it, she'd have to sit up.

If I think about it ringing, it will ring. Bee forced herself to think of other things. Count to fifty in French – but she could only get to ten. Name ten different breeds of dog. Remember all her classmates from primary school. She'd got to the last one, Graham Swinburne, when the car turned a corner, slowed right down, and started bouncing and swaying even more violently than before. It felt more like being in the bottom of a boat than a car. But, then, the brakes squeaked, and they stopped. Bee heard the driver's door open, and the man jump out. The sound of his footsteps got fainter and fainter, until there was only the sound of birds and cicadas left. She sat up, pushing the weight of the tarpaulin off her, and opened the rear door.

Bee was in a clearing between olive trees. The drive they'd come up was behind her, and disappeared back into the gloom. Peering out from behind the shelter of the car, she could see a large log cabin, with a veranda which reminded her of the Deep South of the US, complete with swinging wooden bench and hammock. There were a couple of crumbling stone buildings, which looked like they'd been shaken into place rather than built, a raised vegetable patch, bursting with foliage, and a large wire enclosure, containing twenty or so chickens, who were too busy scratching at the ground to notice an intruder.

There was no sign of the man. No sign of anyone. Thinking of all the police shows she'd watched on television, Bee knew the importance of evidence was crucial. She took out her phone, and snapped a photo of Emmie's scarf draped over the back of the passenger seat. She huddled against the side of the Land Rover, she typed a text, 'I've found Emmie's scarf in this car. Don't know where I am. The car is a Land Rover.' She sent it to Kyriakoulis' number, then took another photo of the registration plate, and sent that, too

"What do you think you're doing?" a Cornish voice called out.

Bee spun around. The man was rushing across the clearing, silver hair billowing out behind him like a steam train.

"You won't get any signal up here."

Bee glanced at her phone. He was right. Neither text message had been sent. Her back was pressed up against the car, the metal cold against her skin. The messages would sit on her phone, until she made it back down the mountain to semi-civilisation.

"Who are you?" The man stopped about five metres in front of her. She hadn't noticed before, but he was dressed in a sapphire blue kaftan and a pair of leather sandals, which looked like they'd been chewed by a large dog. He wore a leather cord necklace, above which bobbed a pronounced Adam's apple around sagging skin and silver mottled stubble. Both forearms were painted with tattoos of ships, dragons, and Celtic patterns.

"I'm here on holiday. I was out walking. I got lost." Even to herself, Bee's voice sounded shaky and unconvincing.

The man tilted his head to one side. He didn't believe her. "Really? Why would you be walking out here?"

"I told you. I got lost."

He stepped closer. She could smell him now, the faint trace of sweat, and feel his breath brush her face.

"Lost, eh? I think you'd better come out the back."

"No, I'm fine. Thank you. I'll retrace my steps."

"You can't walk back to town from here. It's not safe." He put a hand on her arm, his fingers clenching like a vice. Bee wrenched free, backing away towards the trees.

"Don't touch me. I know you've got my friend. What have you done with her? Where is she? Emmie! Emmie!" she yelled, imagining Emmie wherever the dead go, listening to her, unable to help.

"Bee, for Christ's sake."

Bee spun towards the house. From around the back, walked Emmie. She looked exactly as Bee remembered her, like a young, silver birch tree, pale skin, silver blonde hair, pale green eyes, except she was wearing a faded pink, gold, and blue cotton shirt, tied in a knot at her navel, and frayed edge denim shorts. Bee had never seen her look so... scruffy.

"There's no need to get so hysterical." Emmie's face cracked into a huge smile, and she grabbed Bee in a hug.

Out the back, sitting on wooden chairs in a heavily scented garden, Bee was introduced to Gideon Coe, the man, who far from being a terrifying ogre, laughed and joked, and poured her a large glass of homemade lemonade, and his partner, Julia de Montagnac. Julia was similar age to Gideon, black hair streaked with waterfalls of grey. She was still beautiful, with high slanting cheekbones and huge summer sky eyes. She wore flowers in her hair, and long chains of glass beads around her neck. Her feet were bare, the skin as brown as a walnut. It made Bee think this woman rarely, if ever, wore shoes.

"Gideon is a poet and a playwright. A famous one. He was Poet Laureate once back home, and Julia is a sculptor. She makes the most amazing things in her shed," Emmie enthused.

"Oh, no, not really. Just bowls and pots and things," Julia replied. Her voice was heavily accented. French, Bee decided.

"That's why I was in town. Dropping off a specially ordered piece for the art gallery." Gideon leaned forward towards Bee, elbows on his knees. "How did you manage to follow me?"

"I climbed in the back of your car, and hid under a sheet."

Gideon roared with laughter, sitting so far back in his chair Bee thought he'd topple over.

"Proper job," he roared. "Proper job."

"You're mental." Emmie was shaking her head. "Why

would you do that?"

"Because I saw your scarf in the car. I thought you'd been abducted. I thought you were dead."

"Why would you think that? I left you a note."

"No, you didn't."

"Yes, I did. I put it in your suitcase. I didn't want anyone else to find it."

Bee shook her head, picturing her case, certain she hadn't had the need or the thought of opening it since Emmie had disappeared.

"I was going to text you, once we got here, but there's no signal."

"I reported you missing to the police. Everyone has been out hunting for you. There are posters up. And it's all over the internet. You missing, and the dead girl on the beach."

"None of us has been into town since last week, and we haven't had internet since the storm on Saturday night." Gideon's smile had gone. He looked serious. His mouth a straight line, underlining his oversized nose, "What dead girl?"

"British girl, but worked here. She was murdered, and her body dumped on a beach."

"Oh, poor, poor girl." Julia put a hand to her mouth.

"God, Bee. I'm so sorry. I had no idea."

"Why are you here?"

"I met Gideon in town last week. To be honest, Bee, I was crying. We got talking."

"Why were you crying?"

"Because I was about to get married to someone I love and I hate. Someone I know would never let me go, even if I had the strength to tell him. I felt trapped. Pretending to be excited and blissfully happy with you girls. It got too much."

"I saw her sitting at the little fountain, near where you saw the Land Rover."

"Gideon is a sucker for a pretty girl in need of help," Julia added. "His rescue instinct kicks in."

"I poured my heart out to him, and he offered me a way out. Hide up here, until after the wedding, until Warren flew back home. Until I felt ready to leave. Which might be never." Emmie exchanged looks with Gideon.

"My story is not so different," Julia said.

"Did Warren hit you?" Bee asked in a small voice.

"He was good at it. Only places which can't easily be seen. I have photos. Quite a collection."

Emmie passed Bee her phone. Bee scrolled through shot after shot of bruised ribs, blackened hips, purple patches on lower backs.

"It wasn't just the physical stuff. He'd lock me in the flat sometimes. Call me a slut. A piece of dog shit he wished he could wipe off his shoes."

"So, why not just dump him?" Bee handed the phone back. Her thoughts were spinning around in her head.

"Because I love him. And he's always so sorry afterwards. He cries and cries. I know it's a cliché, but it's true. I feel sorry for him. It's not really his fault. His dad beat him when he was little. He doesn't know any other way."

"We have to let everyone know you're alive and okay."

"I can't."

"The police will protect you from Warren. The Inspector who has been looking for you won't let Warren hurt you. He's already overpowered him once. Right in front of me. As easy as anything. Put him on the ground."

"Warren attacked you?" Emmie's mouth dropped open in horror.

"Not me. This other man who's been helping. Mitchell Troy."

"Troy has been helping you?" Gideon stared at her. The

expression on his face mirroring Kyriakoulis' when he saw her with Troy.

"If Warren thinks I'm dead or disappeared, then I'm better off staying that way."

"What? You can't. We have to let the police know."

"And they will tell Warren. They can't protect me forever. And I won't put Gideon and Julia at risk. Warren will blame them. You've seen what he's capable of doing."

"We'll be fine, Em. Don't worry about us." Julia put a hand on her arm.

"But, you can stay as long as you need to," Gideon added.

Emmie got on her knees in front of Bee, and clasped both her hands. "Warren will go home. He'll forget about me, eventually. And then, I'll be free. You've got to promise me, Bee, not to tell anyone. Keep this absolutely secret. Please, Bee. As my best friend. Can I trust you?"

Bee had no idea she was Emmie's best friend, but looking down into her eyes, she could see the fear and the desperation. No one had ever pleaded with her before. No one had ever so completely relied on her before. It was a strange feeling, a warm glow in her stomach. Warren was a thug, no question, and she owed no loyalty to anyone else. From the beginning, the police had been more interested in the dead girl than the missing one.

"Yes, absolutely. I won't tell anyone. At least I know you're safe."

Emmie threw her arms around her, nearly knocking her off her chair. "Thanks, Bee. I will never forget you did this for me."

"Now that's settled, perhaps Bee would like to join us for some food, before Gideon takes her back to town?" Julia got to her feet.

They ate salad, huge tomatoes from the garden, cured meat, and tangy soft cheese. Gideon got out his guitar, and sang.

As they were listening, Emmie sat with her arm around

Bee's shoulders.

"This does mean the world to me, Bee."

"It's okay. It's only I've been so worried."

"I'm sorry. I should have left the note somewhere easier to find. You'll find it when you get back to the hotel. There's something else you could do for me when you get back there."

"What's that?"

"In the hotel safe, is my passport and my mother's wedding ring. I'd really like them with me, especially the ring. Could you get them from the safe, and bring them here? I know it's a lot to ask, but you're the only person who can do it. We'll arrange for Gid to meet you somewhere. This place is a bit out of the way, and I know you don't drive."

Bee nodded, thinking of her adventure on the moped. Emmie had no idea what she'd done in the last few days.

Gideon drove her back into town. He was quiet for the first few miles, but Bee sensed he wanted to say something. As they turned onto the main road, he glanced at her, and gripped the steering wheel so his knuckles shone white.

"You're obviously a good friend to Emmie. Don't underestimate the control her fiancé has over her."

"I don't understand how she can say she loves him when he batters her."

"You've never been in love."

Bee's thoughts conjured up the Detective Inspector, who had been with Kyriakoulis that morning. The way her heart seemed to stutter when she had looked at him. She was sure she could fall in love with someone like that, but no, in her life so far, she'd not been in love. *Could it really make you lose all rational thought?*

"Love will make you do all sorts of crazy things. It's an addiction. As strong as any drug," Gideon added, as if he was reading her mind, "Which is why Emmie has to stay away from

Warren. Go cold turkey. Until she flushes her love for him from her system."

"I won't say anything, I promise." Bee's phone chirruped in his pocket. They were back in signal range again. Her scalp suddenly prickled. The photos she'd sent to Kyriakoulis, the messages which hadn't gone. She got out her phone. The text message was from Mitchell Troy checking she was okay. She ignored it. A couple of swipes of her thumb, and she felt sick. The messages to Kyriakoulis now both said sent. She realised Gideon had been talking.

"I'm sorry?"

"Mitchell Troy. Piece of advice. Stay away from him."

"Why?"

"Because he's not a good man."

"He's the only person who's helped me look for Emmie."

"He's helped you? Why would he do that? What's he asked for in return?"

"Do people need a reason to help?"

"People like Troy do. He always has an agenda. I can't think what he wants from you."

"I haven't got anything to give him. He might have done things in the past, but I honestly think he's just being nice."

"Nice," Gideon snorted. "Just be careful. Now you know Emmie is safe and well, you have no reason to have anything to do with him. In fact, it might be better if you went home."

"My flight isn't until Saturday."

"Best try to stay out of his way, then."

Gideon dropped her a couple of streets from the hotel. They arranged to meet at the same place at 11am the following day, with Emmie's passport and wedding ring.

Walking back to the hotel, Bee felt unsettled by the missing person's posters which now seemed to taunt her, as she passed them. Liar, liar. By the way Emmie had looked and talked about Gideon, and the way Julia had looked at them both. By Mitchell Troy.

"How are you doing, Bee, sweetheart?" Fran was sitting at one of the tables in the hotel's garden, laptop open in front of her. The sound of laughing and squealing and splashing echoed over from the pool, "Any news?"

Bee shook her head.

"The other girls have left for the airport."

"I was always staying until Saturday."

"I know. Of course. I didn't mean… if you wanted to stay longer… until there's news."

"Saturday is fine."

"Okay. Good. If you need anything…"

"No, nothing, thank you. You look busy?"

"Last week's accounts." Fran rolled her eyes.

"Will they take you long?"

"The rest of the afternoon. Still, there's worse places to sit and do admin."

Bee smiled, and went inside. From the reception desk, she could see out into the garden and the edge of Fran's table. If Fran got up and came towards her, she would see her. Bee's palms were sweaty, and she could feel droplets meandering down her back. She lifted the flap, and went behind the reception next. The safe boxes for each room were stacked under the desk. Each room key opened the safe box, but a laminated A4 paper stuck to the wall behind the desk instructed you were supposed to get a member of staff to open them on your behalf. Bee got her room key and crouched down, eyes skimming the boxes for the number 12. She periscoped her head above the desk top. No sign of Fran. She must be still sitting at the table.

She slotted the key into the lock on the third attempt, her hands trembling, refusing to comply with instructions, and swung the little door open. Inside, were two Tupperware boxes.

One with her own passport and reserves of Euros, and the other also containing a passport, plus a small azure blue silk purse. Bee slid the box out and cracked out the lid. She'd never stolen anything in her life, not even a bar of chocolate or a lipstick. Once, when she was about thirteen, a group of girls who lived on her street had invited her shopping. She'd been horrified when they'd gone into Boots, and started slipping eye liners up their sleeves and mascara wands down their jumpers. She'd walked out, and left them. They hadn't invited her again to anything. But, now, here she was, jamming Emmie's passport down the front of her jeans, and the silk purse, with the wedding ring, inside into her pocket. Though, technically speaking, these possessions belonged to Emmie, and it was Emmie who she was taking them for. So not stealing. Not really.

She put the box back where is belonged, locked the safe door, and slipped out from behind the desk, as Fran appeared in the doorway. "Bee?"

"I can't settle in my room," Bee lied. "I'm going to go for a walk."

Bee felt Fran's eyes on her, as she walked past and out of the door.

CHAPTER TWENTY-THREE

Petrakis had looked at him, cold eyed, when Beckett told her he needed to speak to Chrystos. Harper stood near the doorway, ripples of doubt and worry hitting Beckett's back in waves.

"Does it matter what I say?"

"My only other link to Danni in her last few days is Neil Ticknall. You prefer I bring him in?"

"You can't question the Vice Consul, because some kid claimed he's got loose hands."

"Chrystos is the link. I know it."

"I thought you were done with dragging up the past." Petrakis looked sad.

"No one can escape history. However fast you run, it's always there. Like a shadow."

Petrakis looked over Beckett's shoulder. "What do you think Harper?"

Harper hesitated. He looked conflicted. "I think it's a distraction." But there was no conviction in his voice. Petrakis heard it as loudly as Beckett did.

"I need you to speak to the Governor of the hospital. Okay the visit. For this evening."

"I'll authorise the expense of the flights. If you can even get a flight so soon."

"I'll get Faulkner to fly us. He loves an excuse to get in the air."

"He's on the Island?" Petrakis couldn't help but smile. One of his father's undeniable talents was he could make people happy. It worked in reverse, too, for those who were closest to him. His mother likened him to a magpie, attracted to people's emotions, stealing them, and flitting away when something shinier appeared.

"I'm sure he'll drop by, and say hello." Beckett forced a smile. He had a suspicion Faulkner had bedded Petrakis at some point, and she still harboured desire for him. He was just as sure Faulkner had no intention of dropping by. Sometimes, you had to manipulate to get what you needed.

"I'll get on the phone. You will tread carefully, won't you? You know how sensitive this Island is to the past. If it gets out, that you went to speak to Chrystos…"

"If it leads us to Danni's killer, does it matter?"

Petrakis dropped her gaze, and picked up the phone. "It would have been better if the boyfriend had done it," she muttered, almost without thinking.

Leaving Petrakis to arrange the visit, Beckett phoned Faulkner.

"He has a private jet?" Harper stage whispered, as Beckett waited for Faulkner to answer.

"On occasion, he can actually be useful." Beckett hated asking Faulkner for anything. Harper staying at the villa had been a little, petty victory, because he was doing it behind Faulkner's back, but that had been ruined when Faulkner had turned up, and was, of course, delighted.

"Son?" Faulkner's voice chirped in Beckett's ear.

"You busy later?"

"What you got in mind?"

"We need a lift to the mainland."

"Sure. Yeah, of course. It'll be a blast. Boys' trip out. Be good to spend some time with you."

Beckett could feel Faulkner grinning, pleased to be asked, overjoyed to be included. "It's work. But, yeah. Fly out today, back tomorrow morning."

"The investigation?" The tone of Faulkner's voice had

changed.

"I can't discuss it."

"Which airport?"

"Talyeri."

There was silence. "That's the closest airport to Sarabande."

Sarabande was known for only one thing. The secure hospital where Chrystos Spiros had been sent. There had been nowhere for him on the Island.

"You know the way though?"

"Of course I know the way. That's what GPS is for." Faulkner sounded annoyed. "You're going to see the Fiend?"

"Don't call him that, Faulkner. He's not a monster. Or a mythical being. He's a human being."

"Do you need to go? Can't your guy from the Met go? He's seems bright. They wouldn't have sent him, if they didn't think he was capable. I don't mind taking him. You stay here."

"Thought you were looking forward to a boys' trip out? Spending time together." Beckett knew he was being unfair. He didn't much care, though.

"Fine, okay. I'll meet you at the airport, then? I'll let you know the time when I've organised it."

"Good." Beckett rung off. Distracted, Beckett checked his phone – three text messages from Bee. He frowned, and opened the newest – 'Please ignore previous messages. False alarm. Thanks.'

"Okay?" Harper asked.

"Fine."

"What sort of plane has your dad got?" Harper was asking. He looked worried, mouth drawn in a tight line.

"Small Italian twin prop. Why?"

"How small?"

It suddenly dawned on Beckett Harper might not be

relishing the prospect of a night flight on a small plane, piloted by a man who had well-publicized drug and alcohol issues.

"I think you can squeeze six or seven people on it, if that helps. It can get a bit bumpy."

He saw Harper swallow, his skin pale.

"If you get motion sickness, I'd take a tablet. Faulkner loves that plane. If you're going to throw up, he's likely to insist on opening one of the doors and making you stick your head out into the clouds. There's a pharmacy across the road."

"Hilarious." Harper glowered at him, but headed away down the hallway. Beckett opened Bee's older text messages. The message 'I've found Emmie's scarf in this car. Don't know where I am. The car is a Land Rover.' And a photo of a Land Rover and a number plate. He didn't need the registration number to know who the car belonged to. There was only one car like that on the Island.

He dialled Bee's number. It rang out, and then dropped to voicemail. He hung up and redialled. Just as it was about to drop to voicemail again, the phone clicked, and Bee answered, her voice tentative, guilty, even.

"Hello?"

"What am I to make of these text messages and photos?"

"Who is this?" She was playing for time.

"You know who it is. You have caller ID."

"Sorry, Inspector. You woke me up. I didn't see the screen."

"Well?"

"I thought I'd seen Emmie's scarf, but as I said, I was mistaken."

"In Gideon Coe's car?"

"You've already checked it out?" She sounded scared.

"I recognise the car."

"I walked past it in town, after I saw you. Saw a scarf on the passenger seat. Thought it was Emmie's. But, it wasn't."

"How do you know it wasn't Emmie's? You must have been pretty sure to take those photos, which, incidentally, don't look like they were taken in town."

"Honestly. I'm sorry I sent them. The man came back. Explained the scarf belonged to his wife. She'd bought it years ago. I'm getting paranoid. I'll leave the detective work to you from now on."

"Gideon had no idea where Emmie was?"

"None at all. He didn't even know anyone was missing."

Beckett rang off. Bee was lying. He needed to get up to Gideon's place, but it was impossible. They'd be in the air to the mainland in a couple of hours. Surely if Gideon had anything to do with Emmie's disappearance, there could be nothing sinister involved? Gideon was a harmless old hippy—a long-time friend of Faulkner's. His worst crimes were growing marijuana in the woods behind his cabin. There were always rumours about his weakness for women, despite having Julia, who he described as his soul partner. She didn't seem to mind his indiscretions. But, Gideon was knocking on sixty. Emmie wouldn't have been tempted, would she? He couldn't believe Gideon would hurt anyone. Or Julia in a fit of jealous rage? No. It was ridiculous.

He cornered Tomas, who was tidying his desk, ready to leave for the evening.

"Do me a favour?"

"What boss?"

"On your way home, stop off at Gideon Coe's place."

"That's not on my way home."

"Depends which way you go home. You can book it as overtime." *Petrakis would slay him at the end of all this.* "Have a chat with him. Have a look around, if he'll let you."

"What am I looking for? His marijuana plantation?" Tomas disapproved of the drug use, and perhaps more that Beckett chose to overlook it.

"See if he has any houseguests. Show him the photo of Emmie Archer. See if he recognises her."

"You think he has something to do with her disappearance?" As much as he disapproved of Gideon Coe, Tomas couldn't believe he would be involved in abduction, or worse.

"I just want you to drop in. Low key. Then, let me know what you think."

"Sure. Okay." Tomas nodded, pleased to be trusted to have an opinion. "Is it true you're going to interview Chrystos?"

Beckett couldn't help but smile. There really were no secrets in this building. It suited his purposes, this time. He wanted the news out there. He wanted Mitchell Troy to know he was going to talk to Chrystos. Prod the sleeping bear enough times, and he'll swipe a claw at you.

CHAPTER TWENTY-FOUR

The mood on the plane was tense. A different Faulkner to the one Harper had met. Serious. Only the briefest of smiles and greetings, before showing them onto the plane, and doing his pre-flight checks.

Harper hated flying, always had. He had no idea why, but the thought of being inside that thin, metal tube, propelled through the sky, with engines made from thousands of components, knowing only one had to break for disaster to ensue, made his nerves jangle. He could cope with big passenger jets. There were enough people around to get some comfort, but he'd never been on a plane as small as this one.

It was impossible to tell if Faulkner was so serious and monosyllabic because he was pensive about the flight, or for some other reason. Certainly relations between him and Beckett were strained, as they barely looked at each other. The tension made Harper feel sick.

From the outside, the plane looked like something from a Bond movie, all sleek lines and narrow windows. The nose of the plane had two fins, or mini wings, sticking out, which made it look like a hammerhead shark. Harper had never seen a plane like it. He had no idea why this plane needed the extra pair of mini wings, if that's what they were. An idea popped into his head he couldn't shift. They were the plane version of bicycle stabilisers. Perhaps Faulkner needed them to help him fly. Harper pulled his seatbelt even tighter.

Beckett had taken a seat further down the cabin, though the interior was so small, it seemed pointless. If Beckett wanted to isolate himself, this wasn't the environment to do it in. He was deep in thought, but Harper needed a distraction to keep his thoughts away from nose dives into the sea.

"Tell me about Chrystos. What to expect."

Beckett looked at him in surprise, almost as if he'd forgotten he was there.

"Why was he sent to a psychiatric hospital rather than prison? What's his illness?"

"He's schizophrenic, coupled with dissocial personality disorder."

"How successful has his treatment been?"

"He's on anti-psychotics for the schizophrenia. His drug and alcohol use contributed massively to his behaviour. Obviously, he's clean now."

"Will he remember anything about that time?"

"Let's hope so," Beckett replied before looking away. His tone was uncomfortable.

Harper imagined Beckett was reliving that time. Not a time he wanted to travel back to, but circumstances had forced him. Harper had been sure it was a mistake, a red herring. As his bosses had told him, there was no connection to past cases. Chrystos had killed Rosie, raped those women. Of that, there was no doubt. Except, Beckett's doubts were infectious. Harper was sure his bosses would be furious he'd not closed the case down yet, and, even worse, was travelling to the past with Beckett. He hadn't told them, but they would know by now, he was sure.

Harper would argue this trip was necessary to allay Beckett's doubts, to refocus his mind. There were enough connections to warrant a visit. No one could argue any different, but seeing Chrystos would remind Beckett of the monster he was. Harper nodded to himself. Yes, this visit would clear the fog from Beckett's head. Chrystos had clearly horrified Beckett. Seeing one human eat the flesh of another? Harper couldn't even imagine what scar that image would leave. But, it was an image which had faded over time, until the hospitalised Chrystos had become more patient than monster.

The engines spluttered and growled into life. Harper glanced into the cockpit. Faulkner was talking to air traffic control. The lights of the dashboard – if that's what you called it in a plane – were like a fairy grotto. There seemed an impossible number of buttons and switches, dials and levers. All for one small plane, and for one person to operate.

"Do we have an interview strategy?" Harper looked back down the cabin, but Beckett had plugged earphones in, and had his eyes closed. Harper was on his own. He gripped the arms of his seat, and waited for the engines to roar, and the force of the acceleration to pin him back in his chair.

***

They'd picked up a hire car at the airport, and Beckett had dropped Faulkner off at the hotel they were to stay in that night. Beckett could sense Faulkner wanted to talk, to warn him off, but with Harper there, it was impossible. Instead, barely a word was spoken by any of them. Harper had alighted the plane, looking ashen-faced. Small planes were always bumpy, but it had been a rough flight. The sort of flight Faulkner enjoyed the most, but not today. Beckett was thankful for the silence. He felt as sick as Harper looked. He didn't dare hold his hands out in front of him, because he knew they would tremble like a man in detox, and he didn't want to betray himself to either his father, or Harper.

The hospital was an imposing marble-clad building, symmetrical, apart from the addition of a clock tower at one end. The orange tiles of the roof shone in the late afternoon sun, like a heavenly halo, but on closer inspection, many of the windows were shuttered or barred. The building's smile hid the torment inside.

They got through the checks at the hospital without any

201

hitches. Petrakis had pulled the necessary strings, and they were led down a long corridor by a silent man with a clanking bundle of keys – key cards and finger print recognition hadn't yet caught up with a cash-starved Greek mental health system - passing through three double locked doors, and then through another locked door into a large sun-soaked room. They were told to wait, and the man left them to it.

There was a u-shaped cluster of sofas, a coffee table, and large posters on the walls – photos of soaring landscapes, delicate flowers, and flocks of birds soaring over oceans. It was supposed to be a friendly room, but again, there were teeth-like bars at the windows, the furniture was nailed to the floor, and the posters screwed to the walls.

Harper sat on one of the sofas. Beckett was beginning to wish he'd not brought him. He wasn't sure what he was going to say to Chrystos. He wasn't sure of anything now. He stood at the window, peering out through the bars. They were at the back of the building, and below, was an ornamental garden, hedges and flower beds regimentally laid out, terraces and sculptures, fountains and trees. A few people moved about, walking the grassy avenues or traversing the lawns. It was impossible to tell the difference between the patients and the nurses.

The door opening startled him. He turned around, feeling his heart thumping like a prog-rock concert in his chest. A uniformed man came in first, a nurse, broad, business-like. He stood to one side, and a second figure entered. Beckett forced himself to breathe. The beard was neatly trimmed and about five stone in weight had been accumulated, but there was no mistaking the crawling tattoos of gorgons on both forearms, those unblinking charcoal eyes, the bulbous nose, and the mouth, which curled and twisted like a meandering river.

The nurse shut the door behind Chrystos, and locked it. Chrystos shuffled forward, squinting.

"Chrystos. This is Detective Inspector Harper from the

Metropolitan Police in London, and I'm Inspector Beckett Kyriakoulis. Do you remember me?"

Chrystos hesitated, then moved to have a closer look at Beckett, his eyes flickering, taking in the lines of Beckett's face. Beckett wished he could smile, to put himself at ease as much as the man in front of him, but he felt frozen, his throat dry.

"I found you on the Island. Arrested you, and questioned you. Before you came here." His voice struggled out of his mouth. He could sense Harper watching him.

Chrystos shook his head ponderously, as if it was a heavy weight.

"I don't. I'm sorry." He glanced at the nurse, then back at Beckett, "I don't remember much from back then, but I've been told about you, so I do know who you are. I know you were the one who saved me."

Chrystos held out a hand, and stepped forward. His mouth turned up at the corners, an attempt at a smile. "Thank you."

Beckett stared at the hand, the great paw of the man. The hand which had held woman down whilst he raped them, which had held the knife cutting into the face of the man…

Beckett tore his thoughts away from that day and from that place, and focussed on the face of the man in front of him. Just a man. Barely five foot eight. A stocky man, then. An overweight one, now. Stooped in the back and slumped in the shoulders, as if wanting to take up less space in the world. Beckett took the hand, and shook it. The palm was warm, the shake weak but enthusiastic.

Determined to be polite and do things properly, Chrystos nodded and shuffled towards Harper, shaking his hand, too.

"Would you like to sit?" Harper indicated the sofa.

Chrystos nodded, and took himself to the bottom of the U-shape. "Thank you."

He sat back, upright hands on his pressed together knees. Harper looked up at Beckett. He was leaving this to him. Observing. Taking mental notes. *For the investigation, or for his bosses?*

Beckett sat opposite Harper, but turned his body to face Chrystos.

"In what way did I save you?"

"I've been told there were people who wanted to kill me. For the things I did. I was sick." He glanced across at the nurse, "I'm still sick. But, you found me. You didn't hurt me. You could have done. No one would have blamed you. But, you rescued me. And I came here, where they helped me get better. They taught me to paint. I paint all day now. I have an exhibition here. You could go and see it. Later. When we've finished. I wouldn't be here, if it wasn't for you. I wouldn't be anywhere. That's why I'm glad you've come. So, I can thank you." Chrystos leaned forward, hands clasped together half pleading half praying.

He had meant what he said. He believed what he said. But, it sounded like therapy speak. He'd been taught to paint, and taught to accept the events which made up his 'journey.' But, down in the pit of his soul, did he understand it? Did he feel all the emotions of it? Beckett thought not. You couldn't feel what Chrystos had done, and not be revolted by it. Chrystos seemed at peace with himself. Though, perhaps, that was the medication.

"You don't need to thank me, Chrystos. I did my job."

"But, you did it with…" Chrystos searched for the right word, "humanity."

"I'm glad you're coming to terms with what happened."

"I did terrible things. Hurting all those women. My mind was confused. I thought they wanted me. I wish I could say I'm sorry to each one of them. I wrote each one a letter, with my therapist. But, we can't send them. It would upset the women too much, she says."

There was no mention of Panos. Beckett had no wish to

mention his name, either. It wasn't relevant. But, Beckett wondered if he'd penned a letter to him. And if he had, what would it say?

"It's about the women, the reason we are here." Harper filled the silence.

"Do they want their letters?" Chrystos asked, his voice lifting with hope.

"It's about one particular woman." Beckett took back control, "Rosie Payne."

He let the name sit in the space between himself and Chrystos. Chrystos started chewing on a fingernail.

"Do you remember the name Rosie Payne, Chrystos?"

"I'm not very good with names."

"Did you write a letter to her?"

"No." The answer was quick and definite.

"But, you do remember her? I asked you about her at the time. When I found you, you were wearing her bracelet." Beckett fished in his pocket, and pulled out the bracelet. It was still in the evidence bag, but unmistakable. Chrystos turned his head away.

"Please have a look at it, Chrystos. Tell me if you remember it. I found it on your left wrist." Beckett moved closer to Chrystos, and held the bag out to him. Chrystos swallowed. He seemed to shrink into himself like a deflating balloon, "Please look for me. You say I saved you. Now, you can save me."

Chrystos looked at him, those dark eyes, like pits of tar. He took the bag, and studied the contents, turning it over and over in his hands.

"Do you recognise it?"

"Yes. It was Rosie's."

"And when I found you, you were wearing it?"

"Rosie was beautiful. I liked her. She was nice to me."

"When was she nice to you, Chrystos?"

"When I was working. Tidying up. Gardening. Cleaning

the pool."

"Where was that?"

"At the big house. The castle."

"Mitchell Troy's house?"

"I grew up there. Before the castle was built."

"It was your family farm."

"I was glad to be able to work there again. It reminded me of when I was young."

"And you saw Rosie there?"

"She was there, often."

"With Mrs. Troy? Jeanie? You remember her?"

"I remember Mrs. Troy. She was very pretty, but always sad. I didn't see her a lot. She never came outside. I wasn't allowed inside."

"But, Rosie came to visit her?"

Chrystos shook his head. "She came to visit Mr Troy."

"You're sure about that Chrystos?"

He nodded and smiled. "He was very fond of her. I think he was lonely. But, not after Rosie started visiting."

Beckett steadied his breathing, kept his pulse rate even. "I'm going to ask you something that you might find very difficult, Chrystos. About Rosie."

"Okay." Chrystos' voice was small, and he pushed his hands underneath his thighs. The bracelet was balanced on his knees.

"How did you get Rosie's bracelet?"

"I don't remember." Chrystos' left foot started to jiggle.

"Did she give it to you? You said she was nice to you."

He shook his head, eyes fixed on the bracelet, his foot jiggled more violently, so much so he had to put a hand on the bracelet to stop it sliding to the floor.

"If she didn't give it to you, you must have taken it from her. Did you take it from her, Chrystos?" Beckett kept his voice kind, as if he was asking an old lady where she'd left her glasses.

Chrystos gave a nod, then looked into Beckett's eyes. "I'm sorry."

"Why did you take it?"

"Because she was kind to me, and I wanted something of hers to remember her."

"Was she dead when you took the bracelet?"

"Yes," Chrystos whispered. "Do we have to talk about this?"

"Chrystos, did you kill Rosie Payne?"

"No." His answer came out like a plaintive howl. "I wouldn't hurt her. I always said I didn't hurt her."

"But, you hurt those other women," Harper cut in.

"I didn't know I was hurting them. I thought I was loving them."

"Did you love Rosie, too?"

"I wouldn't. I didn't. She belonged to Mr. Troy. I couldn't love her. Not like that. She wasn't mine to love." Chrystos leapt to his feet. "She wasn't mine to love."

Beckett swept Harper with a 'back off' look, and put a hand on Chrystos' shoulder.

"It's okay. I understand. Please sit down."

Chrystos sank back to the sofa, head in his hands.

"Was she alive when you took the bracelet?"

"She looked so beautiful. It was dark, but the moon was bright. It made her skin look silver. I thought she was sleeping. But, her eyes were open. People don't sleep with their eyes open, do they?"

"No, they don't."

"I tried to wake her up, but she'd gone. There was nothing I could do. I saw the bracelet. I thought if I wore it, I'd be close to her. She wouldn't feel so lonely. So, I took it. I know now that was wrong. But, I couldn't have helped her, could I?"

"You could have called someone, told someone."

"I was scared."

"Where was Rosie when you found her, Chrystos?"

"I'm not sure. My head doesn't remember things in order from that time."

"Describe it to me. The place."

"She was by a tree. Sheltered, I thought at least. The trees always protect you."

"Anything else?"

"There was a road. I heard a car go past. Saw its lights."

"Which road?"

"The road down from the mountain."

"What were you doing out there, Chrystos?" Beckett cajoled.

"Nothing."

"In the woods, at night."

"I could never sleep. I liked to walk. I used to explore those woods when I was young. I knew every tree."

"You weren't at the Castle that night?"

Chrystos hesitated. "I heard the music. There was a party. There were always parties. At the Castle. And in the woods."

"You didn't go closer. To watch?"

"Not at the Castle. They didn't like me being there."

"But, you mentioned parties in the woods? You know those woods better than anyone. You could watch and never be seen."

Chrystos started chewing his fingernails.

"You did watch, didn't you? I bet there were lots of girls there."

Chrystos flicked his eyes up to meet Beckett's gaze.

"What happened at those parties, Chrystos?"

"I don't remember." He shook his head, but he blinked and swallowed.

"Try, Chrystos. Was there music? Singing? Who did you

see there?"

"I didn't. I don't remember"

"Did you see Rosie at one of these parties?"

"She was a good girl. Not like the others."

"What do you mean 'the others'?"

"Not good girls. That's what I mean. I'm sorry."

"What do you mean not good girls? Because they were drunk? Taking drugs?"

"Good girls like one man. They don't share themselves."

"Share?"

"Faithful. Good girls are faithful."

"So, there were girls at these parties being 'unfaithful'?" Beckett stressed the word.

"I didn't see. I don't remember."

"Would it have upset you to see Rosie at one of these parties, Chrystos?" Harper jumped in, "Amongst all these unfaithful girls?"

"She wouldn't. Mr. Troy protected her. He loved her."

"What was he protecting her from, Chrystos? Please. I helped you. I need you to help me." Beckett took back control from Harper. "What went on at these parties? I know you watched, Chrystos. You're not in trouble for watching. I just need to know what went on."

Chrystos hesitated, closed his eyes, then opened them, and stared at Beckett, eyes darker than ever.

"Music, singing, chanting, shouting to the gods. Fires, drums. Drinking, smoking, wild women, wild men, laughing, people loving each other. Not hurting each other." His eyes opened wide, and he put a hand on Beckett's knee. "Not really hurting. Sometimes people would pretend things. Pretend to hit each other. Pretend to hang from trees. At least, I think so. I don't remember those bits so well."

"And did you see Rosie at one of those parties?"

"Not her face. Everyone wore masks, you see. But, I saw her tattoo. It was beautiful, not like mine. I knew it was her from the tattoo."

"Did it upset you to see her at that sort of party?"

"I was worried for her sometimes, but I knew Mr. Troy would protect her. He loved her."

"You saw Mr. Troy, Mitchell Troy, at one of these parties in the woods?"

"I saw someone loving her. The man with the silver goat mask. The man they all followed. It must have been him. She belonged to him. She wasn't shared, not like some of the others."

Beckett could hear his heart thumping. He put one fist in another. Anything else would have betrayed his trembling hands. "The night you found Rosie… was that a party at the Castle or in the woods?"

"At the Castle. Then, I heard them in the woods later." Chrystos nodded. "I was checking my rabbit traps. That's when I found Rosie."

"You didn't hear anything? See anyone else? Someone who might have hurt Rosie?"

"No. There was only me."

"Could you see any blood on her, any injuries?" Harper's voice sounded strained.

Chrystos shook his head. "She was beautiful. Perfect."

"And what did you do then?"

"I went home. I had rabbits I'd trapped. I took them home for my mother to cook." He paused, but then his eyes brightened. "But, I felt bad. I didn't like to think of Rosie out there on her own. So, I went back to find her. I was going to bring her home for my mother to look after."

"What happened, Chrystos?" Beckett asked.

"She'd gone."

"Gone?" Harper's voice rose.

"Maybe she wasn't dead after all? Maybe the gods came

for her? I knew I'd gone back to the right place, but she wasn't there. Someone had taken her away."

"He's on medication to keep him calm," a nurse told them, once Chrystos had been lead away to his room. "He was a very disturbed man when he arrived here. Art therapy has helped a huge amount, but he still needs his medication. Do you want to see what he's painted? It's good. So good, the Governor let him have a permanent exhibition in the art room corridor."

Beckett nodded. "Please, if you don't mind."

The nurse led them through locked doors that clunked behind them, and down two floors to a wide, white-painted corridor with double doors at the end.

"These are all Chrystos'."

Beckett stared at the first painting. It was done in oils to mimic a 17th century Baroque style—Greek Gods leering down from the sky over a wooded glade. In the wooded glade were people, humans in animal masks, dancing. There were five paintings in total. All following a similar theme. Greek gods, humans in masks and furs. Dancing, drinking, smoking, eating, bodies coupled together having sex.

Beckett looked at Harper, and then at the nurse. "These are considered good therapy for him?"

"Art therapy is about expressing feelings, and communicating those feelings where the patient doesn't feel able to communicate them verbally. It doesn't mean what you see in the paintings actually happened. It represents feelings the patient has, but has been unable to express. The aim is once emotions are expressed the patient can then understand them, and understand where their behaviour might have been unacceptable."

"So painting these will stop Chrystos from raping women?" Harper said, voice dripping with scepticism.

"Combined with medication, one day, he will hopefully

get to the point where he is not considered a danger."

"But, he won't be released?" Harper asked.

"If the doctors consider him to be no longer a danger, then, yes, potentially, one day."

Neither man spoke until they were outside the hospital gates. Beckett pulled into a lay-by. Dusk was folding in on itself, and a wind whisked up dirt and litter, and sent it dancing in and out of the hire car's headlights.

Beckett seemed to be in another place, hands resting on the wheel.

"You know we can't trust anything he says." Harper broke the silence.

Beckett didn't move. No indication he'd even heard him.

"He said himself he didn't remember much from back then."

"You don't think his recollection of finding Rosie seemed very clear and precise?" Beckett looked at him.

The expression on his face was one Harper hadn't seen before. *Fear? Doubt?* Harper stared out of the passenger window, torn. Eventually, he turned back to Beckett. "Even if he's right. Even if Mitchell was having an affair with Rosie, there's no evidence he had anything to do with her death. The most probable sequence of events is still Chrystos killed her, and then hid her body. Buried her in the woods. He'd know where to do it so no one would ever find the grave. Now, he's just covering up, or maybe he's invented this memory to absolve himself. He believes it, and that's why he's so convincing. If there is a chance he might be released one day, then pinning the murder of Rosie on someone else would help his case."

Beckett seemed to consider that for a moment. "I don't think he's that clever. Or that devious."

But, Harper could sense doubt in his voice. Or was it the thought of Chrystos being released, and returning to the Island?

"We still have nothing to help us with the Danni Deacon case."

"All roads lead back to Troy."

"Why are you so obsessed with him?"

Beckett looked at him about to speak, then changed his mind. "We'd better get back to the hotel, before Faulkner goes on the rampage."

Faulkner was holding court in the hotel lounge bar when they arrived. They heard him, as soon as they stepped through the sliding front doors. Harper saw Beckett physically wince at the loud baritone of his father echoing past the empty reception desk.

The hotel was a throwback to the seventies. Or perhaps, it had never left. It looked like something from one of those sitcoms, which spewed up on one of the random channels Harper occasionally flicked onto, and past. Low ceilings, red, orange and black décor, with multicolour spots, swirls, and chevrons everywhere. It all looked dingy and grimy, but it was impossible to tell if that was because of the colour scheme itself, or because the hotel was in need of a pressure wash. Harper fancied it was the latter. This was not a tourist area. The only guests were there for business, and there weren't many of those. He didn't see how the hotel could ever make money.

"We'd better go and collect him," Beckett said, heading in the direction of Faulkner's voice. Harper followed, but it was too late. As they walked into the lounge bar, Faulkner was settling himself at the faded grand piano in the corner of the room. A couple of hotel staff had pulled chairs up close, together with a smattering of men in shabby and ill-fitting business suits.

"Bollocks," Beckett whispered, and Faulkner started playing. *Waterloo* by Abba. He sang at the top of his voice, and whipped his tiny audience up into a chorus.

Harper glanced across at Beckett. "Is he always like this?"

"Pretty much."

"Whoo hoo… my son's arrived. Ladies and gents, my number one son," Faulkner yelled between verse and chorus, before carrying on, easing from *Waterloo* into *Summer Night City*.

"Abba?"

Beckett shrugged and half smiled. "Drink?"

"I don't really…"

"Tonight, you won't be able to say no."

Beckett was right. Faulkner wasn't going to let any of them off. He bought round after round for all the guests and staff, regaling them with outrageous stories. Eventually, all the other guests and staff crawled off to bed, and there was just the three of them left. Harper's head was swimming. Thoughts seem to take an age to form, and then make sense. It was like being switched to slo-mo. It wasn't that he hadn't ever got drunk before. He had. He knew what it was like, and he hated the feeling of being out of control.

He didn't know how, but he found himself sitting on one side of Faulkner and Beckett on the other. Faulkner had his arms around their shoulders.

"Now, I can sense there is tension between you two. That you don't see eye to eye. I think, tonight, right here and right now, we should clear things up, smooth the waves. What d'you say?"

Harper looked across at Beckett. He didn't seem drunk at all.

"I don't have a problem with him," Beckett said in a tone conveying the opposite.

"You resent me being here."

"I wanted you here."

"So, what's the problem? That I don't just agree with everything you say."

"You're doing as you've been told."

"I haven't been told anything."

"Sure you have. Steer him away from that old case. Steer

him away from Mitchell Troy."

"You're insane. You're obsessed with him. He might be the big crime lord you say, or he might just be a businessman. I have no idea. We need to follow the evidence, not be blinded by your hatred of someone. It's affecting your judgment, and based on what? What concrete evidence have you ever seen on Mitchell Troy?"

"I saw him. When I was serving in Bosnia. With one of the Serb Generals. He was selling them arms and munitions. Arms used to kill civilians. Women and children. He knew what the weapons would be used for. We had to stand by whilst it happened. He sold the weapons, and we watched them being used."

"You saw Mitchell Troy?"

"He was using a different name then, but yes."

"He knows you saw him?"

"No. I was a young soldier. One of many. I doubt he even noticed me. Just a uniform. I had no idea who he was, until I came to the Island, and saw him. There's no record of Mitchell Troy ever having been in Bosnia. I have no evidence, apart from my own word."

"Sounds familiar. Definitely the same man? Memory can play tricks. In times of trauma, we can substitute one face for another. Transference, the men in white coats call it."

"Really? Thanks, Sigmund. It *was* him."

But, Harper could hear uncertainty in his voice. "You're not sure, are you? All those years ago. You've changed. He would have changed. Perhaps it was someone who looked like him. We've all got twins out there."

Beckett said nothing.

"Can you be 100% certain it was the same man?"

"In my heart, yes, my gut, yes."

"But, in your head?"

Beckett's silence gave the answer.

"And you don't agree that your feelings, suspicions, whatever you want to call it, about him are clouding your judgment and affecting this case?" Harper wasn't about to let the conversation drop.

"There are connections."

"To Rosie, perhaps. But, to Danni? She worked at a party at his house. Along with many others."

"She's the only one who ended up dead."

"There were over hundred guests. She didn't disappear at the party. You may not like Mitchell Troy. He might be guilty of crimes, but there is really nothing to put him front and centre in this case."

Beckett was reading a message on his phone. He read then looked up. "They've found Danni's car. The RAV-4. In a ravine, off a track on the coast road. They're going to lift it out in the morning, after forensics have looked at it in situ."

"At last." Harper felt like cheering. "There's got to be something we can use in the car."

CHAPTER TWENTY-FIVE

The next morning at half eight, Beckett and Harper were standing at the top of a wooded slope, where, about 70 feet down, a blue Toyota RAV-4 was resting, skew-whiff against the trunk of a large cypress tree. The path it had taken through the undergrowth to arrive at its resting spot was clear, bushes squashed and branches broken. If the cypress tree hadn't got in the way, it would have ended up 200 feet down in the gully at the bottom of the ravine.

"It looks like whoever drove it here got out, let off the handbrake, and pushed it over the edge," Tomas reported.

"I bet they were disappointed when it got jammed on the tree." Harper remained firmly away from the edge.

"Not a lot they could do about it." Beckett put a supporting hand on the trunk of an olive tree, and leaned over. A chain had been attached to the tow point of the car, and the winch truck was waiting for the okay to start the extraction.

"This track is hardly ever used," Tomas continued. "It was a man out walking who spotted the car and called it in. There were tyre tracks, but forensics reckon not clear enough to get an imprint and tell if they belong to the Toyota, or if there were other cars here, too."

"Whoever dumped the car had to get back to where they came from, somehow. There's a lay-by at the top. Forensics will need to do a search there, a 100 yards in either direction. Where does this track lead to?" Beckett was playing the scene in his head. That scenario would require a second person.

"Nowhere. It peters out after another mile, then it's only passable by foot. Takes you up onto the mountain."

"So, they didn't go that way. It's a bloody long walk back to the nearest habitation."

"About six miles. The yellow bus does go past though."

"So, they might have caught the bus back? Nearest bus stop?"

"About a mile down the road." Tomas was bouncing on his heels, convinced they had the killer in their grasp. "Do you want me to talk to the bus company? See who they remember picking up from that bus stop Saturday night?"

"Saturday onwards. The car might have been dumped later," Harper added.

"Risky, though. Driving around the Island in a dead woman's car." Beckett didn't buy it. He didn't buy the killer taking the bus. "And we know she was killed sometime Saturday evening, and her body dumped by boat early Sunday morning. There's no tow bar on this car."

"So?" Harper frowned.

"The boat was taken to the beach in a trailer pulled by a car. No tow car, no trailer."

"Another car was used to dump the body?"

"And to give a lift home after dumping Danni's car."

"Suggesting there were two people involved." Harper looked at Tomas. "Have we confirmed Sophia and Patrick's story yet? Were they definitely on the mainland?"

"She has credit card receipts." Tomas looked apologetic.

"Let's get this car out, and see what it tells us." Beckett waved at the truck driver, and stood out of the way.

Fifteen minutes later, the car was on the track, with the forensic team swarming all over it.

The boot was cracked open, and after a couple of minutes, one of the white suited forensic officers signalled Beckett and Harper over.

"There's traces of blood here. And hair. Long blonde."

Beckett nodded. "Go on."

"Lots of fingerprints in and around the boot, and in the car itself. We found a mobile phone in the glove compartment. And this was under the driver's seat," He held up an evidence bag containing a used condom. "We'll do a more thorough exam back at base. But, I'll get everything we've got now processed as quickly as possible. Get you some DNA proof of who was in this car."

Beckett nodded thanks. "Can I look at the phone?"

The technician called a colleague over, and Beckett took hold of the bag with the phone. It was a chunky, cheap, and a basic model. Beckett pressed the on-button, and the screen lit up. There was no password required. He stared at it, trying to figure out how to access the memory.

"Let me. One of my sister's kids has one like this. Kept losing her iPhone. Got given one of these as a punishment."

Harper took the phone, and with a couple of button presses, the call log appeared on screen. There was a series of incoming and outgoing calls. The last one dated the Wednesday morning, the last day anyone saw Danni alive. There was only one name – Neil. Harper flicked to the Address Book. Again, only one entry – Neil.

"Neil Ticknall." Beckett pictured the man groping Danni at the Troy's party Tuesday night. Not just Lily Troy stirring things.

"Shall I phone the number?" Harper asked.

"If he sees Danni calling, he's not going to answer. What's the number?" Beckett pulled out his own phone. "No bloody signal. Come on."

Back by the gathered cars at the roadside, Beckett dialled the number as Harper read it out. He put it on speaker phone. It rang and rang, and then jumped to a standard voicemail telling them to leave a message. Beckett hung up.

"Phones are so impersonal. I think a face-to-face meeting

is so much better." Beckett looked at Harper. "Agree?"

"Let's go and have a chat."

The British High Commission was nothing more than a faded wooden door, inset in a pock-marked, four storey terrace. On one side were the offices of a law firm, and on the other, an insurance brokers. Only the brass plaque on the door gave any indication behind the door was a representative of the British nation. Unlike the aging door Beckett thought needed sanding down and re-varnishing, the plaque was polished, and reflected the sun with diamond bolts of light.

Beckett buzzed on the intercom.

"Hello?" The disembodied voice floated back.

"Inspector Kyriakoulis to see Neil Ticknall."

There was a pause and a crackle. "Can I ask what it is regarding?"

"That depends if you expect an answer," Beckett replied. He was tired of this. Tired of people.

There was silence, and then the door clicked.

The girl was waiting in front of the reception desk.

"He really can't see you now, he's very busy. He asks if you can wait."

"Not today. It's okay. I know where his office is."

Beckett side-stepped the girl, and headed up the stairs – old, tight turned, marble clad.

He burst through the door onto the third floor, as Neil Ticknall came out of his office. His secretary blinked, stood up, and opened her mouth.

"Do you want me to call the police?" she stammered to her boss.

"Oh… please do." Beckett smiled at her.

"Inspector… this really isn't acceptable." Ticknall's eyebrows were reaching for his hairline, and his tongue wet his lips. Like a chameleon, he'd turned the colour of the marble floors.

"Nice office, if I remember. View of the harbour." Beckett went past him, and into the Vice Consul's domain. Neatly arranged bookshelves, a carpet so thick you'd lose your toes, large desk, in-tray piled with documents, and beyond the roofs, streets and then the harbour. The sea shimmered with a thousand million sparks. The masts of boats jutted up like skinny white fingers. A hulking, black-windowed yacht was heading out to sea.

"What is this about?" Ticknall followed him in, shutting the door.

Beckett allowed himself a half smile, as the muffled sound of a mobile phone started buzzing from Ticknall's suit jacket pocket.

"That seems to be your phone. You'd better answer it. Might be important."

Ticknall looked at him as if he were insane, but pulled his phone out, and looked at the screen. He blinked and swallowed.

"Please. Don't mind me."

Ticknall raised the phone to his ear, as if he was encased in glue. "Hello?" His voice grated.

Behind him, the office door opened. Harper came in, carrying Danni's mobile, still wrapped in the evidence bag. Beckett caught a glimpse of the secretary, on the phone, looking panicked.

"Hello?" Ticknall said again, but Harper killed the call. Ticknall spun around, and backed up. His head swivelled from one man to the other. "What the hell is this?"

"That's what you're going to tell us, I hope. Bit odd, you see. We recovered Danni Deacon's car this morning." Beckett saw the nerve behind Ticknall's left eye twitch. "And in the car, we found a mobile phone. That mobile phone, in fact."

Harper lifted the evidence bag and waggled it, like a meal

worm to a fish, almost as if he expected Ticknall to reach over and grab it.

"On that phone, there is only one saved number. The only calls made, and received, on that phone are to, and from, this one number. This one number is saved under the name 'Neil.' And when Detective Inspector Harper phoned that number just now, it was your phone that rang. How would you like to explain that, Mr. Vice Consul?"

Ticknall rubbed his hands over his face, and through his hair. His gaze skittered around the room, as if he was looking for inspiration.

"Perhaps you need some help?" Beckett moved in closer. "You were having an affair with Danni Deacon."

"No... no... you've got it wrong. Totally wrong," Ticknall burst out. Beckett noticed a sheen on his forehead, though the room was cool.

"What other reason would she have for keeping a second mobile phone, with only your number on it? Why else would she be making multiple calls to you? Why else would you be calling her?"

"There are lots of reasons," Ticknall gabbled.

"We have a witness that saw you 'groping' Danni at a party last week."

"Groping?" Ticknall was genuinely horrified. "No. No. Why would I?"

"Perhaps our witness was embellishing. Perhaps it was a tender moment."

"But, I wouldn't. Not Danni. She was a friend. Nothing more."

"You'll have to do better than that," Beckett snarled. "I have friends, but I don't have a separate phone for each one. Why did Danni have a phone, with which she only called you?"

Ticknall recoiled away, and sank down onto a sofa, head in his hands.

"It wasn't Danni who was calling me." His voice was so quiet, so beaten Beckett could hardly hear him.

"So who was it, then?"

Ticknall held his phone out to Beckett. He took it, and looked at the source of the missed call. The letters spelt out Nemesis – M. Nemesis the restaurant. M for mobile, or M for Michale. A logic bomb went off in Beckett's head.

"Michale Bakas?" he asked. Ticknall's cheeks were flushed.

"And what is the exact nature of your relationship with Mr. Bakas?" Harper asked. Beckett heard the satisfaction in the tone.

"How would you like me to describe it?" Ticknall sneered, but the feeling was towards himself, not the men in front of him.

"You're in a sexual relationship?" Harper sat on the sofa opposite the Vice Consul.

Ticknall nodded. "I'm not gay. I'm not. I love my wife. I just… I just…"

"Watched *Brokeback Mountain*, and thought, yeah, I'll give that a try?" Harper rolled his eyes.

"Thanks for that, Barry Norman." Beckett shot Harper a shut-up look.

"My wife can't find out. It would destroy her. And my children. Oh, God…"

"So, you are saying this phone… the phone found in Danni's car, which we believed was used to transport her body after she'd been murdered… actually belonged to Michale Bakas?" Beckett asked.

Ticknall raised his head, eyes widening at the implication. "Danni kept the phone for him, so his wife didn't find it." His words raced each other, tumbling over each other like a waterfall. "We had to keep it secret. Both of us. That's why I have it saved as Nemesis. The restaurant. I couldn't risk a second phone. I didn't have a Danni."

"How did Danni get involved?"

"She got us together. I guess she saw the way we looked at each other. I don't know. She had a gift like that, for sensing how people felt. I was at Nemesis one night, on my own. My family were back in the UK, visiting relatives. She served me slowly that night, so that I was the last one there. I remember she leaned into my ear and said, 'Life is short. If you want someone, you have to tell them. Don't wait. Just do it.' She went into the kitchen, and told Michale I wanted to thank him for the meal. He put a hand on my hand. It started there."

"How long?"

"The end of last summer. I want you to know I've never done anything like this before. I can't explain it…"

Harper snorted. "So what happened? Did Danni threaten to expose you both? Is that why you killed her?" He shook his head in disgust.

"What? No. We wouldn't have been together, if it wasn't for her. I told you."

"Maybe that was her plan all along. Get you together, so she could blackmail you." Harper stood up. For a moment, Beckett thought he was reaching for handcuffs.

"You never knew Danni, did you? She wasn't like that. All she wanted to do was help people. We would never hurt her." Ticknall's eyes shone with tears. Beckett thought they were more for himself, and the destruction about to be wrought on his life, than for Danni.

"Where were you Saturday night?" Harper stepped towards Ticknall.

"With my wife." Ticknall shrank backwards.

"All night? She'll verify that?" Harper asked, his voice dripping with scepticism.

"She took a sleeping pill. The storm, you see. She hates

the thunder. So, she thought she'd take a pill, and go to bed early, before the storm hit. The kids were at friends." Ticknall's words were strained with what he didn't want to admit to.

"You went out?" Harper stared hard at Ticknall. "To meet Michale?"

"Sophia was away for the weekend, with girlfriends on the mainland. He shut the restaurant early, because the storm was coming. I knew my wife wouldn't wake up until late the next day. Michale and I were together until the early hours. We talked about Danni a bit. Wondered why she'd gone off, without telling us."

"How did you arrange to meet? Without the phone?" Harper's voice softened slightly. Beckett, watching, knew that Harper had won. Ticknall would tell them everything now.

"With Sophia away, there was no risk. Saturday, we popped in there for lunch."

"We?" Harper picked up a framed photo of Ticknall's wife and kids from the desk.

"My family. I nipped into the kitchen, saw Michale. Made the arrangements then."

"You weren't worried about Danni?"

"We assumed she was making the most of Patrick being away. She'd told us she was seeing someone else. Someone she really loved. We assumed she was with him."

"Who was it?" Harper put the photo back.

"She wouldn't tell us. Said she didn't want to tempt fate. I had my suspicions though."

"Oh?"

"Her neighbour."

"Linus Sang?" Harper glanced over at Beckett.

"That's him. We thought he was a bit weird, but he and Danni were close. I think he was in love with her. I don't think he has any friends. As I said, Danni was all about helping people.

She didn't like the thought of people being lonely. I'd wondered if he was the man she'd been seeing. Michale said that just showed how little I knew about relationships. Michale said Danni was fond of him, but it was sympathy she felt, not love. Turns out Michale was right. As per." Ticknall sighed.

"Why d'you say that?"

"Saturday afternoon, Linus came into the restaurant. Asked Michale if he'd seen Danni. Michale told him Danni had gone off sailing with Patrick. To spare his feelings. He already seemed quite upset."

"So, you and Michale were alone together, the night Danni was murdered?" Harper was studying some of the titles on the bookshelves.

"We didn't kill her. The last time I saw Danni was at Callum and Lily Troy's eighteenth birthday party, over at the Castle. I swear."

Beckett wasn't sure this scrawny little man, even with all his lies and deception, had the nerve to kill anyone. But, Michale… He was different. Cocky with a TV star ego. What the hell had Michale seen in Ticknall? Someone who was in thrall to him? Someone he could control? Or just someone convenient to shag? He wondered if Harper would come to the same conclusion.

"You'll need to come down to the station with us to make a statement, and we'll have to take DNA samples from you, and fingerprints. We'll also have to search your house. And your yacht." Beckett had seen the photo, pride of place on Ticknall's desk. "You have a small dinghy, as well?"

"How will I explain all this to my wife?" Ticknall's head swivelled towards Beckett, as if he'd forgotten he was in the room.

"Tell her you've been shagging the celebrity chef. People love being connected to celebs." Harper opened the door. "Shall we?"

Beckett helped Ticknall into the back of the car. He slammed the door, and Harper looked at him.

"Something in the water here? Is everyone shagging around?"

"It's not the water." Beckett half smiled. "It's the heat."

CHAPTER TWENTY-SIX

As they went into the back of the station, Floros came through waving. "A Fran Kingston is here to see you. Do you have a minute?"

Beckett let Harper take Ticknall upstairs to give his statement and provide his samples, and he went to find Fran. She was waiting in reception, and jumped to her feet when she saw him.

"You look knackered," she said, with a smile offering motherly comfort.

"Long day. Long week."

"You'll need a holiday after this is over."

"I'm in the perfect place."

She mirrored his world-weary smile. "I thought I'd better come and tell you in person. Weird thing, really. It seemed wrong for me to keep Emmie's passport and valuables. As a missing person, I figured the police should have them. When I went to get them out of the safe, they were gone. I know they were there the day before, because that's what had made me think I should bring them in for you."

"Who has access to the safe?"

"Each room has its own safe box. The room key can open the box, but I prefer the guests to ask me. Because people share rooms, and I suppose can borrow each other's keys. It works. Nothing has ever gone missing."

"Bee was sharing a room with Emmie."

"Their things were in the same box." Fran nodded. "And, yesterday, I caught Bee hanging around in reception. She cleared off, as soon as she saw me. She's not a thief, though. She's a nice girl." Fran shook her head, trying to make sense of it, "Why would she want Emmie's passport?"

"Leave it with me. I'll speak to her. Thanks for letting me know. I owe you."

"Come for a drink at the hotel, when this is over. Or, perhaps, we'll go somewhere with a bit of class. Promise you a great night out."

Beckett smiled. When this was over, the only thing he wanted to do was get in a boat, and disappear over the horizon.

Harper reappeared. "Ticknall's being swabbed, and Tomas will take his statement. Forensics will get over to the house, as soon as they can. They're still working on Danni's car. Shall we go and pick up Michale?"

"I'll send a couple of uniforms. I think we need to talk to Linus Sang. According to him, Danni had said she was staying at friends, whilst Patrick was away. He didn't mention going to the restaurant Saturday night. If he thought she was staying with friends, why would he be looking for her? And he downplayed their relationship." Beckett was kicking himself. He'd overlooked Linus. Missed the clues he might be more involved with Danni Deacon than being just a neighbour.

"We've gone from no suspects to a room full of them," Harper commented, as Beckett spun the car down the pot-marked roads, "We think there were two people who disposed of the body, at least. Michale and Ticknall. Both wouldn't want their relationship made public. They had opportunity, and motive."

"Assuming Danni was going to oust them. We've no evidence of that."

"Patrick and Sophia's alibi relies on backing each other up, and some credit card receipts. It's still possible she's lying to cover up for him. She could have got back in time to help him dump the car."

"Forensics won't help us there. Patrick's DNA and prints are bound to be in Danni's car. We need to find the boat her body was carried in."

"And, now, Linus. If he was in love with her, then he could have killed her for rejecting him."

"But, why go looking for her at the restaurant, Saturday lunchtime? Where was she between Wednesday night, and then?"

"With this mystery lover? Perhaps he, or she, was in Danni's flat all the time, and Linus Sang caught them together. We need to DNA match that sperm. I know you think it's Mitchell Troy, but we have no reason to request him to give a sample."

Beckett said nothing. He couldn't disagree. He had nothing, beyond circumstantial, on Troy. He had that familiar feeling, as if his blood was accelerating faster and faster around his veins and arteries, and the image of one man in his mind— Linus Sang.

He parked outside the apartment block. Harper got out, and gazed around. Beckett unfurled his legs, and stood. The cicadas were humming, and a collared dove was coo-cooing in the one of the trees. It was turning into the hottest day of the summer, so far. A day to sit in the shade in a taverna, drink beer, and talk about nothing.

There was a loud crack echoing down from the building. The collared dove burst out from the tree, wings flapping, fleeing from something it didn't comprehend. Another crack. Unmistakable.

"Jesus Christ." Harper was already on his phone. Beckett leaned back into the car, and grabbed his gun from the glove compartment.

"Stay here," Beckett yelled at him, as he ran to the stairwell. His heart was thundering. He took three steps at a time onto the second floor, pausing at the door to the stairwell.

Cautious, he peered out. The corridor between the flats was empty, but the door to Patrick and Danni's flat was open, the police tape ripped and flicked to one side. The door to Linus' flat was also open. Another crack rang out, but it was distant, above him. His radio crackled. It was Harper.

"They're on the roof. You need to wait for back-up."

"Check the flat. Check there's no one in there."

Then, Beckett was running, back into the stairwell, and up. He paused at the door. It had been left open. He edged around, until he could see the men. Patrick was sprawled on the floor, a pool of scarlet liquid spreading out like an oil slick from underneath him. From this angle, Beckett couldn't tell where he'd been shot, but it looked bad. He was groaning. Still alive, but not for long, with the amount of blood he was losing. Linus was standing on the edge of the roof, looking out towards the sea. By his side, gripped by his right hand, was a handgun. It looked like an old Beretta Colt .45 revolver. Old, but still lethal.

Beckett took a breath. Last time he'd been in this situation, on a roof, a man with a gun, someone else shot and bleeding, it had nearly killed him. Torn his body and his career into shreds. But, there was no six-year-old child standing, alone, in danger, this time. This time, there was a man, who'd be dead in a few minutes anyway if no one intervened, the man who'd shot him, and himself. It was a no brainer.

Beckett stepped out onto the roof. He kept his gun low, but ready to use.

"Put the gun down, Linus."

Linus spun around, waving the gun like he was swatting at a fly. His eyes were pinned open, and glittered like a miniature thousand bolts of lightning were exploding inside them. "This is my roof. My building. I suggest you stay away. Stay away."

Beckett glanced at Patrick. The red halo was swelling.

The wound seemed to be in the stomach. "Why did you shoot Patrick?"

"Why?" Linus scoffed. "Because of what he did to Danni. He killed her."

"Patrick didn't kill Danni, Linus." Beckett tried to focus on Linus' face, rather than the gun Linus was waving around. Three shots. Three bullets left, if the gun had been full. A gun enthusiast would know Colts were often left with an empty chamber, as with the hammer resting on the round, the gun had a habit of firing all on its own. Linus didn't strike Beckett as a gun enthusiast, but then again – what was he doing with a vintage revolver? Not that it mattered. One bullet was enough to rip through Beckett's body, and end his life. "Put the gun down, so that we can talk."

"He treated her like a dog. Worse than a dog. He had her put to sleep. And as soon as she's gone, he moves his slut in."

Which meant Sophia was in the flat downstairs. Beckett hoped Harper had followed instructions, and gone to check.

"We know he was cheating on Danni. We know he could be violent. But, we don't believe he killed her."

"She'd still be alive, if it wasn't for him."

"Why do you say that, Linus?"

"She wanted someone to love. He ripped that away from her."

"Did she love you, Linus? We know she was seeing someone else. Was that someone else you?"

"She didn't love me. I loved her. She didn't love me. I tried, but it went wrong. I just thought if I could show her. She was so lovely. But, then, all she could do was cry. She wouldn't stop crying. I think I did something wrong, but I don't know what."

"Did you kill her, Linus?"

"Nooooo," he screamed, and suddenly the gun was fixed and pointed at Beckett. "I'd never hurt her. Don't you understand? Haven't you been listening? I loved her."

Beckett forced himself to keep breathing, to stay calm. He took a step closer. Linus didn't move, the gun still aimed, an almost undetectable tremor in the arm. The muscles of his trigger finger tensed, nostrils wide like a bull ready to charge.

"Do you know who she did love, Linus? Was there someone else?"

"It should have been me. I would have loved her forever."

"Who was it, Linus?"

Linus hesitated, mouth twitching, eyes shining, and gun still aimed at Beckett.

"They might be the person who hurt her. You want me to catch them. Make them pay? Then, tell me? Please, Linus. For Danni."

Sirens screamed into the car park below. An ambulance, followed by patrol cars. Linus looked around. He lifted the gun to his head.

"No. Linus. Please. Don't."

Linus squeezed the trigger. The gun cracked. Brain and blood sprayed into the air. Linus tumbled over the edge, and disappeared.

Beckett sprinted forward. Looking over the edge, his head started to spin. Pinned to the concrete was a misshapen heap of flesh and bones wearing Linus' clothes. Uniformed figures swarmed up to it.

Beckett turned back to Patrick. He pulled off his shirt, and moved to press it onto the blood-soaked stomach, but Harper was there, already applying pressure the wound, trying to stop the red liquid seeping out. Still, it oozed between his fingers—relentless, determined.

"Sophia?" Beckett bent next to him, offered his shirt.

"Hiding in a cupboard. Terrified out of her mind, but

fine."

"Well, that's something."

"Why didn't you shoot him? You had the shot. He could have killed you. Patrick's bleeding to death."

"I needed the truth."

"More than you needed to live?"

Two paramedics scrambled over. Beckett stepped back, Harper also on his feet, furious.

"Don't you care about protocol? Don't you care about doing things properly? You don't wait for back-up, but when you go in, you don't take the shot. I know you're not afraid to fire your weapon. How many people have you killed?"

Beckett stared at the angry man in front of him, fury boiling out of every pore. He didn't understand where such blistering anger was coming from. Harper hadn't been under any threat.

"You're so blinded by what you see as the truth, you forget everything else. You didn't believe Linus killed Danni, and you were happy to die, if there was a chance of proving yourself right. You're dangerous. You shouldn't be a cop. Go be a vigilante, or a mercenary, where rules don't matter."

Harper turned and left. Beckett watched the paramedics working on Patrick, one pounding on his chest, trying to restart his heart. He went back to the edge of the roof. Linus' body was being taped off, uniformed officers ushering a growing crowd backwards. Beckett remembered what it was like to fly through the air. Feel the breeze against your cheeks, as you plunged down. As the world skimmed past you, and the earth rose to slap you in the face. Harper was right. He was blinded. But, the truth had to be outed. And one thing he was 100% sure of – Linus had not killed Danni. He saw it in his eyes. He loved her. *Really* loved her. Love could be twisted and mangled, until all you could do was hurt the one you loved. It drove people to do unspeakable things. Shooting Patrick, shooting himself. Unspeakable. But, in Linus' eyes, when he'd spoken about Danni, Beckett had seen love, sad, full of longing. He would have killed for her, but would never have hurt her.

***

The hospital corridor was bustling. People, porters pushing beds, and wheelchairs, some occupied, some not, doctors striding, nurses chatting or scurrying, shopping trollies full of patient notes being trundled along by crumpled looking clerks; Beckett didn't register any of them. He sat, legs furled under the chair out of the way, or paced to the coffee machine and back again, without ever getting a drink. He had no idea where Harper was, or what he was doing. Didn't really care. He needed to hear Patrick was going to be okay.

"Inspector?" A couple of hours later, the surgeon swung out through double doors.

"Yes?" Beckett got to his feet, studying the surgeon's face for clues. Doctors were well-practised at hiding their feelings. Never play poker with a surgeon, Faulkner always said.

"He's come through the surgery. He was lucky. The bullet missed everything major, and went straight out the back. It looked a lot worse than it was. I've stitched it all back together. He should be fine."

"Is he awake? Can I speak to him?"

"I'd rather you waited. He's very groggy."

"I'll sit with him. Wait until he's a bit more alert."

"He's not in any danger, is he? I heard his shooter head-butted the ground so hard, his head ended up looking back the way he'd just fallen."

"I need to speak to him, as soon as possible. That's all."

"Fine. Please yourself."

Patrick was in a small, private room, which opened out onto a larger ward. He was hooked up to drips and pipes, but was breathing on his own, and his colour was much healthier than when Beckett had seen him on the roof. *That's what a transfusion of a few pints of shiny new blood does for you*, Beckett thought. Every so often, a nurse would come in, check his vital signs, smile at Beckett, and leave. Beckett waited. Occasionally, he'd get up and lean over the bed, hoping to see Patrick's eyes flick open, or some mumble escape from between his lips, which would give him reason to prompt him to wake up fully. But, Patrick slept on.

Beckett got out his mobile, and wondered if he should turn it on. There were no longer rules in hospitals preventing you from using mobiles, but he'd turned it off, because he didn't want to be disturbed. He didn't want to be called back to the station. He didn't want to be involved in the dissection of Linus Sang as the potential murderer.

A coughing from the bed alerted him. Patrick was awake, eyes wide with pain or fear, or simply confusion.

"Drink? Water?" Beckett offered a beaker. Patrick nodded, and Beckett helped him drink. Patrick sank his head back on his pillow, seemingly exhausted from that one effort.

"You know where you are?" Beckett asked. Patrick nodded, but his eyes stayed shut. "If you're in pain, you can self-administer morphine. Press this button."

Beckett folded Patrick's fingers around the PCA pump. Patrick pressed hard, and within seconds, his breathing eased, and his fingers relaxed again.

"Do you remember what happened?"

Patrick's eye lids snapped open. "That bastard Linus shot me. Then, he dragged me onto the roof, wanted us both to jump off together. Bit of bad planning. By the time we got up there, I couldn't walk any further, and he's too pathetically weak to drag me. He should have got me on the roof, and then shot me. Did he jump?"

"Yep."

"Dead?"

"He blew his brains out as he went."

"Good." Patrick's mouth curled into a smile. His thumb squeezed the PCA pump again.

"Why did he shoot you?"

"He thought I killed Danni. Twisted little shit, got that idea from you. Thanks for that."

"We'd released you, without charge."

"Not good enough for him."

"Is that what he said, that he wanted to make you pay for killing Danni?"

"I told him I hadn't done it."

"But, he'd seen you with Sophia. She's fine by the way."

Patrick flushed. "Thank goodness. I thought he was going to kill us both. Fucking crazy. I always thought he was weird. Told Danni to stay away from him."

"Another witness told us Linus was in love with Danni. That he was obsessed with her."

"He was. Told me they were in love. Said whilst I was away that weekend, he slept with Danni. How did he put it? 'That she'd given him her love.' That it had been beautiful. That now his seed was in her, something amazing would blossom. Freak. As if she'd have slept with him…" Patrick's voice trailed off, as he considered what he'd just said. "That's it, isn't it? He raped her. That's the only way. He raped her, and killed her. Then blamed me for making him do it. Twisted fuck."

"I spoke to Linus on the roof, before he shot himself. He said he loved Danni, and that he would never hurt her."

"And you believed him? Is that why you're a copper on an Island where the most serious crime is who smashed Granny Paxos' flower pot? He shot me. Raped my girlfriend. Or tried to. And then, killed her. And now, the bastard will never stand trial, but he's guilty. I know it."

CHAPTER TWENTY-SEVEN

"He hid behind her. Can you believe it? I think the romance is well and truly dead. I think she wishes he was, too." Harper had interviewed Sophia, with the aid of a constant stream of strong sweet coffee for her, and a massive sense of relief for him. "I bet he didn't admit to that."

Beckett shook his head. He'd barely spoken a word since he'd arrived back from the hospital. Harper told himself he must be in shock. Seeing someone blow their brains out in front of you, even if you'd seen many dreadful things before, couldn't leave you unmoved. There was an unsettled feeling in Harper's stomach though, but he did his best to ignore it. Petrakis was ebullient, and he tried to soak up that feeling instead.

"Pity we couldn't arrest Linus Sang, but at least we have our answers now. It will be a relief for everyone, and no more victims."

"No more victims?" Beckett whispered, his voice so low, Harper had to step closer to his desk.

"You think Linus is connected to Emmie Archer's disappearance?" Petrakis panicked, her joy wiped out.

"No. I'm certain the two cases are not connected. In fact, I think Emmie chose to disappear."

"Thank goodness. We can get on with the rest of the summer."

"I meant Linus Sang. You don't think he's a victim?"

"What?" Harper spat.

"You're feeling sorry for him, Beckett?" Petrakis rolled her eyes. "Don't waste your emotions. He raped Danni, and then killed her. All because she didn't love him."

"Is that really what happened?"

Harper prodded the sheaf of papers on Beckett's desk. "Copies of the lab report. Linus' sperm found inside Danni. His DNA found in her car. His fingerprints found in her car. He had motive and opportunity, and we have enough forensic evidence to put him with Danni and in her car. He would have confessed, if he hadn't taken the coward's way out."

Harper meant his last comment to bite. Beckett had done his own plunge off a roof. Not the same, but not that different, either. It hit home. Beckett stared up at him, his blue eyes faded to a winter sky grey, purple-black half-moons underneath, and his chin coated with mottled grey and brown stubble.

"I'm not disputing Linus had sex with Danni. He believed it was with her consent, but we'll never know the truth. But, he said he didn't kill her."

"Well, he would, wouldn't he?" Petrakis sounded as frustrated as Harper felt.

"They had sex, consensual or not. She was upset afterwards, traumatised or guilty," Beckett seemed to be talking more to himself now, working a scenario out in his head, "Where would she go? To her lover. She tells him what happened... he's apoplectic, and he kills her."

"You're making up fantasy stories," Petrakis snorted. "Linus' DNA is in the car. The car her dead body was transported in."

"They were friends. Neighbours. He didn't have his own car. Is it too much of a stretch to think she might have given him lifts? Even lent him the car. Patrick should be able to confirm that. I'll go back to the hospital now, and ask him. We know Danni was seeing someone else. Whose semen is in the condom?"

"We've input the DNA results into the various databases. Nothing local. We may never get a match. But, whoever it was, it wasn't as recent as with Linus. He was the last person to have sex with her, before she was killed. Is this because you didn't spot him before? You interviewed him, and didn't see it?"

"We know whoever killed Danni had help dumping the body. Who helped Linus? He doesn't have any friends. He couldn't have walked all that way on his own. He doesn't have a car with a tow bar, or a boat."

"This island is full of cars and boats, he borrowed or stole one. And, maybe, he did walk home. Or hitched a lift. We can work on all those things."

"He's a small man, small and weak. Danni was bigger than him. He could never have moved her body on his own."

"Why does this feel like history repeating itself?" Harper turned away from the desk. If he hadn't, he would have picked up something – the stapler, hole punch, souvenir snow globe, and thrown it Beckett's head.

"Meaning?" Beckett voice was level; he could have been commenting on the weather, but Harper heard something else. Doubt, fear, the sound of a man starting to unravel.

"I want you to put a report together, collate the evidence around Linus Sang. Tie up loose ends, but by the end of the day, I want to solid case with Linus as main suspect." Petrakis stalked out of the office.

Harper sank into the chair opposite Beckett. "Why are you so bloody minded?" He sighed, exhausted himself, trying to reach out, persuade Beckett to let it go. "Is it so hard to believe Linus would lie to you on that roof? Perhaps he couldn't admit to himself he'd killed Danni. In his sick and twisted way, he loved her."

"Like Chrystos?" Beckett murmured.

Harper shrugged, not wanting to rub it in. "Linus blacked out the part where he stuck her with the blade. Most murders are as simple as that. You know it as well, better than I do. Forensics are all over his apartment. They'll find Danni's blood, and they might even find a murder weapon. Will you be convinced then?"

"Of course."

Harper breathed out and leaned back in the chair. "I know you want to get Troy for something. But, this isn't it."

Without warning, Beckett stood up. "You're right. You'll let me know what forensics turn up in Linus' apartment?"

"Where are you going?"

"I need to clear my head. You can handle things here, can't you?"

"Of course. What do you want to do about Ticknall and Michale?"

"We've got their statements. Send them home."

"Fine. No problem."

Harper watched Beckett leave. He seemed to be limping. But, it was over. He wondered what would happen to Beckett now. Back to snoozing in roadside bars, pretending to catch speeders. Back to his life of semi-retirement. He doubted someone like Beckett would ever slip off the cloak of obsession. He'd fixate on Troy, or rather, whomever the man he saw in Bosnia was, until his memory failed him. He'd believe the guilty were innocent, and the innocent guilty for the rest of his days.

Harper had a sudden, intense sense that no man, especially a man like Beckett, could live like that for long. He'd taken one plunge from a building. How long until the next? It worried him. A good man wasted, but what could he do? This time next week, he might be back home. In the slate-grey grim of London. For the first time, he allowed himself to think of home. Of his bosses being pleased. Of his promotion. Perhaps he'd move stations. Maybe he'd even look at positions in different forces. Be a big fish in a smaller pond for a while. Somewhere more rural. Perhaps with a coastal beat.

Harper wondered if his dad would read the news coverage. Would he finally crack a smile, and acknowledge that he'd done well? At least he'd be able to look his sister in the eye, and feel like he was on an equal footing. Then, his smile faded. He could be promoted to Chief Constable, and he'd never be equal. Not in her eyes, and not in his father's. Some things were too fantastical to ever come true.

CHAPTER TWENTY-EIGHT

Faulkner was waiting for Beckett, swinging in the hammock chair on the veranda.

"You look like hell," Faulkner said. For a split-second, Beckett had an image of his father as a young child swinging on that same chair, dreaming up songs in his head. "I heard what happened."

Beckett eased himself onto the veranda step. His knee was starting to twinge, the effect of the injection wearing off.

"Maybe it's time for you to think about retiring? You've seen more death than any one person should. Your body is fucked."

"And my head is, too?"

"I didn't say that."

Beckett shrugged. Harper had been right about one thing. It did feel like history repeating itself. Rosie and Danni. Official story murdered by men who were obsessed with them. Unobtainable women. Spurned men. Simple. Age old. The rest of their stories just flotsam and jetsam. But, he knew that wasn't right. He knew he'd failed Rosie, and Chrystos, though no one could say he didn't deserve to be locked away. He didn't want to fail Danni. He didn't want there to be another dead girl in another ten years' time for another detective to search for, find dead, or to never find, because the real killer was sitting, smiling, and waiting.

"Harper thinks you're obsessed with Mitchell Troy. That you saw him out in Bosnia selling arms to the Serbs, and that's where all this started."

"You think I'm crazy, too? You think I've seen more than my fair share of death. What about Troy? Death follows him round like a shadow. Rosie Payne, his wife, now, Danni. I can connect them all to him. This is a small Island. You think it can all be coincidence?"

Faulkner looked away, but he brought the hammock chair to a halt. "I think you need to let it go."

"Why?"

"He didn't kill his wife."

"You believe the suicide story?"

"No. I don't believe she's dead."

"What?"

Faulkner sighed. "Go and see Gideon Coe."

And, suddenly, the conversation with Bee popped back into his thoughts. And the missing passport. And going to see Gideon Coe seemed like what he should have done days ago.

***

Beckett found Gideon digging at his vegetable patch around the back of the house. The Land Rover had been parked out front. Beckett had taken a quick look. No scarf. No Emmie. But, he hadn't expected her to be sitting in the car, waiting for him.

Gideon nodded at Beckett. "Beer?"

Beckett nodded. They sat in the shade of two ancient tortured olive trees.

"I expected you before now," Gideon said, licking his lips after a glug of beer.

"I've been a little busy."

"Where is she?"

"Her and Bee have gone up to the waterfall. You remember it? Your dad took you there a few times when you were small."

"I wasn't talking about Emmie Archer. I know she's here. I know she's safe. And I've got a fair idea why she's here."

"Her fiancé – ex-fiancé – is an abuser. She believed the

only way to get him out of her life was to disappear. It was the only way she'd ever feel safe again."

"What about Jeanie Troy?"

The hand clasping the bottle of lager stopped halfway to Gideon's mouth.

"What happened to her?"

"She committed suicide." But, Gideon knew the game was up.

"You helped her stage it?"

"She was desperate to get away. Just like Emmie. I helped her."

"We helped her." Julia came out of the stone shack housing her studio. "She was so scared of Mitchell Troy, she was prepared to leave her kids behind."

"Prepared to let them think their mother had killed herself," Beckett added, thinking how terrified a mother must be to do that.

"I always thought she was a little… selfish." Gideon shrugged. "Highly strung. I asked her what would happen to the children, and she said Mitchell would look after them. Not such an ogre, then. Not if you are blood, she replied. I'm not sure she was ever cut out to be a mother."

"You were crazy about her back then," Julia fired at him, the bitterness not hidden.

Gideon had the decency to flush red. "She asked for help. We helped. Got her on a boat, got her into Italy, with some friends of ours. New passport, new identity. New life."

"Where is she now?"

"Living happily in South America, last I heard. We don't keep in touch."

"And you're going to do the same for Emmie?"

"Another of his pet projects," Julia said. There was such a sadness in her eyes, Beckett wondered why she stayed.

"I think Bee is hoping to persuade her to go back to England. You've met the fiancé. What do you think she should do?"

"I need to speak to her."

"I'll take you, come on." Julia got up, before Gideon could suggest anything different.

The path was narrow and winding, and studded with tree roots. Within a few minutes, they could no longer see Gideon who had gone back to digging his vegetable patch, stabbing the soil with his spade.

"Jeanie was terrified of Mitchell. She was convinced he would have killed her, if she'd stayed. Maybe it was selfish to leave her kids, but she felt she had no choice."

"Did you think she was exaggerating?"

"I think she was manipulative. She'd have said anything to get her own way. Gideon was in love with her. I think he thought she'd stay here with him."

"Where would that have left you?"

"Gideon thought we could all be happy together. But, neither I, nor Jeanie, would have lived like that. She was using Gid as her ticket out. I hated her at first, but only until I met Mitchell, a couple of months later. He came to one of my exhibitions. We only said a few words to each other, but that was enough. I have a great instinct for people, Inspector. Everyone has an aura they can't control. Most people don't even know it's there, but it is the essence of the real person. Not the persona they wear in everyday life. I can see auras, the colours, the moods, as clearly as I can see the flesh and bone. Mitchell Troy's aura is poisonous. I think he would be capable of almost anything."

"Have you been to any of his parties?"

"Me? No…" She laughed, but with contempt. "Those gatherings are for posh, rich folk. Why would I want to mix with that sort? If you want to know about Mitchell Troy's dos, you should ask your father, he went to a few."

Before Beckett could say anything, they emerged into a clearing with a river, a twenty-foot sheer rock jutting upwards, and a waterfall tumbling down into a deep clean pool. Beckett remembered Faulkner encouraging him to jump from one of the large rocks by the side of the pool. Beckett had ignored him, climbed to the top of the waterfall, and jumped in from there.

No one was jumping today. The two girls were swimming across the pool towards them. As they reached the boulders at the edge, Bee saw him, her eyes widening in fear. Emmie simply smiled. She was more striking then in her photos, and as she climbed out of the pool, Beckett had to look away. She was quite distracting. Did Gideon have his heart set on her, as he had with Jeanie Troy? How could Julia see that happening once again, and still want to help the girl?

"Inspector Kyriakoulis, I presume?" Emmie smiled, a half crooked smile, and tilted her head upwards to get a better look at him. "Are you here to arrest me?"

"I should. Both of you." He looked at Bee, who was wrapping her towel around herself, and looked close to tears.

"I'm truly sorry. I didn't know what else to do. I was desperate. No one would have been so worried, I imagine, if that other poor girl hadn't been found murdered."

"I did try to persuade her to give you a call. Or, at least, to let me do it," Bee whimpered.

"But, I refused. I swore her to secrecy. It's not her fault."

"You did lie to me." Beckett felt unkind doing it, but he'd had enough of the secrets and the game playing.

Little Bee's chin started to tremble. "I'm sorry."

"It's really not fair to blame Bee." Emmie's smile was gone, and there was steel in her voice. "I take full responsibility. What are you going to do?"

Beckett left them without an answer. He wasn't sure himself, and it was fitting to let them sweat a bit. He headed back down the hill, his mind full of questions. Mitchell's wife was not murdered. *What other assumptions about Troy had he got wrong?* He so faithfully relied on his instincts, and, in this case, he'd been spectacularly off the mark. But, Julia's words weighed heavily. Troy was poison, and his own father had attended the infamous parties. *Why had Faulkner not said anything? If Faulkner had been to the parties, perhaps he'd met Rosie? What was he hiding?*

Beckett's phone chirped to announce a voicemail. He was back in signal range. The number dialled, and Harper's voice crackled.

"It's Harper. Erm… you're not going to believe this. Or perhaps you will. We've got a partial match on the DNA from the condom. A 50% match to be exact. It came up on the UK database. Seems that Lily Troy was arrested, but never charged, for an assault on another girl at her expensive boarding school back in the UK last year. Which means the DNA in the condom must belong to Callum Troy. He's the secret boyfriend. I'm heading over to the Troy's now. Meet me there, if you get this message in time."

Beckett pulled into the side of the road. His hands were shaking, and he had to grip the wheel hard to steady them. He should have seen it. Lily Troy teasing her brother about Danni. His face flushing red. Mitchell mocking him. *Did Mitchell know? Was Mitchell jealous?* The son had got the girl not the father. Beckett shook his head. He was letting himself be blinded again. But, there was that feeling, right at the pit of his stomach. The creeping gnawing feeling, like a thousand beetles were hunting for a way out. It was a feeling of dread, of fear. He dialled Harper's number, but it rang out, then jumped to voicemail. He wasn't far from the Castle. He floored the accelerator, and got back on the phone. This time, uniformed back-up was a necessary precaution.

At the Castle entrance, he jabbed the intercom. Five times, before it was answered.

"Hello?" An Eastern European accent. The housekeeper.

"Inspector Kyriakoulis, Island Police. Let me in. Now."

"The other policeman has gone. I told him Mr. Callum wasn't here. That he'd gone to the Rock, fishing. I said I would tell Mr. Callum when he got back. He insisted he would wait for him at the jetty at Caspon, where Mr. Troy keeps his boats."

"How long?"

"Ten minutes. Not long."

Beckett stuck the car into reverse, and roared back up the road. The Rock was a tiny, uninhabited wooded island, not far off the coast. It was famous for its colony of monk seals, and its sea caves. He got on the phone again. By the time he'd got to Caspon, Nik was manoeuvring his boat up against the jetty. One of the patrol cars was parked up.

"I'm taking a boat trip out in half an hour. I can't come with you."

"I just need a boat. Take my car, drive back to the yard. I'll pick it up later."

"Perhaps I could cancel. Put them off until tomorrow."

"It's no big adventure. I just need to go and talk to someone. Take your tourists out. Make your money. Give me the keys."

Nik dropped the keys into Beckett's palm. "If I miss out on something good…"

Beckett stepped into the boat. It was the fast speed boat they'd used to find the dumping ground beach.

"Please be careful with her. She is very expensive."

"Cast me off."

He seemed to make no ground on the Rock for the longest time, but eventually, it drew closer. He could make out individual trees, and waterfalls crashing from high cliffs into the sea below. There was a landing jetty, but on the seaward side of the Island. He steered the boat beneath the formidable cliffs, their dark, sea level eyes hiding monsters. He rounded the headland, and there was the jetty, with one small power boat moored up, bobbing in the swell.

He tied his boat up next to it, dwarfing the smaller vessel, though neither were exactly ocean liners. One boat. If Harper had come to find Callum, where was his boat? Perhaps Harper was still on shore, or, perhaps, it was Callum who had never arrived. A movement out beyond the headland, in the shadow of the cliffs, caught his eye. Another boat, dangling its ropes behind it like an errant dog dragging its lead. Harper must not have tied up properly. *Idiot.*

There was no sign of life. If Callum was there fishing, he would most likely be at the fresh water lake. It was famous for its trout. A path led up from the jetty into the woods, and eventually, after a half a mile to the lake. It was the only path from the jetty, and the one Harper must have followed.

Beckett jogged, the path corkscrewed through the dense forest, climbing steeply at first, and then levelling off. The birds were silent, eerily so. Even the cicadas were hiding. A few metres from the lake, he heard voices, talking. He could hear muffled noise, but not detail. Then, a yell. Panicked. Beckett sprinted out into the clearing. The lake stretched like a mirror in front of him, the size of a football pitch, twisted into a dinted and damaged oval.

Two figures on the fishing jetty at the far end. They were hugging, it seemed. But, it felt wrong. Unnatural. One let go. The other teetered on the edge of the cracked and faded wooded slats. *Harper.* Beckett recognised the shape, the height. And then, Harper fell, backwards, into the lake. The splash like a whisper, the ripples rolling one over the other, distorting the reflection of the trees, and then sinking back, as if they'd never been there. The other figure ran, scampered across the jetty, and into the dark of the forest. Beckett's muscles readied to chase, as he looked back at the lake, expecting Harper to bob to the surface, to splutter and rage. But, there was nothing.

"Harper?" Beckett yelled. The lake was deep and cold. But, Harper could swim. The image of the hug and the parting. "Shit." Beckett yelled, but to himself now. He knew no one was there to hear him.

He kicked off his shoes, and dove into the water. Within a few strokes, he was at the point Harper had disappeared under the sharp cold surface. He plunged down, forcing his eyes to stay open against the clawing of the water. And there, he saw Harper, on the bottom of the lake. Motionless, apart from his hair, those curls, billowing around his head like anemones. And spewing out from his side and spreading through the water, like an oil slick, was black ink. *Not ink.* Beckett made sense of it. *Blood.*

He grabbed Harper, and dragged him up and up. He seemed impossibly heavy for a slight man, as if the underwater world did not want to release him. It seemed to take a life time, but Beckett broke through the surface, took a huge breath of beautiful, pure fresh air, and kicked for the shore. He pulled Harper onto the grass. His skin was translucent. Lips the colour of putty. He looked like one of the marble statues of the Greek Gods. Beckett put his ear to Harper's mouth. Felt nothing. He started chest compressions. Thirty. Then, he pinched Harper's nose and blew life into his chest. He looked. Nothing. Two more breaths. Nothing. Thirty more chest compression. Another breath. And a cough, and water and a groan. Not conscious, but not dead. Not yet.

Beckett saw the scarlet pool start to form at Harper's side. He ripped Harper's shirt, exposing the wound. A circular wound, only a few millimetres across, puncturing the skin, going in deep. He'd seen one just like it—on Danni Deacon's body. He put his hands over the wound, iridescent crimson liquid oozed between his fingers. He turned his head away and pressed hard.

In the distance, he could hear the sound of an outboard engine starting and fading. He fumbled his phone out of his pocket. Water rippled down the screen. He wiped it on his shirt, and squinted at the screen, through the fog. No signal. He would have to hope Nik would direct back up to the right place.

It seemed like a lifetime. The cold crept up on him like a shadow, caressing his skin at first, before digging its claws in deep. His hands were numb, holding back the flow of blood. Harper seemed a distance away, still breathing, but in shallow tentative waves that seemed to drift further and further apart.

Then, suddenly, noise and people. Uniforms and authoritative voices. A blanket wrapped around his shoulders. Being led away. Looking back to see people swarming and crouching over Harper's body.

CHAPTER TWENTY-NINE

Back at his car, Beckett refused a trip to hospital. He did not want to know Harper's fate, not yet. His only medical need was to get warm. He had a change of clothes in the boot, and a heater in the car. Air temperature was approaching 85 degrees. He wasn't about to die of hypothermia, despite the concerns of the paramedics and Welsh Nik, who was now taking the whole thing very seriously.

He didn't expect anyone to be waiting for him at the Castle, but that was the direction he headed in. It was a place to start. Nik had wanted to come, drive him even, but Beckett had refused.

He'd got within a mile or so, when he had to jerk in the steering wheel to avoid a car hurtling around a bend towards him. Too fast, too reckless. A red car, hatchback.

"Shit." Recognition rattled around Beckett's head. He three-pointed the Evoque, and went after it. The red car was a Ford Focus. Being driven fast, but not as fast as the Evoque could go. Beckett soon caught up, and flashed his lights. The Focus didn't slow. Beckett waited for a straight section of road, then gunned the accelerator, pulled alongside, and then executed a perfect hard stop, turning in front of the Focus, forcing the driver to slam on the brakes, and turn the nose of the car into the side of the road.

Beckett was out of his car, and at the driver's door of the red car, before the driver had time to open it. Beckett yanked it open. Callum Troy was staring out at him, face crumpled with distress. Beckett was way beyond feeling sympathy. He grabbed hold of the lad, and dragged him out on the verge.

"I have to find Lily," Callum whimpered. "Please."

"Before she hurts anyone else?" Beckett growled.

Callum looked at him wide-eyed. "What has she done?"

"You tell me Callum?"

"Nothing." But, he could look anywhere, except at Beckett.

"Did she kill Danni?"

Silence.

"We know you were sleeping with her. We've got forensic proof. We know from her friends she'd been seeing someone, other than her boyfriend, Patrick. And we know she had sex with Linus Sang, not long before she was killed. Perhaps it wasn't Lily. Perhaps you killed her? Jealous that she'd slept with Linus."

"No," he roared back, face dissolving into tears. "I loved Danni. I would never hurt her. She was brilliant. I couldn't believe she was even interested in me."

"And Linus Sang?"

"She said she felt sorry for him. But, he drugged her, and then took advantage. She blamed herself. She felt so bad, she came to tell me."

"You were angry. Betrayed."

"Lily was raging at her. Told her I'd suspected she was only using me to get back at Dad."

"What d'you mean get back at Dad? Mitchell?"

"It's what he does. He sees someone, takes a liking to them. Buys them things. Piles on the charm, until they can't say no. Patrick and Danni started coming to Dad's parties."

"The ones in the woods?"

Callum nodded. "'Just a bit of grown-up fun,' he'd call them. 'Not your sort of thing, Cal. Far too sensitive.'"

"And Patrick and Danni came to some?"

"When they first came to Farou, Lily told me. That's where Dad saw her. He started bringing her to the house. They couldn't go out in public, because of Patrick. Then, one day, he freaked out. I was next door. He lost it. Was yelling about a bracelet she was wearing. It was her favourite. She always wore it when we were together. He didn't see her again after that. But, I missed her. I started hanging around at Nemesis. We got friendly. And then more…"

"Mitchell had a relationship with Danni," Beckett said more to himself than Callum.

"I loved her. But, I got jealous. Lily winding me up, threatening to tell Dad, but then saying he'd never believe me. And reckoning Danni was shagging around. After all, how could I hope to keep her happy? I took Danni's tablet. She didn't know. Thought she'd lost it. Or Patrick had sold it. I wanted to see who she was emailing. She'd saved all his emails. And photos of them together. I thought she still wanted him, but she wasn't emailing him or any other men. I was so happy, but then, when she came and told me about Linus…"

"What happened? Who killed her?"

"I don't know. I wasn't in the room."

"Just Lily and Danni?"

"When I came back, Dad was there… and Danni was on the floor, bleeding. I don't know what happened." Callum's face disappeared into itself, and he stumbled back against the car.

Beckett stared at him, no idea whether to believe him or not. *Lily or Mitchell? Or Callum himself?* "Who dumped the body?"

"Me and Dad. No one ever goes there. He thought it would be months before she was found. But, I didn't want her left alone there."

"So, you phoned it in. And you left the flowers and the bracelet at the roadside?"

"The bracelet must have fallen off back at the house. Lily

reckoned Dad hated it, because of Mum. She used to make bracelets like it. When we were little. I don't remember, but Lily has one, too. She won't wear it. But, she still has it… somewhere."

"What the hell are you doing?" A voice made them both spin around. Mitchell Troy, his car parked a few feet away. Callum recoiled. "Get in my car," Mitchell spat at his son.

Beckett stood between them. "I'm about to arrest him. And you."

Mitchell's face split in a roar of laughter. "You really think so?" He looked past Beckett to Callum. "I said get in my car, and wait there."

Callum shot around the two men, and climbed into the Porsche, but as he passed Beckett, he whispered, "Aphrodite," and nodded towards the back of the red car.

"And your daughter, Lily, will make a nice trio."

"You won't be arresting any of us, Inspector."

"DI Harper was stabbed earlier this morning."

"Sorry to hear that. Fatally?"

"Too early to say."

"I'll send a card. We do have the greatest doctors on this Island. As you know."

"Where is Lily?"

"You can't think either of them have anything to do with Harper's misadventure, surely?" Mitchell scoffed.

"And the death of Danni Deacon."

"You're wasting your time. Callum doesn't have the cojones to hurt anyone. Plus, he was with me all morning. Meeting with the architects for the new hotel. Brand new development. The biggest hotel built on the Island for twenty years."

"And Lily?"

"That, I don't know. You know what girls are like. I expect she's been out shopping. Spending more of my money.

Too much like her mother. As soon as Lily gets in touch, you'll be the first to know." Mitchell could have been talking to him about the weather. "But, I can assure you, they both have rock solid alibis."

"For when?"

"Whenever they need one."

"Does that apply to you, too? Were you sleeping with Danni Deacon?"

The smile evaporated from Mitchell's face.

"Did you kill her, or was it Lily?"

Mitchell took a step forward. Beckett could smell his peppermint breath.

"I know Lily stabbed DI Harper. I was there. I recognised her. The way she ran. And I think Lily killed Danni. Did she think she was she protecting Callum? Or perhaps, she was jealous. Twins. That's how it works, isn't it? Incredibly close. More than normal brothers and sisters. Do anything for each other."

Mitchell pushed Beckett against the side of the car, the genial businessman gone. When Beckett looked at him, he was the man in Bosnia, standing next to the General, shaking hands on the deal. Cruel. Ruthless.

"Or perhaps I'm wrong. Perhaps it was you who killed Danni. Like you killed Rosie Payne. You picked them, used them, had sex with them, and then, once you'd gotten bored, you killed them. Or maybe you just hated the fact Danni had moved onto your son.

Mitchell tilted his head back and roared with laughter. "Really? That's what you want to throw at me? I thought you were smarter than that. You honestly think you can come after me?"

"I have a witness who says you were sleeping with Rosie,

and the last time she was seen alive was at one of your little parties in the woods."

"Lots of people attended my parties. You'd be better looking closer to home. Ask Faulkner what happened to Rosie Payne."

"What?"

"You come after my family, and I will come after yours. It's a question of what means more to you. Destroying me, or destroying your father."

"I don't understand."

"How did those old BT adverts go? 'It's good to talk.' We all keep secrets from our pasts. Mistakes we've made. Things which can't be undone. But, if you insist on bringing my past misdemeanours out into the open, then you'd better make sure you know all the facts. Talk to Faulkner. And then, we'll talk again. When you're in a more reasonable mood."

"You'll jump in your plane, and disappear."

"I'm confident you'll make the right decision. And this is my home. Why would I go anywhere else?" Mitchell shrugged, and walked to his car. Callum stared out through the windscreen.

For a fleeting moment, Beckett felt worried for him, but even Mitchell wouldn't hurt his own children. He watched Mitchell drive away, and could not push his words from his head. *Ask Faulkner about what happened to Rosie Payne.* It hung there like a raven black storm cloud. He hated to follow Mitchell's instructions, but had no choice. He had to find out.

He turned to close the car door, and spotted something glinting in the sunlight on the passenger seat. An iPad, wrapped in a grapevine printed case. *Danni's.* And Callum had given him the password. Beckett picked it up, and slipped it into the glove compartment of the Evoque. He had a good idea what he would find on it, but that was for later.

CHAPTER THIRTY

aulkner was sitting on the terrace, looking out over the sea. It struck Beckett how similar a setting it was to Mitchell Troy, sitting on his terrace, surveying his domain.

"How's Harper?" Faulkner asked, as soon as Beckett stepped out of the house. His face was lined with genuine concern.

"No change." Beckett wasn't in the mood for small talk. He'd called the hospital on the drive over. Harper was out of surgery, and on life support. Critical condition. Beckett felt sick, the worry about Harper creating a great pit in his stomach, and the Faulkner-shaped storm cloud pulsating in his head.

"But, the surgery went well?"

"They've stitched him up."

"Have you any idea who did it?"

"I know exactly who did it. Lily Troy. Callum was sleeping with Danni. I think Lily got jealous, or overprotective. Killed Danni, and then Harper, when he came to talk to Callum."

"Jesus. Well there you go. Good. Good that's excellent news. Then, perhaps, you can forget all this. Take a holiday. Have a normal life."

"It's not that easy though, is it?"

"No... no... that's true. You did think there was a connection to Troy from the beginning, but not him. His daughter."

"I don't think he's innocent in this. He helped dump the body. I may have it wrong. It might have been him who killed Danni. I'd have to prove it, of course. Not sure I can."

"Forget the past. Whatever Troy is, or isn't, best to move on. I expect he'll have spirited Lily off the Island by now, anyway."

Beckett figured he was probably right. Mitchell proudly saying he and Callum wouldn't be doing a flit, probably because his plane was busy already.

"You're right. I was wrong about him having something to do with his wife's disappearance."

"You spoke to Gideon?"

Beckett nodded. "I spoke to Mitchell, too. Asked him about Rosie Payne." He watched his Dad's face for a reaction. There it was. A slight frown, a twitch of the eyebrow. Gone before you'd even imagined it was there. "He said I should ask you."

"Ask me what?" Faulkner laughed, but turned away.

Beckett knew, without any doubt, his father knew something. He felt sick. He'd still hoped Troy was stirring up trouble, playing with him. "What happened to Rosie Payne?"

"How would I know?" Faulkner picked up a drinks coaster, and started rolling it around on the table.

"You were at the party. The last time she was seen alive."

"I don't really remember."

"Yes, you do. Who were you with?"

"You don't want me to tell you this."

"What? Why would I not want to know the truth? This has been haunting me for years. For God's sake, Dad, just tell me what happened."

"Yes, I was at that party. Lots of alcohol. I didn't touch the drugs. I'd given up by that point. Plenty were partaking, though, including Rosie Payne. And, yes, Rosie and Mitchell were together. She'd started out as a friend of Jeanie's, but when Mitchell clapped eyes on her, that was it. They were happy. His feelings for her were real. Believe it, or believe it not. But, they had a fight at the party. She was talking to another man. Mitchell didn't like it. She stormed off. Excitement over, but I was knackered, and I needed to get home. I was getting in my car, but I was totally wasted. Ed Hefferman offered to drive. Sebastian Wolf came with us. Not that you ever saw Ed and Sebastian far apart. He was always Ed's shadow."

"They were at the party?"

"They were doing some business on the Island. It's not unusual. Ed wasn't a Cabinet Minister, then. Sebastian was organising all sorts of meetings. I think they thought Troy might be useful. Ed had had a few drinks. Not as much as me, but he shouldn't have been driving, and I shouldn't have let him. But, you know what it's like here. People do it all the time. I was in the back. Asleep. I was jolted awake. The car had stopped. Sebastian had got out. He came back. Said we'd hit a deer. It was dead. Nothing to be done. Ed carried on. Dropped me off at home. End of story. But, then, a day later, Rosie was reported missing. Sebastian came to see me, brought the car back. It wasn't a deer we hit. He'd got rid of the body. Begged me to keep quiet. It was an accident. Nothing we did now would change the fact she was dead. Ed was on the verge of a post in the Cabinet. Tipped to become party leader one day, and then Prime Minister. He was a good man, who could be a great leader. All that talent, all that passion, would be wasted if this came out."

"And you agreed?"

"He's proved himself, hasn't he? One of the most popular politicians around. He's making a difference in the world."

"He got pissed, and killed a girl."

"It was an accident. It could have happened to anyone. It should have been me driving. The ends justify the means. I thought you'd understand that better than anyone."

"If you believed that, you'd have told me years ago."

It all made sense. Chrystos finding the body, and then

going back, and it was gone.

"There's no proof any of this happened. Not without a body. Mitchell can't prove anything. And even if he could, they – the Government – wouldn't let him."

"And these are the people you call 'great'?"

"Country before individual."

Beckett knew he was right.

"We never knew how Mitchell found out. Guessed. Pieced it together, somehow."

Spoke to Chrystos, no doubt, Beckett thought, *but how did he know it was that particular car which had hit her?*

"So, Mitchell Troy has a hold over a senior British politician?"

"He has no evidence."

"Someone told him what happened. Perhaps there was another witness? He has more than enough to blackmail him. Someone like Troy, he's not a nothing police officer like me. He could exert massive influence on government policy."

"If he was going to do it, he would have done it by now."

"How do you know he hasn't already? How do you know it's not happening right now, every day, every business deal?"

Faulkner looked at him, panic creeping into his eyes.

"And there's absolutely nothing we can do about it."

"If Mitchell is as bad as you say, you'll get him on something else, won't you?"

Beckett laughed. "And if I have something now? Something to connect him to Danni's death?"

Faulkner stared back at him. He suddenly looked all of his seventy years, and more.

"He sent me here with the message. If I come after his family, he'll come after mine."

"Me?"

"You think? Suddenly, it'll have been you alone in the car that night. You, the pissed driver, who killed the girl, and then disappeared the body. What did happen to the body?"

"Sebastian sorted it. He never told me. Or Ed, I don't think." Faulkner's voice was a whisper. The full consequences filling his thoughts.

"What would you do? Blame Hefferman? Who do you think the authorities would believe? The pissed up, drugged out old rock star, or the Secretary of State, backed up by his faithful advisor with the whole weight of a Government and country behind them?"

Beckett turned to leave. "If I arrest any of the Troy's then you'll get accused of the manslaughter of Rosie Payne, plus the disappearance of the body. You'll go to prison. For something you didn't do."

"So, what are you going to do?"

"Nothing. What choice do I have?"

"I'm sorry, son."

He heard Faulkner's words, as he left.

Beckett sat at Harper's beside. The younger man looked like a chameleon, colour changed to match his white surroundings. But, he was alive, and would stay that way.

Harper's eyes flickered open.

"How are you feeling?" Beckett asked.

"I've been better."

"You look terrible."

"Thanks. You look pretty crappy yourself."

"It's been a bad week. Nice card." There were a few cards behind his bed already, but one huge one. "From your Dad?"

"No. From yours. Doubt mine gives a toss."

"Mine's great at the big gestures."

"Seems you are, too. You saved my life. They tell me."

"I'd have done the same for anyone."

"Not quite true."

"These days."

"I'm grateful, anyway. She got away, though? Lily Troy? Left the country, Tomas told me. But, who helped her with Danni's body? Callum? Mitchell? When are you going to question them?"

"Tomas has. They claim they don't know anything. There's nothing more we can do." He avoided Harper's gaze. He knew he sounded like he'd given up too easily.

"I guess we'll never know what really happened. You were right about the connection to Troy, though. You bastard." Harper coughed, in pain but surprisingly buoyant. Wait until he was Beckett's age.

"Righter than I thought. This is Danni's tablet." He had the grapevine encased iPad in his hands.

"How did we not find that?"

"Callum had it. He passed it to me."

Harper looked suspicious. "Passed it to you, but couldn't help our enquiries? What's going on Beckett?"

"Seems Danni came to Farou, with an ulterior motive. To get close to the Troy's, and report back on the kids."

"To who?"

"She was emailing a woman called Jenny Daniels, formerly known as Jeanie Troy."

"The dead Mrs. Troy?"

"Who staged her own suicide, with a bit of help, to escape from Mitchell, and is safe and well living in Rio, where she met Danni."

"Jesus. I take a day off, and all hell lets loose. At least you know Mitchell didn't kill his wife, but come on. His daughter kills Danni, and he doesn't know about it. I don't buy it, do you?"

Beckett shrugged. "Time I moved on. Time I retired."

"Yeah. Okay." Harper grinned, and again winced in pain. "Olive farming? I can't see it."

"I can't think of anything I'd rather do right now. What about you? Back to Blighty, and your promotion?"

"After a few months' rest and recuperation. At least I'm in the right place for a holiday. Faulkner says I can stay on at his."

"He'll like that."

"Give me chance to buy you dinner. As a sort of thank you. For not getting me killed whilst I was here."

The door squeaked open, and Tomas' head appeared. His eyes were wide, and energy coursed through him like a firework about to pop. "Boss, I've been trying your phone."

"I turned it off. So as not to disturb Harper. What is it?"

"You need to come back to the station. It's your Dad. It's Faulkner. He's handed himself in."

"What?"

"He's confessed to killing Rosie Payne. In a hit and run. Years ago. Says he couldn't cope with the guilt of keeping it a secret any longer. I think he's lost his mind."

Beckett slammed to his feet.

"Jesus Christ. Beckett?" Harper tried to sit up in bed but failed, groaning, "What the hell is going on?"

Beckett looked at Tomas, and then at Harper, his mind racing. Suddenly, there was everything to play for, once again.

The End

ACKNOWLEDGMENTS

Thanks to all the amazing crime writers who have inspired me along the way. To my fellow writers, editors and producers in the world of television who taught me how to tell a story. And thanks to Richard who had the faith to support me in the writing of this book.